Jody Gehrman

confessions of a
Triple
Shot
Betty

Dial Books

DIAL BOOKS
A member of Penguin Group (USA) Inc.
Published by The Penguin Group
Penguin Group (USA) Inc., 375 Hudson Street, New York, NY 10014, U.S.A.

Penguin Group (Canada), 90 Eglinton Avenue East, Suite 700, Toronto, Ontario, Canada
M4P 2Y3 (a division of Pearson Penguin Canada Inc.)
Penguin Books Ltd, 80 Strand, London WC2R 0RL, England
Penguin Ireland, 25 St. Stephen's Green, Dublin 2, Ireland
(a division of Penguin Books Ltd)
Penguin Group (Australia), 250 Camberwell Road, Camberwell, Victoria 3124,
Australia (a division of Pearson Australia Group Pty Ltd)
Penguin Books India Pvt Ltd, 11 Community Centre,
Panchsheel Park, New Delhi - 110 017, India
Penguin Group (NZ), Cnr Airborne and Rosedale Roads, Albany, Auckland 1310,
New Zealand (a division of Pearson New Zealand Ltd)
Penguin Books (South Africa) (Pty) Ltd, 24 Sturdee Avenue, Rosebank,
Johannesburg 2196, South Africa
Penguin Books Ltd, Registered Offices: 80 Strand, London WC2R 0RL, England

Designed by Nancy R. Leo-Kelly
Text set in Weiss
Printed in the U.S.A.
1 3 5 7 9 10 8 6 4 2

Library of Congress Cataloging-in-Publication Data
Gehrman, Jody Elizabeth.
Confessions of a Triple Shot Betty / Jody Gehrman.
p. cm.
Summary: Sixteen-year-olds Geena, Hero, and Amber
spend their summer working at a Sonoma, California, coffee shop,
experiencing romance, identity crises, and newfound friendships.
ISBN: 978-0-8037-3247-6
[1. Interpersonal relations—Fiction. 2. Friendship—Fiction.
3. Summer—Fiction. 4. Identity—Fiction.] I. Title.
PZ7.G25937Co 2008 [Fic]—dc22 2007017128

For my mom, Sherry Garner,
who knows the power of a good caffeine buzz.

Thursday, June 5
8:10 P.M.

Great. So much for my summer. I should have known. School's not even out yet, and Operation Girlfriend is already in tatters. Amber, Hero, and I were going to be glorious; armed with big sunglasses and supersized iced mochas, we were supposed to take this crazy, tourist-trap, sun- and wine-soaked town by storm. I could see us so clearly, laughing happily as sunlight doused our brown shoulders and pooled in our bouncy, naturally highlighted hair. We were supposed to spend lazy afternoons lounging in bikinis on Hero's deck, and long, giggly nights painting our toenails in sorbet hues. But what are we doing instead? Enduring awkward pauses and thinly veiled snarkiness.

Fabu. Just what I had in mind.

Tomorrow, after a mercifully brief half day, school's officially out. When that final bell rings and we're released en masse from those stifling, fish-stick-scented halls, I should be the happiest girl on Earth. I mean, come on, this is my sixteenth summer; it should be epic. I've read enough coming-of-age novels to know this is the magic moment when even we late bloomers get to shed our ugly duckling baby fat and emerge as triumphant, nubile swans. I wanted to share this historical turning point with my two best girls: my cousin Hero, and my friend Amber.

Just one tiny glitch in that brilliant plan: Hero and Amber are on the fast track to hating each other's guts. They met for the first time like four hours ago, and already they're constructing voodoo dolls.

What was my first clue that Amber and Hero weren't exactly hitting it off? Oh, let's see, maybe it was when Hero stopped by Triple Shot Betty's today and Amber called her a scrawny little beeatch.

I honestly have no idea how this happened. There I was, wiping up coffee grounds, nursing a mocha, and bursting with almost-summer excitement. Triple Shot Betty's is a drive-through coffee stand about the size of a shoe box; if you don't clean constantly, it's like working in a mine shaft. I guess the caffeine and chocolate hit my system all at once, because I found myself chattering incessantly to Amber about Hero while I cleaned.

This, I suspect, was my first mistake.

"She's a total girl-genius," I said, scrubbing at the espresso machine. "She speaks fluent Italian—her mom was from Milan—and now she's learned French too, and last summer she taught herself Latin for *fun!* Can you believe that? I just know you two are going to get along *so well.* She's flying in from Connecticut today. Her sister's picking her up. Bronwyn. You're going to love her too. She's a sophomore at Berkeley and she's so insightful about the human condition—picture Michelle Pfeiffer with a psych degree. Okay, only half a psych degree, but she's going to be the best therapist *ever.* She's been practicing on Hero and me since we were five, analyzing our dreams and asking us how decapitating Barbie makes us *feel*. Anyway, sorry I'm babbling, I just can't wait for you to meet Hero!"

"Cool." Amber toyed with the straw in her drink. She didn't look very excited.

"What's wrong?" I paused in my frenetic cleaning and studied Amber. Her long red hair was draped around her face, so it was hard to tell if she was mad or tired or what.

"Nothing." She still didn't look up. "What kind of name is *Hero*, anyway?"

"Oh, that. Our moms were totally crazy about Shakespeare—it's a long story."

"And she goes to, like, a boarding school?"

"Yeah. She has English with Virginia Woolf's great-grandniece."

"Who's Virginia Woolf?" Amber asked.

I searched her face for signs of irony. Nope. Not a trace. "Nobody—just a writer." I racked my brain for something that might impress her. "Plus, her roommate's mom is Johnny Depp's agent."

Amber looked up. "Has she met him?"

"Who?"

"Johnny Depp."

I shook my head. "No. The school's in Connecticut. Johnny's in L.A." Strictly speaking, I guess I don't really know *where* Johnny Depp lives, but it seemed a reasonable guess that he wasn't camped out in Connecticut.

"Oh." Amber went on twisting her straw in listless circles. I'd never seen her like this. She was acting like this was Labor Day, not Summer Vacation Eve.

"Aren't you psyched? School's out tomorrow! No more legalized torture at the hands of sadistic algebra Nazis!"

"Yeah. I'm psyched."

Usually Amber is the most vivacious, in-your-face, outrageously funny coworker on the planet. Get a double latte in her, she's like your own in-house comedy channel. Today she was acting more like the Grim Reaper on downers. I didn't have time to investigate further, though, because right then a familiar blond head appeared at our window.

"Hero!" I dropped my sponge and almost knocked Amber over as I lurched past her. "Oh my God! You're home!" I wrenched the window open and squeezed my body halfway out, pulling her into an awkward hug.

"Geebs!"

As I clutched at my cousin, I smelled her familiar scent: apple shampoo and baby powder. We hadn't seen each other since Christmas, which seemed like forever. She looked a little different: Her usual B cup seemed to be inching toward the C range, and the rail-thin, hipless body she'd inhabited throughout our childhood was filling out into curves. Her nose was still slightly freckled, though, and the miniature rhinestone barrettes she'd been wearing since junior high were still struggling to stay attached to her blond, baby-fine bob. She was dressed in her usual: a gossamer-thin skirt paired with a filmy tank under a barely-there cardigan.

"I'm so glad you came by!" I said. "Come around back—I'll show you the inside."

She ran to the back door and I let her in. As she crossed the threshold, she said, "Wow, this place is so small!"

"Welcome to our pygmy sweatshop."

"It's kind of cute," she said, wide-eyed. "Like a doll's house. Bronwyn just went to Sonoma Market. She'll pick me up in a minute." Hero nodded at Amber, then quickly cut her eyes to me.

"Oh—sorry . . ." I looked from Hero to Amber and back again. This was the moment I'd been looking forward to—finally, our trio would magically come together—but now that it was really happening, I found myself going all awkward and shy. "Hero, this is my friend Amber. Amber, my cousin Hero."

Amber didn't get up; she just sat there, fiddling with her straw, looking glum. "Hey." She gave Hero the once-over. "What's going on?"

"I'm fine, thank you. And yourself?" Hero has such impeccable manners, you'd think she was employed by the royal family. It can be embarrassing.

"Can't complain." Amber looked mildly amused. "Geena was just telling me all about you."

Hero glanced at me and tucked a strand of hair behind one tiny, translucent-pink ear. "Oh, really?" She giggled nervously. "Like what?"

Amber leaned back against the counter, her knees splayed out immodestly in her distressed-denim mini. "Like how you're roommates with Johnny Depp's daughter."

"His agent's daughter," I corrected.

Hero nodded, setting her tiny Prada purse on the counter. "Oh, yeah. Mallorie. She's really nice. She's spending the summer in Tuscany," she said to me. "Dad said we might go there for Christmas again."

"How nice for you." Amber's sarcasm was obvious to me,

though Hero's bland expression made me wonder if she detected it.

What was happening? "Um, Amber moved here from Lake County," I blurted. "Last fall."

Hero nodded politely. "Do you miss it?"

"Not really. I mean, you know, if you like hippies, tweakers, white supremacists, and born-agains, it's paradise. Otherwise it pretty much sucks ass."

Hero's lips tightened, like she'd just sampled a lemon. "And how do you find Sonoma?"

I wanted to shake Hero—she was being so stiff and aloof—but then, Amber wasn't doing much to put her at ease either.

"I find it . . . quaint."

"So you like Sonoma Valley High? I never went there."

Amber squinted at her. "It's like most high schools. You've got your jocks, your emo-kids, wangsters, FFA freaks. I seem to have found my niche right away, so that was nice."

I knew what was coming; I wanted to close my eyes, like before a car crash. I started to say something—anything—but it was too late.

"Oh, well that's good, that you feel—you know—comfortable," Hero said, nodding.

"Uh-huh. I even have a nickname at school. They call me Blowjob Beezie."

Hero's eyes went wide. I winced. Amber smirked.

Cue extremely awkward pause.

Just then Bronwyn's bright red Jeep pulled up and she hollered through the window, "Hey, little cuz—what's up?"

Only then did I realize I'd been holding my breath.

"Bronwyn! Love the new haircut." She'd chopped her hair really super-short, and it made her eyes look even bigger and grayer than usual. She's so beautiful. If she weren't my cousin and incredibly useful when it comes to psychological insights, I'd have to kill her.

"Thanks." Bronwyn looked at her sister. "Come on, Hero. We gotta fly. I told Dad I'd get you home for dinner. Elodie's making millefeuille just for you."

My mouth actually watered slightly. Elodie, their French chef, makes the best millefeuille in the world.

"Millefeuille," Amber said, still smirking. "*Quelle* yummy."

"Okay, just a sec." Hero looked at Amber uneasily. "Nice to meet you."

"Same here."

I grabbed Hero's hand and squeezed. "I'll call you soon as I'm off."

"Okay."

The minute they'd driven away, Amber blew a couple strands of hair out of her moody green eyes and looked at me. "So that's Hero . . ."

"Was that really necessary?"

Amber raised her palms. "What?"

"'Blowjob Beezie'?"

"What? That's what they call me. Is that supposed to be a secret?"

I sighed. "Hero's sheltered. She's—"

"The chick's got a phone pole up her butt—is that my problem?"

A black convertible Saab full of tourists cruised up to the window. You could tell they'd already sampled a few too many Pinots and Chards, because the women were laughing like hyenas. The driver looked at me over his Ray-Bans and ordered four cappuccinos in a sulky tone. I got them their coffees; predictably, they didn't tip, and I swore at them under my breath.

When I looked at Amber, she was back to twisting her straw in slow circles. She looked as miserable as the stingy Saab guy.

"I was hoping we'd all be friends," I said.

"Don't hold your breath," she said.

"What don't you like about her?"

She looked at her watch. "How much time you got?"

"Seriously." I knew from her expression she was getting annoyed, but I wanted an answer. "Name one thing that's wrong with her."

"She's a stuck-up, rich, bony-assed beeatch."

I sighed. "That's three things."

"That's the abridged version."

"Why are you being like this?" I put a hand on my hip. "She's not stuck-up. Just because her dad owns Monte Luna doesn't mean—"

"Wait a minute . . ." Amber looked like she was trying to remember something. "Her dad owns Monte Luna Winery?"

"Yeah." I tried not to sound defensive.

"So Alistair Drake is their new neighbor?"

I looked at her blankly. "What are you talking about?"

"Hello! Alistair Drake? Former drummer for Stalin's Love Child? Founder of Floating World Tattoos in Santa Monica?"

"If you say so."

"Duh, he just bought a huge place right by Monte Luna."

I was steadfastly blasé. "Oh. So?"

She made an impatient sound. "So he's the most amazing tattoo artist on the *planet,* and he's going to open a second Floating World up here."

Amber's big dream is to be a tattoo artist. At first I thought that was kind of sad. I mean, we're young, we can do anything we want, and her mission in life is to drill ink into the pores of hippies, bikers, and giggly trendoids? But the more she told me about it, the more I started to respect her vision. She says it's body art; skin is her canvas. And anyway, who am I to judge someone who knows what she wants? I'm so indecisive, I'll probably still be a barista when I hit thirty.

"Alistair Drake studied tattooing in Japan for years. He's a genius. Anyone who apprentices at Floating World has respect and job security for life." She bit at a cuticle on her thumb, looking suddenly small and scared. "It's going to be totally competitive. I bet everyone in northern California's going to apply. Still, I have to work there."

"Well, maybe Hero could introduce you, then. I mean, if they're neighbors . . ."

Amber arched an incredulous eyebrow. "Yeah. Like *that's* going to happen."

"What? It's not a big deal. I'm sure she wouldn't mind."

She didn't look convinced. In fact, she was staring at me like I was pathetically slow. "Girls like Hero don't do favors for girls like me, okay? We're from completely different worlds."

"Oh, come on—you don't even know her."

"I know how much money it takes to buy a winery like Monte Luna."

I shook my head. "Uncle Leo didn't *buy* it. Hero's mom inherited it—it's a family business."

She eyed me suspiciously. "So then, your family owns it too?"

"No. Hero's dad is my dad's brother—my parents aren't rich, you know that." Hero and I don't talk about money, but it's pretty obvious her side of the family has a lot more than mine. They live in a sprawling, vineyard-enshrouded nouveau villa up on Moon Mountain, while Mom and I inhabit a tiny Craftsman-style bungalow in town. I never really think about the differences between us that much, but obviously these distinctions were important to Amber, and for some reason that irked me. "So what if Hero's family has money? It's not like that's who Hero *is*. Monte Luna doesn't affect her *personality* or anything."

"Right." I'd never heard her sound so bitter. "And I suppose boarding school is just a way to ensure she's *well-rounded*. It's got nothing to do with being too good for us townies."

I hesitated. Sure, I was bummed when Hero decided to go away to school. And yeah, sometimes I wondered if she didn't feel a tiny bit superior, now that her classmates were chummy with Johnny Depp. But Hero was still my cuz; it bugged me that Amber was so sure she had Hero pegged five minutes after meeting her.

"You know, she could have gone kayaking this summer in Patagonia, like her dad suggested," I said. "But she decided to work here, with me. She likes Sonoma." Of course, Hero also vetoed the kayaking thing because she considers camping a form of ritualized torture, but Amber didn't need to know that. "She hates it when people assume she's different just because she's rich. She just wants to be normal."

"Normal?" Amber made a sarcastic sound in her throat. "That's pretty funny."

"What do you mean?"

She took out a compact and applied a fresh coat of lip gloss. "I doubt her idea of normal and my idea of normal are even in the same universe."

I watched as she pressed her lips together, spreading the sparkly orange lip gloss evenly. Her point wasn't exactly lost on me. When Amber showed up last fall at Sonoma Valley High, I took one look at the tattoos, the tight, cleavage-baring clothes, the pierced belly button she never failed to display, and I thought what everyone else did: *Who's the new hoochie-mama?* But then we started working together at Triple Shot Betty's, and I got to know her. I was fascinated by her in-your-face attitude and her total disregard for social norms. You can learn a lot about someone when you're stuck together in a box the size of a broom closet, and Amber's the type of girl who'll tell you about her dad's meth habit, her mom's obscenely hot twenty-year-old boy toy, and her avid interest in pornographic manga within the first ten minutes of meeting her.

I guess since I like Amber and Hero both, I assumed they would instantly hit it off. Until today, it never occurred to me that they have absolutely nothing in common. I mean, Amber's an uninhibited trailer-trash goddess, and Hero's this perfect little Rhodes-Scholar-to-be. Maybe it was a mistake to get Hero this job.

"Just keep an open mind," I said, hiding my second thoughts

with an encouraging grin. "I'm sure you'll love her if you get to know her."

Amber snapped her compact closed and shrugged.

"Are you going to graduation tomorrow?" I asked.

"Yeah, I guess." She didn't sound enthused.

"Cool. Let's go together. Maybe Hero can borrow her dad's car."

Amber's glossy lips went all pouty. "She doesn't even go to school here. Why would she go?"

I tried to hide my exasperation. "She grew up here—of course she'll want to go. Come on, Amber, lighten up. We'll have fun."

She looked away. "You're not going to like . . . spend the whole vacation with her, are you?"

I took a step toward her. "I was hoping we'd all spend it together. Is that so crazy?"

"Yeah." Our eyes met and she softened her tone a little. "I don't know. Maybe not."

"Give her a chance. We're going to have a great summer."

"If you say so . . ." She definitely didn't look convinced.

Suddenly, neither was I.

Friday, June 6
4:15 P.M.

I am *so* never getting married. What's the point? All you get is screwed. Take my mom, for example. I came home from school today and there she was, gripping the phone with white knuckles, speaking in her *I won't let this get to me* voice.

"Oh, here she is now, Jen. . . . Yep, she just walked in the door." She covered the receiver with one hand and said, "Your dad's girlfriend. You want to talk?"

I leaned my skateboard against the wall and dropped my messenger bag on the kitchen table. "Jen?"

"Yeah. Do you want to talk to her or not?" Mom's eyes were bulging a little; she was trying to stay calm, but I think she really wanted to pitch the phone across the room. I'm afraid she's still a little hung up on her ex (aka Dad). He left us last year—moved to L.A. with this Jen person. I've met Jen a couple times, but she's never actually called me. I figure our best policy is to deny each other's existence whenever possible.

Mom gestured impatiently with the phone.

I took it from her. "Hello?"

"*Hi*, Geena. How *are* you? Enjoying your *summer*?" She has this really annoying habit of emphasizing random words; it makes every sentence sound strangely significant, even if it's just inane babble.

"I'm okay."

"That's *so* great. I'm *really* glad. I need to ask a *favor*, sweetie. Would you be really *mad* if your dad didn't come to visit this weekend?"

"Uh, well . . ." I didn't like where this was going.

"Because I just booked the most *amazing* trip to Maui, and I rearranged his work schedule, but then I found out he's supposed to see you, and I felt so *bad*—I mean, what awful timing—but then I thought, you know, Geena is such a *sweetheart*, she'll definitely understand that this is a once-in-a-lifetime opportunity and I'm sure you want your dad to have *fun*, since he's been working so *hard*—not that he wouldn't have fun with *you*, but you know what I mean." I don't think she took a single breath in that whole run-on sentence.

"You can't go to Maui another time?"

There was a tiny, shocked pause. "Honey, I already *booked* it. I can't get a refund."

"Well, I guess if it's already booked . . ."

"Thank you, Geena, that is *so* nice of you! Oh, and it's a surprise, so don't *tell* him, okay?"

"Yeah," I said, "got it."

After I hung up, Mom's eyes were shooting me questions, but I didn't feel like talking. I just grabbed my bag and trudged off to my room, where I could pout about this latest development in peace. I've been foiled once again by my father's bimbo (did I say bimbo? I meant extremely sweet and nurturing life partner). I just hope this isn't a sign of things to come. I don't think I can take another summer filled with Sloane family drama.

Last year I got a crash course in Why Love Sucks. Dad moved out in May, and by June Mom was transitioning from total bewilderment to middle-age rage, which wasn't pretty. Dad didn't actually take off for L.A. until September, which gave us three whole months to run into him and the bimbita everywhere we went. We'd see them kissing in the aisles of Safeway, nuzzling each other at Blockbuster, holding hands at Longs. We'd even see them at Starbucks, which really broke Mom's heart. Her Frappuccinos were her only real comfort back then, and seeing Dad kicking it in the corner with one hand on his grande cappuccino and the other on his scantily clad bimboccino sent her off on a caffeine-fueled rant every time.

Obviously, my formative years haven't left me with

many romantic illusions. Everything I've seen so far has just convinced me not to trust any guy ever—at least, not unless he comes with a bulletproof dossier detailing what makes him completely different from the rest of the male species. Not that they're exactly beating down my door. I'm just not the kind of girl they go for. My usual uniform is a ratty tank top, cutoff Dickies, and worn-in sneakers. I skateboard everywhere—have since I was thirteen—and I always wear my hair in two long brown braids. I've got boring-but-big brown eyes and a body that is completely unnoticeable in every way, except for my boobs, which I fear are turning into the Uniboob, a hereditary trait (thanks, Mom). Right. Enough about me. Now I'm totally depressed.

Amber's always telling me I spend way too much time reading obscure novels and scribbling in my journal—that I should try indulging in normal teen activities, like drinking beer, smoking bud, and having sloppy sex in parking lots. Well, I'm sorry, but I just don't see it happening. I'm simply not capable of tittering brainlessly at my male contemporaries. From what I've seen, a girl's got to behave like a mental midget before she'll get any action in this town. If resisting that makes me a freak, so be it. I may die with my hymen intact, but at least I'll have my dignity.

Saturday, June 7
1:20 A.M.

So there we were at graduation, watching the seniors bouncing beach balls in the air while the band geeks played "Pomp and Circumstance" ad nauseam. We were squirming uncomfortably on the hard wooden bleachers as the last of the grads filed onto the football field and took their seats. The warm June breeze carried the smell of hot dogs and popcorn. I had Amber on my right, Hero on my left, and I was stuck in between, desperately trying to make them like each other.

"Hey, Amber, did you know Hero's an amazing pianist? Isn't that cool?"

Amber smirked and brushed a strand of hair from her eyes. "Wow. I've never met a penis. Isn't it hard?"

Hero stared straight ahead. "How original—never heard *that* before."

Code Red: If there's anything Amber can't stand, it's the thought of being less than original. "Actually, I play an instrument too," she said.

"Really?" I was all smiles, thinking, *Great, they have something in common.* "I didn't know that. What do you play?"

Amber leaned around me and looked right at Hero. "The skin flute."

I laughed, and Amber let out a throaty giggle as I shoved her gently. I was hoping to hear at least a chuckle from Hero, but even without looking I knew she was sitting ramrod straight, staring directly ahead, her lips pressed tightly together.

"Excuse me, pardon me. Coming through." I spotted PJ walking with a stranger and Ben Bettaglia. They were navigating the stadium rows, sidestepping paunchy parents and squirmy little kids, heading in our direction. PJ was in the lead, strutting with cocksure *I'm the man* attitude in his sagging jeans and tight black T-shirt. The stranger was long and lanky with shaggy hair and a friendly smile. Behind them Ben had his hands shoved into the pockets of his chinos, and his dark eyes peeked out from under long lashes every now and then. As they drew nearer, he glanced up at me and I saw his lips tighten into the Ben Bettaglia trademark smirk. He'd been shooting me that look since we were kids; it seemed to say *I know something you don't know.* All these years, I still hadn't quite cracked whatever secret he thought he had on me.

"'Sup, ladies?" PJ took a seat next to Amber. The new guy sat next to Hero, and Ben sat down on the bleacher directly behind me. "You all having a safe and sober graduation?"

"Way too safe," Amber said, "and definitely too sober."

PJ chuckled. "We can fix that. Party at the Inn tonight."

I looked at him, surprised. "Seriously? How'd you swing that?" The Sonoma Mission Inn is this huge, super-posh resort in Agua Caliente, just a few minutes north of town. There are rooms there that'll set you back more in one night than the grand total of my college fund.

"Friend of my dad's owns it. We booked four rooms. Should be a rager."

PJ's official name is Pedro Jamieson, but people call him DJ-PJ, or sometimes The Prince. The DJ bit is his claim to fame; he's got an awesome sound system, and he spins at parties all the time. He's got an unusual knack for getting along with everyone, not just the Pretty People. Maybe that's because he wasn't always a member of Sonoma royalty.

Up on the stage, Principal Hardbaugh was fumbling with the mike, sending out an eardrum-shattering wail of feedback. We were still cringing when we heard him announce, "It's my pleasure to introduce to you valedictorian and student body president, John Jamieson."

All the seniors and half the crowd began chanting, "You the

Man! You, you the Man!" They got louder and louder as John strode across the stage to deliver his graduation speech. John (aka "the Man") is PJ's half-brother, and he's a big deal around here. He's been in like four commercials and played the lead in every drama production at SVH for years. Supposedly he has the highest SAT scores to come out of our school *ever.* He's headed for Yale in the fall. Basically, every male in Sonoma wants to be him, and every female wants to do him.

John took the mike from Mr. H and surveyed the audience as they screamed and chanted his special cheer. He stood there with his white-blond hair gleaming, his eyes hidden behind mirrored sunglasses, soaking in the waves of adoration. When the explosive mantra finally gave way to an expectant hush, he raised the mike expertly to his lips and spoke in a voice so deep and intimate, it actually gave me chills.

"Winston Churchill once said, 'Success is the ability to go from one failure to another with no loss of enthusiasm.' I'm sure we've all experienced failure in the last four years, but I can see just by looking at your faces, fellow seniors, there will be no lack of enthusiasm tonight."

The senior class roared their approval. This was John's genius; he didn't need to say anything profound or even particularly original to have everyone in the stands love him. It was his style—his bone-deep confidence—that kept him moving in a spotlight at all times.

As he continued with his speech, pausing periodically for spasms of applause, I looked over at Amber. When she moved here last August, she and John had an end-of-summer fling. As she watched him now, her jaw was clenched, her hands gripping the edge of her seat, and I saw her throat move as she swallowed. I wondered what she was thinking. She glanced over, caught my eye, and instantly her tense expression turned into crossed eyes and a flash of tongue.

I hazarded a quick look at PJ, who was watching his half brother with a strange mixture of pride and wariness. He and John are so different, it's hard for anyone to think of them as brothers—including them, from what I hear. Their family situation's a popular source of gossip. About three years ago, Mr. Jamieson, one of the wealthiest men in town, left John's mother and married PJ's mom, a petite Mexican woman who's a dead ringer for Salma Hayek. Evidently, she used to work for Mr. Jamieson washing dishes at one of his world-famous restaurants. They had an affair, she got pregnant, and thirteen years later he left his wife for her. It was a big scandal. People say John's never forgiven his father. Or PJ.

My thoughts were interrupted by a voice at my ear. "How'd you do on that algebra final, Sloane?"

I didn't have to turn around to know that Ben Bettaglia was leaning forward, his elbows on his knees, his lips inches from my ear.

"No problem," I said. "Piece of cake."

"Oh yeah? Piece of cake, as in A plus, or piece of cake as in, *Bombed it, but at least it's over?*"

Ben and I have been vying for top academic ranking since we were in the fifth grade, when I beat him at the county-wide spelling bee; it's been war between us ever since. In two years, we both want to be where John Jamieson is right now, spewing valedictorian rhetoric, packing our bags for a full-ride scholarship to an Ivy League college. We've been leapfrogging every semester, our GPAs passing each other by a fraction of a point each term. Ben knows algebra is my Achilles' heel; I know he sucks at science, mainly because he's squeamish about dissecting anything with a face.

"What did you get in biology?" I asked.

Out of the corner of my eye, I could see he was frowning. "None of your business."

"Oooh," I whispered. "Did I hit a *nerve*?" A couple weeks ago, he was so pale and shaky during the fetal pig dissection, he blanked on Mr. Patel's question about the central nervous system, which lost him something like three points. This is the sort of minutiae Ben and I keep track of in our ruthless race to the top of the college admittance ladder.

"Very funny." His breath smelled of cinnamon. I snuck a glance at him, and noticed that already his olive complexion was starting to tan. He's a cyclist, so he spends a lot of time outdoors, trying to be Lance Armstrong. He's so dedicated, he even shaves his legs; the one propped up on the bench beside me was smooth as a girl's, though his ropey muscles were hardly feminine.

"I'm sure the fetal pig was moved by your sensitivity."

"What are you doing this summer?" he asked, ignoring the jab. "Going to brush up on that quadratic formula?"

"Actually, I thought I'd intern at the morgue. Care to join me?"

Ben and I exchanged barbed comments for the duration of John's speech, snickering rudely at each other's expense, drawing pinched looks from neighboring adults now and then. When John wrapped it up at last, the crowd erupted in thunderous applause, most of the girls and women screaming like wild beasts in heat.

Mr. H mumbled into the mike a bit more, and then they began the long, tedious process of handing out diplomas. As I watched the graduates slouch or swagger their way across the stage, one by one, I felt strangely sad. While the popular seniors were baptized in showers of rapturous screams, lots of kids were acknowledged only by a faint smattering of polite clapping. I couldn't help but wonder who would be cheering for me when my time came. Would Hero make it back from boarding school in time to see me walk, or would she be too caught up in her glamorous friends by then to bother? Would Amber still be here, or would her pack-it-up-and-move-on mom drag her away? Could Dad extricate himself from the bimbo-monster long enough to attend?

Luckily, PJ's voice tugged me back from my morbid reflections. "By the way, you guys, this is Claudio." He nodded at the shaggy-haired guy. "He's from Italy. He's studying viticulture there, but he's staying at our place this summer 'cause he's doing an internship in Sonoma."

"At a winery?" I asked.

"Yeah," PJ said. "I forget which one."

"Where's your internship?" Amber asked Claudio. He looked blank; his smile was open and pleasant, but he clearly had no idea what she was saying.

Hero mumbled something shyly in Italian, and his face lit up with astonishment. He carried on in rapid-fire Italian for a few minutes, turning fully toward her. Hero's cheeks flushed bright pink and her mouth quirked up at the corners, her eyes darting from his face to her lap to his face again. Even I understood the gist of his reply: He was interning at Monte Luna. From that point on, we completely lost the two of them; they were locked in animated conversation, with Claudio doing most of the talking, and Hero tucking her hair behind her ears a lot.

"*Quelle* exciting," Amber grumbled. "A global exchange."

"So, you guys coming out to the Inn later?" PJ asked.

Amber gave him a sly look. "Depends. Will there be any hot guys?"

PJ held his hands out, palms up. "Hey—I'm going to be there. Isn't that enough?" PJ's a shameless flirt, but everyone knows he has a girlfriend in the Bay Area he's totally loyal to.

"Let me rephrase that. How many hot, *available*, heterosexual guys will be there—"

"Who aren't puking more than they're dancing," I added.

"Picky, picky," Ben scolded. "What's the matter, Sloane, don't you find beer barf sexy?"

I made a face. "Gross."

"Oh, come on," Ben persisted. "I hear Corky can burp the national anthem once you get a six-pack in him."

"Charming," I said. "The height of masculine appeal."

"I suppose you're saving yourself for Mr. Darcy?" I did an oral report last month called "Scoundrels and Studs in *Pride and Prejudice*"; Ben's been teasing me about it ever since.

"No, but I do have standards."

He looked intrigued. "Such as?"

"I'd rather make it with Mr. Hardbaugh than a guy who shaves his legs."

"Ouch!" PJ reached over to high-five me, laughing. Amber snorted. Ben folded his arms across his chest and tried to look bored.

The amplified voice of Mr. H suddenly cut through our

banter. "And now, I present to you, the class of two thousand and—" Only he didn't get to finish his sentence. Corky Daniels, a big muscle-bound senior, released a primal shriek of joy, cuing his classmates and the entire crowd to follow suit.

Just then I felt Ben's knee brush lightly against the bare skin between my shoulder blades, and for a weird second I felt inexplicably light-headed.

∘ ● ∘ ● ∘

Hero's dad let her take the Merc to graduation, and surprisingly, he didn't say no when she called to ask if she could drive Amber and me to "a small gathering at the Inn." He's usually pretty overprotective, especially of Hero, his *baby*, but since the Sonoma Mission Inn is barely more than a mile from Moon Mountain, and since it's about as far as you can get from a seedy hotel or a parking lot kegger, I guess he figured we wouldn't get into too much trouble. Luckily, my mom didn't require a phone call, since I'd already told her I was staying at Hero's, and Amber's mom was in the city with her boy toy—not that she ever cared what Amber did anyway.

What with the end of school, the frenzied sentimentality of graduation, and the balmy June weather, there was palpable electricity in the air, and it was infectious. We didn't want to be the first ones at the party, so we cruised around town for about an hour, playing Mac Dre at top volume, putting on makeup, inching through the drive-through at Taco Bell for a round of Cokes, and generally just behaving like stupid, giggly girls. Well, Hero and I were, anyway. Amber was in the backseat, staring out the window, lost in thought. Every now and then I'd spin around and squeeze her knee, and once I pulled her up with me so we were both hanging out of the moonroof, our arms flailing like strippers erupting from a cake, but generally she was sullen and withdrawn, two adjectives I'd never connected with her until now.

It was almost eleven thirty when we finally found room 68, the number PJ had scribbled on the back of my hand with a ballpoint pen. There was a bass beat throbbing through the door—sounded like reggae. We knocked, but nobody answered. Hero and I looked at each other, hesitating, but then Amber stepped between us, tried the door, and, finding it locked, pounded as hard as she could with the palm of her hand. Within seconds the door flew open and there was Dog Berry, nodding his scruffy, sun-bleached head to vintage Bob Marley, toking on a cigar-sized spliff. Dog's a junior with a sweet smile and a brain so saturated with bong hits, he's been voted *Most Likely to Become a Vegetable* three years running. Behind him, the room was packed with people, and the air was opaque with smoke.

"Good evening, mamacitas," Dog said with a lazy smile. "You looking for smoking, thizzing, Jell-O, or sixty-nine?"

"S-sorry?" I stammered.

He leaned back and gazed at us from under heavy lids. "This here's the smoking room. Next door's for Jell-O shots, and next to that's where you get your thizz." He was moving his arms around like a stewardess indicating exits. "Over here's room sixty-nine, and that's for—well, I guess that one's self-explanatory."

Beside me, Hero giggled nervously, and I found myself doing the same without meaning to. Amber just grunted in disgust and strode past us, into the smoky haze. Considering our other choices, I thought a little smoke sounded pretty benign, so I clamped a hand over my mouth to stifle my own childish laughter and followed Amber's roving red hair, pulling Hero along by the hand.

"Whoa, whoa, whoa." An arm shot out of the smoke, stopping me in my tracks. "Skater Girl, hey. Who's your beautiful friend?"

The arm was attached to John Jamieson. I was shocked; I couldn't remember him ever addressing me directly. I was surprised he even knew—well, not exactly my name, but Skater Girl meant he had *some* idea who I was.

"Um, this is my cousin Hero. Hero, this is John. He's . . . a senior, and . . ." I racked my brain for something intelligent to add. "He's got amazing SAT scores." I closed my eyes. Had I actually said that?

Lucky for me, John wasn't paying any attention to my mortification. "Hero. Cool name. You like Shakespeare?"

She tilted her head this way and that, blushing. "Yeah. I guess."

He offered her a red plastic cup filled with beer and as soon as she had taken it he struck a theatrical pose. "'In mine eye she is the sweetest lady that ever I looked on.'" He dropped the pose and treated her to a flash of his blinding teeth. "That line's about Hero. Remember that? I never met a Hero before. Seriously. You're the first." His icy blue eyes drank her in as he added, "You look like a Hero."

She blushed again. "Thanks?"

He nodded slowly. His expression made me think of an artist assessing his model; he searched her face with a feverish intensity, as if committing the pink of her lips, the slant of her cheekbones to memory. "You don't go to school here, do you?"

"No." She was having a hard time meeting his gaze. I could see why—his eyes were so piercing and intense it was like trying to look directly at the sun.

"She goes to a boarding school back east," I offered.

John smiled at me, surprised; apparently he'd forgotten my presence entirely. "What are you up to, Skater Girl? Training for the X Games?"

Having his 100-watt stare rotate in my direction, especially combined with a familiar, teasing tone when we'd never even spoken before, made my mind go totally blank. Luckily, an interruption saved me from blurting out anything I'd have to beat myself for later.

"Ah, *ciao bella!*" The lanky form of Claudio emerged from a smoky corner and clasped Hero's shoulder warmly.

Hero's face went from shy to radiant as she turned away from John and kissed Claudio on both cheeks, Euro-style. The two of them launched into a bright, musical exchange in Italian that left John and me blinking.

"I see you've met Claudio," John said, slapping the taller boy with considerable force on the back. "He's staying with us this summer. His parents manage a restaurant supply company in Sicily." I thought I caught the slightest whiff of condescension as he added, "Dad gets all his garlic presses and cheese graters there."

Claudio nodded and smiled uncertainly. "Restaurants— yes. Very good."

Hero said, "We met at graduation."

"And you speak Italian—impressive!" John hooked his arm around Claudio's neck in a chummy way, though it looked like it might hurt a little. "I'd learn every romance language if it scored me points with girls like you."

Just then Natalie Coleman, the blond, statuesque captain of the basketball team, came over and punched John playfully in the shoulder. "Good speech tonight, Mr. Smooth."

"You think I'd let you down, gorgeous?" John ruffled her hair affectionately.

Behind Natalie a whole gaggle of senior girls followed, each of them long-limbed and svelte, reeking of beer and designer perfume. They seemed to take John's response as a cue to swarm around him like a cloud of gnats, each of them eager to share an inside joke or catch his eye with a flash of push-up bra.

Even engulfed in this cloud of hot girl pheromones, John's eyes sought out Hero. She didn't seem to notice; her voice was bright and animated as she locked into the Italian groove with Claudio.

"So, Hero," John said, breaking away from a skinny redhead's manicured clutches. "You in town for long?"

The redhead cast a testy glance over her shoulder at Hero before laughing hysterically at something her friend mumbled.

Hero looked uncomfortable. "Most of the summer."

"We should hang out." He puffed his chest out slightly, and though his tone was casual, the challenge to Claudio was hard to miss. "Maybe go to the coast?"

"Uh, my Dad's sort of . . . protective."

Calling Uncle Leo "sort of protective" is like calling Hitler "a little unstable."

"I could talk to him," John assured her. "I've got a way with 'rents."

Hero shot me a split-second furtive glance.

"He's pretty much impossible," I put in, trying to help. "Believe me."

The situation was quite hilarious. I'd never seen any girl try to get out of a date with John. Hero's excuse about Uncle Leo was true, but I could also see she wasn't exactly melting under John's piercing gaze like every other female in the room. John must have sensed it too. He looked positively bewildered.

Before he could pursue the point further, though, Corky, his muscle-bound sidekick, tackled him with an animal roar, sending plastic cups of beer flying in every direction. The two of them wrestled on the floor, forcing the people around them to scatter as best they could. John was obviously trying to extricate himself and continue the conversation with Hero, but all he could manage was a sheepish *what can you do?* grin in her direction before more thick-necked jocks joined the fray.

Can anyone say *obnoxious?*

"Yo, G!" I heard Amber calling out to me from across the room. "Get over here."

I left Hero chatting happily with Claudio and found Amber pillaging the minibar. "What do you want? Crantini? Screwdriver? Cuba Libre?"

"I don't know," I said. "Something not too nasty."

"Did you lose the little princess?"

I rolled my eyes. "She's not a princess."

"You're right. She's probably really cool when she's not

surrounded by her minions." Amber poured some vodka and cranberry juice into two clear plastic cups.

"No fancy umbrellas?" I complained.

"You're lucky I was able to find this before the crowd did. I hate beer. Cheers." We knocked our plastic rims together and drank. She downed half of hers, while I took a cautious sip. Alcohol's not exactly my friend. The only time I've ever been drunk was at my parents' anniversary party—the one they had the night before Dad freaked out and left. I had too much sangria and was busy throwing up while Dad packed.

"So." She studied me with her cool, green eyes. "I saw John talking to Hero. What was that all about?"

"I think he was hitting on her."

She blew her bangs out of her eyes, irritated. "Really?"

"Yeah, but she didn't seem interested. I think she likes that guy Claudio. You should have seen the look on John's face when she turned him down. I bet no girl's ever done that before."

Amber threw back the rest of her cocktail and poured herself another. "She won't resist for long."

Corky cried out to the room at large, "Behold, I shall christen him!" and poured half a bottle of frothing champagne on John's head while everyone cheered. "You the Man," they chanted. "You, you the Man!" John just laughed, occasionally turning his face up to swallow some of the foaming liquid.

Amber watched him, her eyes narrowed to slits. "He's irresistible."

"Even if she liked him," I said, "Uncle Leo doesn't let her date."

Amber seemed to perk up a little at this. "Really? So she's never had a boyfriend?"

I shook my head. "And she won't until she's thirty, if Leo has his way."

"Yeah, well, John gets everything he wants." She watched as John's buddies hoisted him into the air, passing him from arm to arm like a rock star.

I studied her over the rim of my plastic cup, and her expression was so wistful, another tiny red flag popped up in my brain. "You're not still into him, are you?"

She scoffed. "Me? Yeah, right. The only thing guys are good for is occasional comic relief. John Jamieson is no exception."

I noticed, though, that she went on sneaking peeks at John the rest of the night—or until Hero and I left, anyway, which was only about half an hour later, when Uncle Leo called and reminded us that curfew was fast approaching. I didn't really like leaving Amber there, but she assured us she'd find her own way home.

I wonder what really goes on inside her head. She talks a big talk, but is she truly happy playing the hoochie-mama? Sometimes, the way she looks at John, I can't help but wonder.

Monday, June 9
2:30 P.M.

I came into work this morning at the usual time (five a.m.— the zombie hour). Amber showed up ten minutes late looking even grumpier and more zombified than me, if that's possible. She grunted at me, pulled out a compact, and started painting her lips a plum so dark it looked almost black.

"What?" She got all defensive when she caught me looking at her. "I'm in a death-rocker mood. Is that *okay* with you?"

We both had on our Triple Shot Betty tank tops, the ones our boss, Lane, insists we wear. They're white spaghetti-strapped numbers with pink rhinestone letters. They totally show bra straps—something Lane obviously never considered—and white is insanely impractical in this filthy little hovel. Then again, we could be those poor girls at Hot Dog on a Stick wearing big striped hats and up-the-butt shorts; Howdy Doody meets Hooters. Yuck.

After the morning rush hour, things slowed down a little, and Amber slumped onto a stool with her sketchbook, frowning in concentration as her fingers gripped the pencil and flew over the page in light, feathery strokes.

"What are you working on?" I asked.

She grinned without showing any teeth—her sneaky smile. "Your tattoo."

I snorted. "Yeah, right. Mom would have me locked up." Her comment made me curious, though—if I did get a tattoo, what would it be? And what did Amber consider a fitting icon to brand into my skin forever? I tried to look over her shoulder, but she pushed me away, laughing.

"Not yet!" She put on a fake Jedi-knight voice and commanded, "Do not disturb the master before she has summoned you."

A few customers drove up then, and I momentarily forgot about Amber as she sketched away in the corner. When I finally turned my attention back to her, she held up her sketchbook, eyebrows raised high.

"What do you think?"

I leaned in closer and peered at the drawing. It was me on my skateboard. There were little lines shooting out behind my body to show how fast I was going. I looked tough; my braids were flying and my mouth was set in a hard, determined line. In graffiti-style letters that wrapped all the way around the portrait she'd written TRIPLE SHOT BETTYS RULE.

"That's cool." I grinned. "I love it."

She turned it around and examined the page. "When you get the balls and I get the needles, we'll make it happen."

Thursday, June 12
1:45 P.M.

I planned to stay at Betty's later than usual today so I could train Hero. I figured that would be easy, seeing as she's got an IQ higher than Paris Hilton's Visa bill; I think she can handle a little steamed milk.

I was hoping Amber would skip out a few minutes early, as usual, so we could avoid any virgin-whore awkwardness, but wouldn't you know, she lingered today, performing an elaborate grooming ritual that involved plucking, painting, and plumping for what seemed like an hour.

I was getting nervous as the minute hand inched toward eleven and Amber was still glued to her compact, checking her teeth for lipstick.

(Side note: I'll be the first to admit Amber's hot. She's got miles of flaming red hair, perfect, creamy skin, river-green eyes, and boobs that scream *voluptuous* without being so huge that they qualify her as Dolly Parton freaky. She's definitely not skinny, but she wears her curves with such attitude, nobody would dare call her fat.)

At precisely eleven o'clock there was a knock at the door. Obviously it was Hero, because no one around here ever knocks. I called out, "Come in!" while Amber rolled her eyes.

In walked Hero. She had on the Triple Shot Betty tank top, like us, only she'd paired it with a white cashmere cardigan with tiny pearl buttons, a gauzy pink skirt, and brand-new pink suede ballet flats. Her blond, wispy bob was pinned back with shiny baby barrettes, and she was wearing such a serious, earnest expression you'd think she was showing up for her new position as a nuclear physicist, not a coffee-slinging minimum-wage slave.

"Hey, Hero, whattup?" I squeezed her hand in what I hoped was an encouraging you're-still-my-cuz-even-if-Amber-doesn't-like-you gesture. "Ready to learn the ropes?"

She just nodded and nibbled on her bottom lip.

Amber pocketed her lip gloss. "Hi, Hero. Aren't you kind of warm?"

"No." Hero's voice was clipped and stiff. "Why?"

"Oh, I don't know, it's like a *hundred* degrees out there and you're wearing a sweater. Just thought you might be uncomfortable. Call me crazy."

"Well, I'm not."

"Good for you. Guess you're an ice queen as well as a princess."

One of our stalkers drove up in his retina-searing yellow monster truck and revved the engine a couple times. I had to crane my neck to see past the wheel wells. We call him Mr. Little. Amber says anyone willing to spend that kind of money on *tires* is overcompensating for *something*. He favors muscle shirts, too-tight denim cutoffs, and aviator sunglasses. I feel a little sorry for him. He suffers from an all-too-common form of thirtysomething dementia. He obviously believes it's still 1985. And that he's cool.

Anyway, seeing as the temperature in our tiny workspace had just dropped about thirty degrees, I seized the opportunity to serve Mr. Little. He always gets the same thing: a large caramel shake and a glazed donut. He always tips exactly the same too: thirty-five cents. From the smug look he always shoots me, it's clear he expects me to swoon over his loose change, then beg for a spin around town in his monster truck. As usual, I offered him a tight-lipped grin and a reluctant "Have a nice day."

Once he was gone, I turned my attention back to the girl-fight-in-progress. These two were like toddlers; you couldn't look away for a second or they'd go for the jugular.

"What's wrong with my outfit, anyway?" Hero's sharp chin jutted out defiantly.

"It's perfect." Amber couldn't resist adding, "For a Moral Majority meeting." She can be so mean! "Look, this job's like working in a coal mine. You get covered in coffee grounds, especially when you're training."

"I'm careful," Hero said in her conversation-over tone.

"Of course you are. Plus, Daddy will get you another cashmere cardigan when you ruin that one."

I held my breath. The one thing Hero hates more than anything is being dissed because her family has money.

"You might be white trash and proud of it, but that doesn't mean you can make assumptions." Hero's hands were twitching at her sides, and I was terrified she'd try some of the karate she's been learning on and off since she was seven.

"Maybe we should just—" I began, but Amber interrupted.

"Listen, princess, your shit might not stink back at boarding school, but you don't insult me here. I work in this dump because I have to, not because my mommy thinks it will—"

"My mom's dead."

Okay, that stopped her cold. An uncomfortable pause ensued.

"So, you ready to start?" I asked Hero, trying to sound cheerful.

"Is that your trump card? You pull that one out when all else fails?" Amber leaned back against the counter, her eyes a challenge.

Hero looked from her to me. "Can you believe this? She won't stop!"

"I just wouldn't do that," Amber said.

"Do what?"

"Use my mom's death to defend myself."

"I don't *use* her death! I just corrected you—"

"You guys, this is stupid." I edged closer, even though what I really wanted to do was burst out the door and skate as far from these two as I could. "Just stop, okay? Seriously. You're giving me a headache."

"You're defending her? Did you hear what she just said?" This from Hero.

"I refuse to take sides. You're both being childish."

Hero looked a little contrite, but Amber grabbed her purse and launched herself out the door with a highly irritated "What*ever*." As the door slammed we heard a car horn honking, and Amber let out a string of curses that would make Dr. Dre blush.

"What's *up* with you two?" I said to Hero. "I thought you'd like each other."

Hero sniffed. "You thought wrong." I could tell she wanted to cry, because her neck was all blotchy and her voice was tight, but she had too much pride to break down, even in front of me.

"Hey . . ." I went to her and wrapped an arm around her shoulders. "It's okay. She has wicked PMS. She'll get over it."

Hero nodded, and swallowed hard. I think a tear slipped out, but she wiped it away so quickly with the back of her hand, it was hard to be sure.

Saturday, June 14
3:15 P.M.

I was working with Amber this morning when Hero cruised up to the window behind the wheel of her dad's antique Jag. It's a convertible XK140. Uncle Leo loves that car so much, I've actually heard him serenading it. He was riding shotgun, looking a little anxious.

"I can't believe he's letting you drive his baby," I teased as I opened the window.

"It's taking years off my life," Leo said. "Believe me."

"One small coffee and one small iced soy chai—actually, make them both larges," Hero said. "We'll need energy. We're going to interview event planners. My birthday party's only fifty days away!"

Hero's actual birthday was back in May, but since she was in Connecticut then, she and Uncle Leo decided to have her long-awaited sweet sixteen party this summer instead. It's kind of a big deal for her. I got their drinks and tried to ignore Amber's strenuous eye-rolling.

"Have fun," I said.

She beeped the old horn twice in answer and lurched away while Leo yelped, spilling coffee on his white linen shirt. She hadn't quite gotten the hang of the stick shift yet.

Amber's arms were crossed in front of her chest when I turned away from the window. "Ooh, goody. Planning a party in Daddy's Jag. *Quelle* amusing," she quipped.

Just then I heard a tremendous roar behind me, but before I could even turn around, Amber rushed past me and leaned out the window, blocking most of my view. "What are you *doing* here?"

Curious, I tried to peek around Amber without being totally obvious about it. I saw a big chili-red Harley with a twentysomething guy driving and a rail-thin woman perched behind him. They were both dressed in leather pants and jackets, with tiny black skullcaps strapped to their heads. The guy was a total Brad Pitt look-alike; the woman looked older, with slightly leathery skin, volumes of bleach-blond hair streaming out from under her cap, and major boobage displayed beneath her skin-tight, black leather vest.

The woman said to Amber, "I need that twenty back."

"Are you kidding? I already spent it on groceries."

The blonde teased her hair with her fingers while the guy revved his motor a couple times. "What do you got on you?

We need gas money. We're going to visit Grandma."

Amber sighed and dug into her pockets, then handed her a limp bill. The woman studied her over the rims of her wraparound sunglasses. "This all you got?"

Amber nodded.

"Okay, sweetie. Thanks. See you later."

"Are you coming home tonight?" Amber asked.

The blonde hesitated. Brad Pitt glanced over his shoulder at her impatiently. "Maybe. Depends how your grandma's doing. I'll call you." Then the two of them roared off, leaving only the stink of exhaust behind.

Amber didn't move. She stood there, bent over the counter, watching them.

"You okay?" I asked.

She spun around. "Yeah. Why?"

"Just wondered." Neither of us said anything for a little while. "Was that your mom?"

"Yeah."

The funny thing with Amber is she'll talk about her family and all their problems like it's a soap opera she tunes in to every day; she's totally open about it. That's part of why I feel like I know her so well. But when it really comes down to it, I've never been anywhere near her house, never met her parents. Actually, I can count on one hand the number of times she's even been to my house. It's like our friendship exists only at school and at work—like we're having a secret liaison or something.

"You upset?" I asked.

"Of course not." She started sweeping—something she never does. "I'm fine."

"You want an iced vanilla latte with whipped cream?"
She shot me a sideways glance. "Sure. Thanks, G."
"No problem."

Tuesday, June 17
Oneish (I think) P.M.

After work, I skated to the health food store for a sandwich,
then here to Geevana (Geena+Nirvana = Geevana). I love
hanging out here; it's so peaceful, and the view makes me feel
like Julie Andrews in *The Sound of Music*—it's all rolling hills
and grazing cows and miles and miles of vineyards. I discovered Geevana when I was eleven. Back then I was into anthro-
pomorphizing everything, so most of the trees and flowers
here have names. The three oaks sitting in a half circle in
the grassy meadow are Gloria, Maxwell, and Albert. There's
a wild iris that blooms every spring right in the center of the
oaks I call—somewhat predictably, yes—Iris. There's also a
large, lichen-covered rock sitting all by himself at the edge of
the meadow; his name is Hudson. I realize at sixteen this all
seems pretty childish, but I can't help thinking of them as distinct entities, even if I have outgrown such games. I don't talk
to them out loud or anything, but it is nice to sit on Albert's
low, mossy, muscular branch and feel like I'm among friends.

I don't dare describe Geevana's exact location here for fear
that my information-obsessed mother (she always thinks I'm
on drugs—should I be offended, or flattered?) will read this
and show up here unannounced, dressed as a federal agent.
With my luck, it'll be the one day I do decide to toke up or
drop acid.

I worked with Hero all morning. Not to be mean, but I assumed she'd have a much steeper learning curve—it's taken her like four days to steam milk properly. I figured a girl who already speaks fluent French and Italian, knows the names of every bone in the human body, and can play Chopin like— er, well, like Chopin, I guess—could whip up a macchiato in her sleep by now. Not the case. Apparently, being book-smart doesn't automatically make you barista-smart. I don't know, maybe it's because she's so distracted by Claudio these days. He started his internship at Monte Luna last week; if it's possible to stalk someone on your own property, she's definitely guilty.

By mid-morning I'd downed two hefty cappuccinos and believe me, I was feeling the buzz. Also, I was feeling some semi-seismic activity brewing below the belt. Amber and I have like twenty different euphemisms for this by now, some of them so gross I'm not sure they qualify as eu-phemistic at all, but the one we use in polite company is: "Somebody's knocking on my cellar door." This is occa-sionally upgraded to "Somebody's pounding on my cellar door."

Now, BMs in public places are awkward at best, but to make things worse, Triple Shot Betty's is too small for even the most claustrophobic of restrooms. Add to this our habitual caffeine-pounding, which tends to get things moving, and you've got yourself a human rights violation.

The good news: Pedal Pusher, the bike shop next door, lets us use their bathroom.

The bad news: Ben Bettaglia's dad *owns* Pedal Pusher, and Ben works there like *constantly*, and the bathroom there is *unisex,* meaning the chances of Ben *smelling* the less desirable aspects of my personality are—well—*catastrophically high.*

You see the quandary.

Today was really the first day Hero and I'd gotten in a groove since she's been back. I don't know if it's Amber or what, but something's been slightly off between us lately. I guess in Connecticut all her friends have million-dollar wardrobes and horses and vacations in the south of France, so hanging out with me again in Slow-noma is no doubt mind-numbingly boring. But today we finally got back in sync, and it was pretty much like old times. She was there steaming milk for the uptight housewife in the Hummer who always wants her double latte half-soy, half-milk, and half-caf (where do these people come from?!?). As soon as she drove off we burst into a fit of giggles because the chick had lipstick all over her teeth, and every time she'd flash us a smile we'd almost lose it.

That's when I felt it. The little knock-knock-knocking on my cellar door.

I've been known to skate two blocks to KFC for their bathroom, which is hardly ideal, but at least it's a little more anonymous than the Pedal Pusher. Today, though, the urge was going from a tiny tapping to a booming voice going, "Let me OUT!!!!" within a span of fifteen seconds. I would never make it to KFC. It was Pedal Pusher or the pants. So I bolted across the parking lot and raced into the bike shop, running smack into—yep—Ben Bettaglia. He was dressed in baggy Levi's and a pale green T-shirt that brought out the golden undertones of his olive skin. His dark eyes were shining at me, amused.

"What's up, Geena? You in a hurry or something?"

I squeezed my butt cheeks together and forced a casual pose. "No. Why do you ask?"

"You practically ran over me, is all."

"I . . . um . . ." I couldn't very well say I needed the toilet, or the situation would be painfully obvious. "I need some . . ." —I looked wildly around the store—"lubricant." As soon as the word was out of my mouth I regretted it.

Ben's smile spread across his face so slowly, it was like watching a big blob of butter melting on toast. "Lubricant?" he echoed.

"Yeah. For my . . . uh . . . gears."

"Do you cycle? I thought you only skated."

I shrugged. "I ride a bike now and then." A cramp in my lower abdomen was almost blinding me with pain, but I made myself breathe as Ben led me to a shelf of brightly colored bottles.

"Here they are," he said. We studied them together. "I like this one, but lots of guys use—"

"Ben? Can you ring this up?" Oh, thank God. Ben's dad was calling him from somewhere near the register.

"Sorry," he said. "I'll be back in a sec." His eyes are like melted chocolate, with these long black lashes that would be almost girly if he weren't so completely, 100 percent Guy. He let his gaze linger on my mouth for a quick beat before he turned around and jogged toward the register.

Finally! My moment of escape. I slunk as quickly as I could toward the bathroom, trying to avoid sudden, jarring movements that might accidentally jolt something loose. The minute I got the door locked behind me I dropped my shorts, sat on the pot, and let go.

Oh, yes. Praise the gods of indoor plumbing, I'm free at last.

After my initial rush of gratitude subsided, though, I started having little pangs of remorse. Did I make any noise? Had an incredibly loud *plop-plop* echoed throughout the store? Were Ben and Company out there now, trying not to laugh at the indelicate sounds reverberating off the walls?

Then a new, half-titillating, half-disturbing thought seized me: My butt was sitting where Ben's butt sat. Our bare skin touched the same surface. Not just our skin, but our butt-skin. My God, it was so intimate.

And then I realized: This is where Mr. Bettaglia's butt sat too.

Aack! I sprang from the seat and wiped quickly, pulled my shorts up, flushed, and washed my hands. I studied my reflection, scanning for fresh zits or sticking-out hair. I pulled my braids forward and tried a smile.

Suddenly there was a knock. On the door. Oh my God.

What if it was Ben? If I opened the door, he would be hit with a wave of nauseating foulness. What if it was Mr. Bettaglia—would he see right away from my expression that I'd been thinking about his butt-skin?

"Just a minute," I squeaked. Another glance at the mirror confirmed that I'd gone beet red. I waited for the sound of footsteps retreating, but there was only an expectant silence. I sniffed the air. To me, the smell wasn't totally putrid, but I guess everyone thinks that about their own foulness.

I resolved to open the door, scoot on out, and shut it before my most intimate odors could escape.

I opened it a crack, slipped out, and slammed it so loudly

that every customer in the store swiveled around to get a good stare. Ben was standing there, smirking like he could see everything: my desperate need to evacuate my bowels, my foolish ploy to cover up by pretending to shop for lubricant (*lubricant?*), my shameless butt-skin musings that connected me not only to him but to his father in a bizarre, semi-incestuous psychic love triangle.

"Hi Ben," I said. "How's it going?"

"Okay. Mind if I use the bathroom now?"

I leaned against the door, barring his entrance. "I wouldn't."

This time he smiled outright. He was *enjoying* this. I wanted to strangle him.

"No?" he said. "Why's that?"

"Because studies show that allowing at least five minutes to pass before you enter a small, enclosed space that someone else has recently . . . entered . . . or exited . . . can be an effective deterrent in the spread of germs. And bacteria. And stuff."

He let this sink in. I folded my arms in front of my chest. "In other words, just wait," I said.

"You're really a nutter, aren't you?" He said it like he'd always suspected as much, and was mildly gratified now that his hunch had been confirmed.

"What, you don't believe me?"

"I'll take my chances, okay? I've seriously got to go." He reached for the doorknob.

"Five minutes!" I pleaded. "That's all."

But it was too late. He was already wrenching the door open, and a fog of noxious gas swept over us. "Oh," he said, wrinkling his nose slightly. "Wow."

I was blushing so furiously, I thought for sure my cheeks would burst into flame. "I tried to warn you," I said, and with that I scurried toward the exit.

Just as I was escaping, I heard him calling out in a voice that choked back laughter. "Hey, Sloane! Aren't you forgetting your lubricant?"

Hardee-har-har. Just you wait, Ben Bettaglia. Two can play at *that* game.

Saturday, June 21

10:00 P.M.

Hero's gone insane.

She's been home two weeks, and already she's in love.

Please. When it comes to boys, I'm starting to think Amber's got the right idea: Use 'em and lose 'em. (Not that I've ever used anyone—or been used, unfortunately. Hell, I'm probably the only sophomore-nearly-junior on the planet who hasn't been to third base. Even second is questionable in my spotty, mortifyingly innocent sexual career. Todd Crossman put his hand on my boob once, but it was more like he was helpfully removing a piece of lint than feeling me up, and I think PJ dared him, so I'm not sure that counts.) Anyway, I'd much rather have Amber's winner-take-all attitude than Hero's starry-eyed listlessness. There are people in *comas* more responsive to external stimuli than Hero is right now.

We were at her house earlier today when I realized just how far gone she is. First off, we were in her room, which I have to say is even more annoyingly pink than I remember it.

In my opinion, it's more suited to a fairly slow second grader who is still enamored with Barbie than a sixteen-year-old—that's how ruffle-infested and cutesy it is. Ever since Aunt Kathy died, Hero's refused to change a single aspect of her childish sanctuary, even though it completely clashes with the rest of the house. Walking through that place—passing the enormous windows and vaulted, exposed beams of the living room, the stainless steel appliances and bamboo floor of the kitchen, up the great, cold sweep of marble stairs to the glass fountain and river-rock moat of the hallway, the last thing you're prepared for is pink ruffles. It's like stepping through the sleek world of the future and then stumbling into My Pretty Pony Playland circa 1995.

Bronwyn, our resident psychologist, says Hero won't redo her room (or change her hair, for that matter) because she suffers from arrested development brought on by severe trauma. She says that emotionally, Hero is still eight, which I have to admit makes some sense, since I may be the only sophomore-nearly-junior who's never made it past second base, but Hero is surely the only one who's never even gotten to first.

"Hey," I said, eyeing her pink satin comforter and matching shams. "Don't you think it's time for a new look in here?"

She didn't respond; she just lay there on her bed, staring dreamily out the window. If I'd had a camera right then, I would have captioned her photo *"Teenage Lobotomies: Are They Worth the Price?"* There was an arrangement of daisies in a crystal vase on the bedside table, and she absently selected one before slowly, deliberately yanking the petals off one at a time.

"What's up with you?" I asked, sitting next to her on the bed. "Why are you maiming that poor flower?"

She paused in her petal yanking long enough to look up at me. "Dad won't let me go out with Claudio."

"Aha. And this is surprising because . . . ?"

She kicked at one of the elaborately scrolled bedposts. "His rule is *so* stupid. Just because Bronwyn got burned doesn't mean I will."

Uncle Leo has a firm commandment: No dating until college. This law was passed on Moon Mountain when Bronwyn fell for Tad Wollner the summer she was sixteen. At first Uncle Leo was pretty open to the idea; the guy was an Eagle Scout—how bad could he be? Then she missed her period, and made the mistake of confiding in her father. It turned out to be a false alarm, but Uncle Leo was livid; he wasn't taking any more chances.

"I bet he'll let you guys have lunch or something," I said.

She looked incredulous. "Have lunch? Have *lunch*? I want to share the secrets of his soul for eternity, not a measly hour over french fries and shakes."

"Oh, come on." I laughed. "You just met him a couple weeks ago. Is he really all that?"

Her pretty little mouth went into indignant pout-mode. "You don't get it."

"What's that supposed to mean?"

She propped herself up on one elbow. "Love is completely foreign to you. I bet that journal you're always writing in has more about skateboards than guys."

"That's not true!"

"Oh yeah? Name the last guy you were into."

I thought for a second. "Ashton Kutcher?"

She nodded with an annoyingly wise expression. "I rest my case."

"No, I mean, I think lots of guys are cute. I just . . . can't really see myself with any of them. So far, anyway." I decided to change the subject. "If you really like Claudio, you'll just have to convince your dad that you're not going to get knocked up."

"It's hopeless. I've been trying for weeks." She got a puzzled look on her face and added, "Except he's not consistent. When John Jamieson called a few days ago—"

"Wait, John called you?"

"Yeah. He wanted me to go to the city with him . . . Something about his friend has a sailboat or—"

I let my jaw drop. "John 'the Man' Jamieson asked you out on the *yacht* and you didn't even tell me?"

"I never said yacht."

"Hero, that boat is legendary. Any girl at SVH would *kill* to set foot on it."

She furrowed her brow at me. "What are you talking about?"

"If you went to school here you'd totally get the magnitude of this. Last year John took Lexa Davis out there after junior prom—people were talking about it for weeks. She was an instant celeb. Until he broke up with her, that is."

Hero rolled her eyes. "You think I care about John and his Love Boat? I don't even like him. Apparently, though, you're not the only one around here who thinks he's God. Dad actually seemed impressed when I told him who'd called."

Outside, wheels crunched gravel as a car pulled up. She

jumped up and ran for the far window, tripping on the rug and nearly falling flat on her face, but recovering just in time. "He's here!"

I walked up behind her and looked over her shoulder. Uncle Leo was explaining something to Claudio and about five others. Behind them, the vineyards sloped out and down in a rolling carpet of lush green. The view was amazing from up here. Hero obviously saw nothing but Claudio.

She nibbled her bottom lip. "Isn't he unbelievably sexy?"

"Sure, he's cute I guess." I was noncommittal. It hardly mattered. I don't think she even knew I was there anymore.

"He has the most beautiful green eyes."

"Have you talked to him since the party?" I grabbed my board, plopped down on her pink rug, and started examining my trucks. I'd been meaning to replace the bearings. It just wasn't riding smoothly these days.

"Yeah, we've been IM-ing. Every night. For like five hours at a time." She did a giddy little dance. Then there was laughter outside and she suddenly ducked. "Oh God," she breathed, still crouching below the windowsill. "I think he saw me."

"So? It's your house. Can't you look out your window if you feel like it?"

"I'm so embarrassed," she said. "My hair was sticking out all over the place." She crawled over to me and collapsed onto the rug. "Do you think it's weird I'm so into him?"

"No, not at all. I mean, personally I see love as a social construct designed to enslave women in the institution of marriage—remember how Bronwyn explained all that?"

"Ohh!" Hero flopped violently onto her back. "I don't *care* what Bronwyn says about it."

"Not that you would even think about *marrying* Claudio—
I mean, obviously. You should just have a hot summer fling,
get some sexual experience in, and then sail away to boarding
school before the relationship gets boring and confining and
your identities get blurred. Sounds perfect."

She stared at the ceiling. "You don't understand, Geebs.
This is serious. I have to be with him or I'm going to die."

"Can anyone say *drama queen*?"

She ignored me. "You have to help me convince Dad."

"Yeah, right." I was still concentrating on my trucks. "You
got any WD-40?"

"Are you even listening to me?"

I looked at her, surprised. "'Course I am."

"I'm totally serious. You have to help me convince Dad
that Claudio's not like other guys."

"I don't even know Claudio!"

"So?"

I spun the wheels on my board aimlessly with one hand.
"So what can *I* do?"

"Please?" she begged. "Dad respects you. He might listen."

I shrugged. "Okay, I'll try, but I'm not making any
promises."

She sat up on her knees, leaned over, and hugged me. "Oh,
thank you, thank you, thank you!"

"Go on," I said, nodding at the daisy that was still dangling,
half-mutilated, from her fingers. "Finish dismembering it
already. The suspense is killing me."

She pulled the remaining five petals off slowly, deliberately,
whispering to herself. When she got to the last one, a radiant
smile lit up her face. "He loves me."

We decided our chances were best with Uncle Leo right after lunch. We enlisted Elodie's help, who, being French, was eager to conspire in matters of romance. She uncorked Leo's favorite Petite Syrah, and we kept refilling his glass when he wasn't looking. We ate out on the back patio, where the view of the vineyards, the smell of lavender, and the trellises overrun with wisteria always put him in a good mood. Elodie cooked up a delicious meal of grilled ahi, seared asparagus, and fresh tomatoes with basil and mozzarella. Uncle Leo loves a long, indulgent lunch alfresco. It's one of his favorite pastimes. The afternoon was particularly beautiful, with big bumblebees dipping drunkenly in and out of tiger lilies and the Tuscan fountain gurgling a bright little rhythm nearby. Luck was on our side.

Uncle Leo took a long, satisfied draw from his wineglass and leaned back in the teak lawn chair. He closed his eyes, letting the sun warm his face. Leo's older than my dad by three years, but they look more like ten years apart. His face is pinker than Dad's, his hair is thinner, and his jaw is covered with salt-and-pepper stubble. There's a certain distinguished charm to him, and I know for a fact that he's considered quite a catch around town. He took off his spectacles, studied them for smudges, and set them next to his wineglass. Hero kicked me under the table.

"So," I said, spearing another bite of mozzarella. "Uncle Leo. What do you think of your new intern Claudio?"

His eyes popped open. "Are you going to start on me now too?"

Hero's head slumped forward in frustration.

"He seems like a really nice guy." I tried to infuse each word with innocence and objectivity.

"You know my rule, Geena. No boys until college."

Elodie came out then carrying a tray filled with crème brulée, crystal glasses, and a chilled bottle of Gewürztraminer. She raised her eyebrows like *Did it work yet?* and I shook my head.

Uncle Leo spun around and barked at Elodie, "Are you in on this? My God, it's a conspiracy."

Elodie just made a very French sound (something like "boef"), set down the dishes of crème brulée, poured the dessert wine into fresh glasses for all three of us, and disappeared. For some reason, Uncle Leo never minds if we have a little wine—as long as it's top quality (i.e., his). Crack open a Coors, and he's ready to put us in rehab, but a finely crafted Gewürztraminer in the right stemware is a totally different thing.

After he'd finished half his dessert, I decided to try again. "You know, in many ways, Italian boys are more sophisticated than Americans."

"All these punks are after one thing."

Hero made a breathy, indignant sound. "Maybe he *likes* me—did you ever think of that?"

I shot her a *stay out of it* warning glance and she shut up.

"And anyway, Uncle Leo," I persisted, "Hero's smart. She's got values. It's not like she'll just hop into bed with him."

He almost spit out his Gewürztraminer at that.

"And you can totally trust Claudio. I mean, you trust him with your wine, right?"

"He's an intern—I'm not exactly handing him the business."

"Yes, but you must trust him a little, if you hired him."

"It's not that I've got anything against Claudio—or John Jamieson, for that matter. Did Hero tell you he asked her out?"

I couldn't help but notice the proud little grin as he said this. John had that effect on people. Even old guys like Leo wanted to be associated with him.

"I'm not interested in John!" Hero blurted out.

"Leo, come on, you were sixteen once." I looked him in the eyes. "Didn't you ever fall in love?"

"Look, Geena, if it was you, I'd be fine with it." He wiped his mouth with his napkin and studiously ignored Hero's slack-jawed indignation. "Really. You're level-headed, you know what insufferable pricks they can be. But Hero's full of romantic ideas. I don't want to see her get hurt."

"Dad! That is so unfair."

He reached over and touched her hand with surprising tenderness. "Honey, I'm your father. It's my job to be unfair." He leaned back in his chair and considered me with a sigh. "Maybe we can reach a compromise."

Hero's eyes sparkled. "Really? Like what?"

"So far, he seems like a decent guy. But then, I thought Bronwyn's Eagle Scout was decent too, and look what happened with that."

"God," Hero moaned, "why do I have to pay for Bronwyn's mistakes?"

I kicked Hero gently under the table. Uncle Leo was leading up to something, and it sounded like he was getting ready to cave—at least a little. "So, what's the compromise?" I asked.

"Here's what I propose," he said, turning to Hero. "You

can go out with Claudio, on a probationary basis. And only if Geena tags along."

We both just stared at him. Hero spoke first. "Why would that help?"

"Because she's your cousin, she's a straight-shooter, and she's just enough of a hard-ass to talk you out of doing anything stupid."

I shook my head. "I don't know . . . I'm not a babysitter."

He tossed back the rest of his Gewürztraminer and licked his spoon. "That's my offer. Take it or leave it."

"We'll take it," Hero cried, then grabbed my hand and pulled me away from the table before I could protest further.

Monday, June 23
6:10 P.M.

Hero hasn't stopped hounding me since Saturday. I can't believe Uncle Leo did this. He knew I'd hate the idea, but he also knew it would get Hero off his back and onto mine. What tyranny!

Thursday, June 26
4:00 A.M.

Mom came into the kitchen, where I was nursing a cup of chamomile tea (hideous, by the way—I suspect it "soothes" by knocking you out with its indescribably sucky flavor— tastes like compost). She was all squinty-eyed in her huge, baggy T-shirt, wondering what in the world I was doing up at three in the morning.

"I'm having a moral dilemma," I said.

"What kind of moral dilemma?"

I explained the situation with Hero and Claudio and Uncle Leo. When I was done, she put an arm around my shoulder, and her skin felt cool against mine. "I see. That is a tough one, isn't it?"

"I mean, why should *I* be their chaperone? It's embarrassing."

She tilted her head away from me and studied my profile. "I guess it means Uncle Leo trusts you."

"Yeah, to be the sex police! How flattering is that?"

She chuckled. "Well, you should listen to your feelings."

This is a tiny taste of my mother's patchouli-scented past—this "follow your feelings" bit. Mostly she's annoyingly logical, but I happen to know that before she became an English professor, she was a full-time hippie. I know this because one time she got a little wasted on red wine and burdened me with the following secrets:

A) I was conceived in a tepee
B) While she and Dad were tripping on acid
C) His nickname for her was Ruby Tuesday

Oh, horror! Why does my brain refuse to store useful information, like, say, bus schedules or algebra formulas, but when it gets its claws into a hateful picture like my parents doing it in a tepee with long, greasy hair, and my father crying out "Ruby Tuesday!" it simply will not let go?

"So you think I shouldn't do it, then?" I asked, trying to block out this grotesque image.

"I'm just saying you should trust your intuition. You want a little of Uncle Leo's Merlot?" She poured herself a glass. "I've found it's a more effective soporific than chamomile."

"Sure." I took the glass from her and sipped. "What's up? You don't want to drink alone?"

"No, I'm trying to get you to stop banging around in the kitchen so I can get some sleep."

"Selfish, selfish," I said, smiling. "I should have known."

We sipped our wine in silence for a few minutes. When she'd finished hers, she stood up and carried her empty glass to the sink. "How are you doing with your dad gone?"

Bit of a non sequitur, but whatever. It was after three; I guess I had to cut her some slack. "Um . . . I guess I'm fine."

She turned the tap on and washed her glass out. "You miss him?"

"Sometimes." I hesitated. "You?"

She shrugged, her back still to me. "Occasionally." She turned and looked at me, leaning against the counter. "Well, don't stay up too late."

I looked out the window. "Yeah, okay."

The weird thing is, I don't really miss Dad. Not actively, anyway. I mean, he wasn't around all that much, even when he was here. He worked a lot. He's preoccupied by nature.

Still, it would be nice if he called more than once a month.

Friday, June 27
1:00 P.M.

I was skating to work today when I noticed a truck slowing down behind me. When I heard a heavy bass beat and an Ice-T riff pouring out the windows, I knew exactly who it was.

"Hey, Geena. Hold on."

PJ was idling behind me in his electric blue truck. He still had the music blaring so loud it made my chest thrum. I skated over to his window, shielding my eyes against the brilliance of his paint job in the sun. He did me the honor of turning down the music.

"Cool shoes." He nodded at my Pumas.

"Thanks."

"Hey, does Hero have a boyfriend?"

"No, why?"

"Here's the deal," he said, leaning a little out his window. "Don't tell anyone, but you know Claudio?"

I nodded, rolling my board with one foot.

"He's so into her. The dude's obsessed. Either we hook them up, or I'm going to kill him, because he's driving me nuts."

"I think the feeling's pretty mutual."

He flashed his crooked grin and turned his music back up. "Cool. I'll tell him to go for it."

I added, "Except her dad's got this rule: No dating until college."

"Oh, yeah?" He backed down the volume again.

"She can only go out with Claudio"—I kicked my board vertical and rested it on one shoe—"if I go too."

"No, really?" He laughed. "That's pretty funny. What are you, the virgin patrol or something?"

I cringed. "Shut up."

"Well, it wouldn't be so bad if you got something out of it, right? Just take her out with someone you're into—like a double date." I think he could tell from my expression there weren't big lightbulbs flashing in my brain. He gave me a playful shove. "I'd ask you out, but my girlfriend wouldn't like it." Then he got a mischievous sparkle in his eye. "My homie Ben's single, you know."

"Don't even think about it," I warned. "I'll date Ben Bettaglia when hell freezes over."

He laughed. "Okay, okay. I'll tell Claudio the deal. Good news and bad news, I guess." Then he winked at me, cranked the music back up, and revved his engine. "You never know, Skater Chick. Hell might freeze over soon."

"Ha, ha," I said.

He drove away, and I ignored the uneasy feeling his last comment left in the pit of my stomach.

11:00 P.M.

Hero and I got to work at the same time. We took over for Lizzie and Sarah (aka the Sandalwood Sisters—they both have straw-colored dreads down past their shoulders, pierced tongues, and they reek of sandalwood. Thank God I never have to work with them or I would choke on that stench. Though I bet they're really nice people, once you get past the odor issues).

"So," I said to Hero when they were gone. "I ran into PJ on my way here."

"Yeah?"

"He says Claudio really likes you."

She turned to me, suddenly excited. "He did? What *exactly* did he say? Tell me everything!"

Just then Amber burst in. She was wearing a bikini top with a mesh tank thrown over it, Daisy Dukes, and huge red sunglasses. "Oh my God, I am so bored," she announced. "I could scream."

I was surprised to see her. "You don't work today, do you?"

"No. My stupid mom was supposed to lend me the car, but then her boy toy called and *bam*—she was out of there. Not having your own ride totally sucks." She flung her sunglasses and sketchbook onto the counter.

Hero turned her attention back to me pointedly. "Anyway, Geebs, tell me—come on!"

Amber looked a little miffed at Hero's lack of interest in her car deprivation, but she started making herself an iced vanilla latte without lashing out. The place was so small we could barely move with the three of us in there.

"I believe the exact phrase he used was 'the dude's obsessed.'"

I don't know what swept over us—it was like Hero and I were momentarily possessed by the ghosts of crazed Beatle groupies. We found ourselves jumping up and down, squealing at the top of our lungs.

Of course, right then our boss drove up in his Mini Cooper, wearing a serious sourpuss frown. "Girls, girls, girls," he scolded. "What is this, cheerleading practice?" Then he softened a bit. Lane likes to act tough, but he's a sucker for my cappies. "Geena, make me a double cappuccino, will you?" He handed me his high-tech to-go mug that matched the green of his Mini perfectly.

"Sure thing," I said.

Hero glowed with joy while I made Lane his cappuccino. I whispered that she should clean something, since Lane likes us to look busy at all times. She stood there beaming into the sink, swishing a sponge around in slow motion like she was doing Tai Chi.

As soon as Lane drove off with his cappy, she dropped the sponge and said, "Oh my God. I can't believe PJ used the word *obsessed!*" She stood on her tiptoes and let out a high-pitched squeal.

Amber broke the spell. "Yeah, cool. Geena said you wanted to get it on with that guy. That's awesome."

I glared at Amber. "I didn't—I—Amber!"

The beatific smile slid right off Hero's face. She turned to me with accusing eyes. "You said I wanted to 'get it on with him'?"

I looked back and forth between the two of them. "I might have mentioned that you think he's cute, but I never said 'get it on with him.'"

"My bad," Amber said. "Wrong choice of words. Obviously you're hot for him, though."

Hero's nostrils flared. "Whatever's developing between Claudio and me is really none of your business."

"Oh, well, excuse me, but wasn't it you who was shattering my eardrum two seconds ago? If you don't want people to know, don't run around screaming at the top of your lungs."

I was so not in the mood for this. "Amber, be cool, okay?"

"Me? Why do you always side with her?"

I put a hand over my eyes. "I don't."

"I'm out of here." Amber grabbed her sunglasses and sketchbook from the counter and slammed out the door.

After she left, Hero stood there glaring at me.

"What? You never said it was a secret."

"I'm taking my break," she said, and for the second time in five minutes, I had a door slammed in my face.

Hero was gone for what seemed like an hour. In the meantime, Ben Bettaglia drove up in his ancient Volvo station wagon with Claudio riding shotgun. Claudio ordered a large iced coffee and Ben ordered a milkshake. I couldn't believe it. Hero was totally missing out by pouting. Probably she'd blame me for this too.

"So, uh, doesn't your cousin work here?" Ben asked.

I nodded, hating everyone for putting me in the middle of things and making me look like the beeatch. "Yeah, she's on break right now. What's it to you?"

"Having a bad day?" he asked.

I put a hand on my hip and yelled over the blender, "Why do you say that?"

"You just seem kind of . . . grumpy."

"What, like I'm supposed to smile all the time?" I glanced at Claudio in the passenger seat. He was grinning broadly and nodding, but I could see it was more from a lack of fluency than any comment on my moodiness, so I ignored him and turned my attention back to Ben. "Do you know, by the way, that espresso milkshakes are the biggest pain in the butt to make out of everything on our menu?"

He eyed the large wooden sign that listed our offerings. "Harder than the double chocolate cheesecake?"

"Yeah, duh, all we have to do is slice that."

"Harder than the tropical island smoothie with bee pollen?"

"Yes! I have to scoop the ice cream, which is hard as a rock, and brew the espresso, then hope it doesn't melt the ice cream too quickly. It's a total drag."

Ben appeared to consider this. He turned to Claudio. "Did you realize there was such a strong sentiment against milkshake lovers?"

Claudio looked from him to me and back again, still beaming and nodding.

Ben shrugged. "I guess Claudio knew about this too. It's a conspiracy." He leaned toward me as if to share a secret. "Ever get that lubricant, Sloane?"

I fixed my gaze on Claudio and ignored the cretin beside him. "Claudio, don't you find it tragic the way some guys fixate on childish double entendres and repeat them ad nauseam like toddlers who have just discovered the thrill of farting noises?"

Claudio just blinked at me.

Seeing that I had the advantage, I pressed my point. "Personally, I think it's a pathetic attempt to connect with members of the opposite sex. In lieu of any actual social skills or maturity, boys often resort to infantile tactics in a desperate plea for attention."

Just then, Hero stormed back in, and froze when she saw Claudio.

"It is Hero!" he called to her as I was handing them their

drinks. "Hello! *Bon giorno!*" His smile was so huge, I thought his face might crack in half.

While Ben handed me a ten and I got change, Hero stood at the window, speaking in halting Italian with Claudio. I could tell she was nervous, but after a few phrases she warmed up, and then they were off, bantering in that musical tongue, laughing like children.

Ben said to me, "Look, I'm sorry, but I like milkshakes. What can I say?"

"You like milkshakes, I like lubricant," I told him. "There's someone behind you. Better go."

He handed me a dollar. "For your trouble," he said.

"Thanks," I said flatly.

I waited on the customers who had lined up behind Ben, then turned to face my cousin. She tried the silent treatment for about ten seconds, but she was so happy after talking to Claudio, it was no use. "Okay, look. You messed up. Fine. I'll forgive you."

"You're so generous," I said.

She grinned. "As well as brilliant. I have a really stellar idea."

Uh-oh. I had a feeling I knew what was coming. "What?"

"How would it be if you, me, Claudio, and Ben all went out sometime?"

"Not."

"Come on, you guys have been flirting since we were in preschool. Plus he's totally hit it off with Claudio. They go everywhere together."

I stared at her, aghast. "I've never *flirted* with Ben Bettaglia in my life."

"What do you call ten years of practical jokes, play-fighting, and in-class debates where you always take opposite sides? You two are like the classic couple-who-won't-admit-you're-a-couple."

My mouth hung open. "That's insane. Ben and I are . . . barely even friends. In fact, we're archenemies." I squinted at her. "You're trying to con me into liking Ben so you can get with Claudio."

"Not at all. I just want you to have a little summer fun, is all."

"Uh-huh," I said. "You, me, Ben, and Loverboy."

"Exactly!" She slapped my arm. "Now you're getting it."

"Look, I'm not going to pretend I like some guy just so you can have your precious fling." She looked hurt, so I softened my tone. "I was really hoping to spend time with you and Amber this summer. You know, girl time."

"Girl time with *Amber*?" she sneered. "Joy. Like getting your nails done with Cruella DeVille."

"She's cool when you get to know her."

She went back to her *I've got a really good idea* face. "Okay, listen, how's this? If I make an effort with Amber, will you make an effort with Ben?"

"It's different. I'm not suggesting you *date* Amber!" I protested.

"Just be friendly. That's all I'm asking."

I shrugged. "I'm always friendly."

She made a sarcastic sound.

"What?"

"Nothing," she said.

Saturday, June 28

2:40 P.M.

When I went to Moon Mountain today, I found Hero in her room. She was glued to the window, gripping a pair of binoculars. I said her name and she jumped halfway to the ceiling. "Don't *do* that," she scolded.

"Hero, you're stalking the poor guy."

She looked indignant. "I am not! It's only stalking if the person wants you to stop, right?"

"I guess . . ."

She held out the binoculars, eyes shining. "Look!"

I took them from her and trained them on the tiny figure standing amidst the rows and rows of grapes. He was holding a piece of ragged cardboard with the words *Hero is Beutiful* scrawled in dark ink.

"Cute," I said. "Too bad he couldn't spell-check that."

"Ha, ha," she said.

Friday, July 4

(i.e., time to celebrate our freedoms as Americans by eating hormone-laden farm animals and blowing shit up)

6:00 P.M.

Today my dad showed up with his girlfriend, Jen. I know it's a cliché to hate your dad's girlfriend, and for that reason alone I'd like to give her a chance, but let's face it: Bimbohontas doesn't give me much to work with. Bronwyn told me once that the reason I hate her so much is because of this weird thing Freud was all into called the Electra Complex, which basically means I'm attracted to my dad and therefore view his girlfriend as a rival. Usually, I respect what Bronwyn says, but that time I had to just cover my ears and go "La-la-la" because really, how disgusting can you get?

Originally, I was supposed to go camping with Dad this weekend in Santa Cruz, but that got changed because he had a huge project at work. As I waited for him and Bimbotissima to drive up, I tried not to be mad that our long weekend in Santa Cruz had been downgraded to an afternoon barbeque among geriatrics. This is the third time he's changed plans at the last minute since he moved to L.A., and it's getting on my nerves. They were a couple minutes late and Mom kept looking at her watch, trying to be all casual about it, but driving me batty anyway. She was picking lint off the couch and wiping crumbs that weren't there and generally being a really super-annoying mom-on-the-verge-of-a-nervous-breakdown type. I've already learned from experience not to snap at her in this situation, though, because it'll escalate instantly into a fight, and we won't be able to stop even when Dad gets here, which will inspire Count Bimbula to stand there with a smug *Aren't you glad you've escaped all this?* expression on her face, and I'll want to slap her.

As I was waiting, I saw Ben Bettaglia ride by on his bike. Ben's a serious cyclist, so usually when I see him out riding he's all bent over, drenched with sweat, scowling at the road, his legs pumping so fast they're just a blur. Today, though, he wasn't even touching the handlebars, he was just gliding

along at a snail's pace, looking around like, "La-di-dah, just
out for a little spin, don't mind me."

I decided it was time to go outside and look for our dog.
Tragically, our dog is nonexistent, since my mother is extremely doggist and refuses to give in, saying I can have a
fish if I promise to take care of it, but obviously I don't want
a fish (otherwise why would I beg for a dog? Hello!). Fortu-
nately, Ben couldn't possibly know any of this, so searching
for our nonexistent dog struck me as the ideal ploy to find
out what he was doing cruising past our house.

After checking for nose-shine in the mirror, I ventured
outside, casually calling, "Auggie! Auggie!" at the top of
my lungs. I decided long ago that if I ever do get a dog I'll
name him Auggie (short for Augustus) so that, in moments
of particularly affectionate bonding between said canine and
myself, I can cry, "Auggie doggie!"

After a few minutes of this, Ben slowed to a stop at the edge
of our lawn. "Hey, Sloane," he said. "You lose someone?"

I shielded my eyes against the sun and feigned surprise at
the sight of him (Academy Awards, here I come). "Ben! Didn't
see you there. You didn't notice a dog out here, did you?"

He looked around. "Nope. What kind?"

"Oh, you know, just a . . . dog. Kind of . . . golden . . . with
spots."

"Is he a golden retriever?"

I didn't want to describe a dog that looked even remotely
like any in our neighborhood—that might lead to an
embarrassing misunderstanding. "No, he's part Australian
shepard, part Great Dane, part poodle. He's got a reddish
head with white paws and a black tail."

"I thought you said he was golden with spots?"

"Right," I said, thinking fast. "His body's golden with spots, but the rest of him is . . . multicolored."

He smirked. "Where'd you get this thing, a genetic lab?"

I stiffened. Ben Bettaglia had no right to insult Auggie doggie, even if he didn't exist. "He's a great dog."

"I'm sure he is," he said, holding up a hand in the *No offense, back off* gesture. For some reason that made me mad.

"Why, what do *you* have? A purebred something-or-other?"

He shrugged. "A Chihuahua."

A high-pitched trumpet of laughter escaped from me before I could cover my mouth with one hand.

"What?" he demanded. "Mr. Peabody's the coolest—"

"*Mr. Peabody?* Does he wear little glasses?"

"Very funny. What's *your* dog's name?" When I told him, he started looking around the yard calling, "Auggie! Come here, Augster!" very loudly.

Of course, Dad and Madame Bimbette chose this particular moment to drive up. Ben kept calling for Auggie as Dad got out of the car. I wanted to run into Dad's arms for a big, crushing bear hug, but I thought that would look pretty childish to Ben, so I just waved. The bimbocile extended her incredibly long legs from Dad's Porsche, and I saw Ben do a double take.

Dad walked over and wrapped one arm around me in a kind of half hug, which seemed like a decent compromise. "Who's Auggie?" he asked. No hi, no anything, just honing right in on my lie-in-progress.

"Um . . ." I offered.

Ben nodded to my father in a manly, businesslike way and

said, "Hello, Mr. Sloane. I was just helping Geena look for her dog."

Dad's eyebrows jerked in surprise. "Her dog? Did you get a dog, Geena?"

Lightbulb-style brain wave: Dad doesn't live here, how does he know if I have a dog or not? Later I can just say it got run over, or—I don't know, get one, maybe. "Yeah. He's, um, lost, though. Can't find him."

Dad looked skeptical. "Mom gave in?"

I gave him my Screen Actors Guild–worthy Innocent Look, infused with slight undertones of *Not now, Dad*. "Yeah. Anyway, I'm sure he's around here somewhere." I turned to Ben. "Thanks for your help."

"Everything okay, babe?" Dad called toward the car. I looked over to see Bimborama's butt sticking straight up in the air as she dug around for something in the Porsche. There was no reply.

"We have to go to some stupid barbeque," I mumbled to Ben. "I guess I'll see you later."

"Hey, maybe your 'friend' Ben would like to come along." My dad injected the word *friend* with tiny, barely audible quotes, and I could feel myself going beet red.

"Oh, uh, thanks Mr. Sloane," Ben said, "but—"

The bimbomaniac came striding up to us then, looking all dewy-fresh and inhumanly tall, stopping Ben mid-sentence. She was wearing a floppy straw hat and a white spaghetti-strapped sundress that showed off her shiny brown shoulders and her ample cleavage. I've never actually worked up the nerve to ask my dad about the bimbocita's age, but I'm guessing she's either a Botox miracle or she's a long way from thirty. As much as it pains me to admit it, the woman's a dead ringer for Julia Roberts circa *Pretty Woman*. If I were Mom, I'd seek vengeance.

She flashed her big white teeth at us, saying, "Hey *Geena*," then turning to Ben with, "Hi there, I'm Jen. Are you Geena's *boyfriend?*"

Oh, God, I thought. *I wonder if they still have nunneries.* All the blood surging to my face at once was giving me an ice cream headache.

"We—um—we were just looking for Auggie," Ben told her, obviously flustered.

Bimbo-san looked puzzled. "Auggie?"

"Geena's dog," Dad offered.

Would this never end? Either we were calling Ben my boyfriend or we were dwelling on Auggie doggie, who, through absolutely no fault of my own, didn't exist.

"Anyway," I said, giving Dad a meaningful look, "Shouldn't we get going? Aren't Bim—*Jen's* parents expecting us?"

Dad looked at his watch. "Not for a little—" But then Mom walked out to greet us and he mumbled, "Yeah, maybe we should."

It's not that my parents can't be civil to each other. It's just that their heightened state of niceness is exhausting for everyone involved, like smiling for a picture when the photographer is taking way too long.

"Hello, Jen," Mom called, friendly as could be. "Dan." She gave my father a quick, impersonal kiss on the cheek. The tepee scene flashed through my brain like a pornographic film strip spliced into a Disney movie; thank God it disappeared as soon as I blinked.

Mom was wearing her new red halter top, startling red lipstick, and bright white wide-legged slacks. She'd blown her auburn hair dry and had even applied some mascara. She was no Julia Roberts, but I thought she looked elegant, in her own way, and I was torn between being proud of her for making an effort and feeling sorry for her, dressing up like that just so she could wave good-bye without looking like a slob.

"Hi, Mrs. Sloane," Ben said.

"Hi, Ben. Did you come by to see Geena?" Mom gushed.

Soon I'd be discovered, imaginary dog and all. I had to act fast. "Dad, we better get going." I started moving toward Dad's Porsche in an urgent, *Let's get out of here* fashion. Dad seemed willing enough to follow my lead, but the Bimbomeister lingered.

"Sure you don't want to come, Ben? It's a *pretty* drive." I turned to see her beaming at him enticingly.

"Oh, no, thanks," he said. "My parents would wonder . . ."

She whipped a tiny silver cell phone from her purse. "You could call them. I'd *explain*."

I stood there, flabbergasted. My dad's girlfriend was flirting with my not-even-boyfriend. I'd be on Jerry Springer any minute now.

"No, really," Ben said. "I was just helping Geena look for her dog."

He'd said it. My life was over.

Mom blinked. "Sorry, I thought you just said you were helping Geena look for her *dog*."

Ben nodded. "Yeah. Auggie."

My mother's head swiveled slowly in my direction. "Geena doesn't have a dog," she said, eyeing me.

I laughed nervously. "Of course I don't! I was just . . . joking."

Now everyone's heads turned in my direction.

"I thought that was kind of odd," Dad observed, and then, to Mom, "I didn't think you'd give in."

Mom got a flinty look in her eye. "It's not a matter of 'giving in,' Dan. We're just not set up for a dog."

"Oh, you could have a small one and you know it," he said.

"That's not true. Don't make me look like the bad guy."

"Come on, Joan, you hate dogs."

"I don't hate dogs! I put up with your smelly little cocker spaniel for seven years."

They were off, then, bickering over the ancient dog issue like they'd never even gotten divorced. Ms. Bimbonstein hovered nearby, looking like she wanted to contribute but didn't quite know how.

Ben walked over to me, his hands in his pockets. "So you don't have a dog?"

"I was just playing around," I said, barely able to look him in the eye. "You know, like a July Fourth joke."

He nodded. "Okay, Sloane, if you say so."

"Shut up." I was so mortified, it was the only thing I could think of to say.

"Lubricant, imaginary dogs—what'll you think of next?"

"You're just mad 'cause you fell for it." I folded my arms and leaned on one hip, hoping I looked defiant instead of lame.

"Yeah," he said, not looking convinced. "I'm real mad about that. Later on, Sloane." Then he got on his bike and rode away, calling, "Here, Auggie! Auggie!" all the way down the street.

Still Eat-Dead-Things-and-Blow-Shit-Up Day
11:50 P.M.

Luckily, we got back from the Geriatric Meat Fest in time for me to skate down to the high school for the fireworks. On the way there, some little punks on boards—probably freshmen—stopped and stared as I bombed a hill. When I got to the bottom one of them yelled, "Show us your tits, Skater Girl!" I did an ollie instead and flipped them off when I hit the ground.

Skating always makes me feel a little more right with the world. I got my first board when I was thirteen, around the time when my parents started fighting a lot. There was a practical element; I needed a way around town, and bikes just didn't appeal to me aesthetically. But there was something deeper too. I was shopping for an identity. I refused to go in for sparkly eye shadow and bubble-gum pink lip gloss, like most girls. In my mind, that was the fast track to misery. The hereditary Uniboob was just starting to come in, so already men were looking at me—not just boys, but father types, which creeped me out. I guess it's not totally logical, but skating made me feel tough, invincible. Like I could defy everything: lip gloss, heartache, gravity.

I got to the high school just as the first round of fireworks was exploding against the dusky blue sky. There was barely enough light left for me to see people's faces. I wandered about, feeling conspicuously alone, looking for Amber or Hero.

I spotted Amber sitting with PJ, Claudio, and Ben on a big plaid blanket. She was wearing a bright orange tube top and a short denim skirt; she looked like a night-blooming orchid in the middle of their white T-shirts and faded jeans. I was kind of torn—after the Auggie doggie incident, I wasn't exactly dying to interact with Ben, so I didn't head straight over. That's when I felt delicate little fingers squeezing my arm, and I turned to see Hero beaming at me.

"You're here! Finally!" She was wearing a cute yellow sundress with one of her trademark, barely-there cardigans, apparently knit out of dandelion fluff. Next to her, my none-too-clean cutoffs and Sector Nine T-shirt probably made me look like a big-boobed boy.

"Yeah, sorry I'm late. Had to hang with Dad and his midlife-crisis-arm-charm. I swear to God, if she becomes my stepmother I'll move to Uzbekistan and join a cult."

She kept glancing furtively over my shoulder, and it didn't take a genius to figure out why she was so happy to see me. Now she'd have an excuse to go sit with her dreamboat.

I turned and looked pointedly at their blanket. "Ohh, you want to go over there?"

She put on an absurdly innocent face. "No, why?"

"Oh, I don't know—you can't stop looking at them for three minutes—just thought you might want to see what they're up to."

She smoothed her hair. "Well, okay, if you feel like it."

I'd have to face Ben at some point, imaginary dog and all; it might as well be sooner rather than later. We started walking toward them and were only about four feet away when I was enveloped in a cloud of Calvin Klein cologne.

John Jamieson was suddenly in our path, blocking our way with loose-limbed confidence.

"Hey girls." He held a can of Mountain Dew in one hand, and he raised it slightly in greeting. In the weeks since graduation, his tan had deepened to a perfect golden brown, and his eyes looked even bluer than usual. "It's my two favorite heartbreakers: Skater Girl and the pretty little pixie Hero."

"Hi, John." I still wasn't used to such a celebrity addressing me directly, and I tried not to look too dazzled.

"Hey, John," Hero echoed, though she sounded more annoyed than impressed.

"Missed you out on the water the other day," he told Hero. "I really think you'd like sailing. There's nothing like the feeling of wind in your hair, watching the sun go down behind the Golden Gate. It's amazing."

Hero offered a polite smile, then snuck a furtive glance over his shoulder. "Yeah, well, too bad I couldn't go."

John's look darkened as he glanced back and saw Claudio on the picnic blanket. He didn't let his irritation show for long, though; he covered it with a smile so luminous, I could see why he got cast in that Aquafresh ad last year. "Maybe I should swing by sometime and talk to your dad? It's criminal he keeps you locked up like that."

Hero shook her head. "I wouldn't bother. He's pretty set in his ways."

"Worth a try, though, huh?" John's smile looked slightly strained now.

"Actually, no." Hero didn't even try to hide her impatience. "It's not."

I was shocked. Nobody talks to John like that—I mean,

he's John Jamieson, for God's sake! He *invented* charisma. Most girls would give their right breast just for a three-minute flirt-session with the guy, and Hero was treating him like an annoying freshman with food caught in his braces.

"Hey guys." Amber sauntered up to us then, her hips swaying. "Happy Fourth." She raised a paper bag in a toast, clinked it soundlessly against John's Mountain Dew, and took a swig.

"'Sup, Ginger?" He slung an arm around Amber's shoulder casually and she looked up at him with starry-eyed delight.

"When do you head off to Yale?" She sounded so unlike herself—perky and alert, like she was auditioning for something. She even twisted a strand of hair around her finger. *Gag.*

"Probably leave in August." He offered her a lazy grin. "You gonna miss me?"

"Duh!"

Was it my imagination, or was John sneaking sideways glances at Hero? She raised an eyebrow as she watched them, but said nothing.

A truck screeched to a stop at the entrance to the field, and we all turned to look. It was Corky's Ford Explorer, and its tinted windows rattled with bass. There were at least three other senior guys piled in back. Corky leaned his head out the window and bellowed over the music, "Yo, Jamieson! Come on, we're late!"

John started to back away from us. "Party at Salmon Creek if you feel like it. There's a bottle of Jack reserved for you Bettys, okay?"

His friends started chanting at him, "You the Man, you, you the Man!"

He flipped them off, but loped over to them and jumped in the Ford before it peeled out and roared away.

"You guys want to go?" Amber followed the Explorer with her eyes as it disappeared around the corner.

"Naw." I knew Hero couldn't, and even if she could, it sounded like a disaster in the making. Amber was obviously not 100 percent over John, and he was starting to seem a little too interested in Hero. None of this bode well for my girly summer aspirations.

Amber looked at Hero, one hand on her hip. "So what's the deal with you and John?"

Hero addressed her shoes. "There is no deal."

"A word of advice," Amber said, her green eyes boring into Hero's. "He's impossible to resist, and a pain in the ass to get over."

"I'm not even remotely interested, so don't worry." Hero sniffed and stared off into the distance.

Okay, this was leading us nowhere sisterly, I could see that right away. Eager to distract them both, I led my little virgin-whore posse over to PJ, Ben, and Claudio.

"Hey Sloane, how's Auggie?" Ben asked as we approached. I expected the other guys to erupt in snide giggles, but they didn't. Amazingly, he must have kept it to himself.

"Auggie's good," I said, sitting on the blanket. "How's Mr. Peabody?"

"What, are we talking in code here?" Amber demanded. "Who are these people?"

"Nobody," Ben and I both said, and exchanged a look.

A truly impressive round of fireworks exploded overhead then, and the crowd oohed and ahhed; some whooped in approval. We just kicked back in silence, too cool for exclamations.

Hero was sitting next to Claudio, and I overheard her saying, "I'm having a birthday party at the beginnig of August. PJ's doing music. I was wondering if you would . . . you know . . . be my date? Dad said it was okay."

Unfortunately, Amber overheard this too; she collapsed against me, whispering, "What is she, *seven*? 'Be my date'? 'Dad says it's okay'?"

Hero shot us a sidelong glance and I shushed Amber. It was a little geeky, yes, but Claudio probably just figured this was how Americans did things. The last thing I wanted was to embarrass Hero in front of him. Apparently, he didn't have any problem with the formality of her request, because he was nodding yes with the urgency of a wind-up toy.

Thank God. Maybe now she'll stop hounding me about dating Ben.

A particularly huge boom of fireworks went off just then, followed by cascades of gold that lingered in the sky like fistfuls of glitter falling through water. I glanced at Ben just as he was looking at me. We both looked away, embarrassed.

When the finale kicked in, the whole sky erupted in a massive series of explosions while the crowd around us went wild. I lay flat on my back and watched the mad orgy of color as it peaked. Streaks of violet, blue, red, gold, and green spiraled and swirled like the brushstrokes of a Van Gogh painting. I let myself be swept up in the heart-pounding beauty of it. It was so violent and anarchic up there, and at the same time Disneyland-sweet, especially when all the explosions ceased and there were just the fizzy remnants of fairy lights spiraling slowly toward the earth.

"Well," Amber said when it was over. "That was good, wholesome fun." She turned to me. "Now I think I'll go home and listen to my mom having sex with her boy toy."

Thursday, July 10
2:30 P.M.

Being a Triple Shot Betty is a lot like being an animal in a zoo. Without the perks. We can never loll about doing nothing. There's always something to wipe or wash or scrub or sweep or stock, even if business is slow. And when people try to rattle our cage, we never get to roar; we have to smile sweetly and suggest through gritted teeth that they have a nice day.

Mr. Little had been skulking in the parking lot in his gigantic monster truck, peering down at Amber and me through the windshield. The guy is way sketchy. He hangs out around the shop at least two or three times a week, more than that when the weather's nice. He's got sad, lank hair chopped into a mullet, a bushy mustache, and these huge, mirrored aviator sunglasses.

"I'm going over there," Amber threatened for the third time in ten minutes. "We're not TV. He can't just sit there and *stare*."

I shook my head. "I know, it's disgusting."

She threw down her sponge. "Okay, here I go."

"Wait!" I grabbed her arm. "What if he yanks you up into his truck and drives off? Next thing you know, you're a face on a milk carton, and I'm scarred for life."

"Why would *you* be scarred?"

"Duh! Helplessly watching your best friend get abducted by a monster-truck-driving-mullet-guy scars you for life."

We turned our attention back to Mr. Little. He did something disgusting with his fingers and his tongue.

"Ooh! What a—" Amber called Mr. Little a string of epithets that would have been rendered as one long, screaming beep on the air. Luckily, at that moment, a distraction appeared to keep her from racing across the parking lot and getting in his face. An old yellow VW bus pulled in with three beat-up surfboards strapped to the roof. When it stopped in front of Triple Shot Betty's, the window rolled down slowly and a cloud of smoke poured out that was so thick you could taste the THC.

"The stofers," Amber and I said simultaneously.

"Morning, dude. How 'bout a big mocha? Better make it a double." It was Dog Berry behind the wheel. Also in the car were Virg Pickett and George Sabato, his constant companions. They were stoner-surfers, but that was a mouthful, so Amber and I shortened it to stofers. It was, more or less, a term of affection.

Virg leaned over from the passenger seat until he was practically in Dog's lap. He had a digital camcorder glued to his face. "Smile, Bettys," he said. "You're on *Candy Camera*."

"*Candid*, man," George called from the backseat. "It's *Candid Camera*."

"What are you talking about? It's *my* camera," Virg told him, indignant. You never saw Virg when he wasn't filming something. Hardly anyone knew what his face looked like, because all you ever saw was the lens. Once, at school,

I'd watched him from the window of my geometry class for an hour; he was out in the senior parking lot, filming clouds.

Dog turned to his passengers. "You Barneys want anything?"

"Strawberry shake," George called.

Amber went to get the ice cream from the freezer.

Dog turned to Virg. "Hey, kook, what do you want?"

"I want her to take her top off," Virg said, nodding at me, the camera still stuck to his face.

Dog shoved Virg back into his seat and turned to me with an apologetic smile. "Sorry, Geena. He's a real turd in the morning."

"It's okay," I said. "I'm used to being sexually harassed at work."

Just as I was handing them their orders, John Jamieson drove up in his silver convertible with Corky riding shotgun. He nosed the Beemer as close to Dog's rear fender as he possibly could—so close that he actually tapped it slightly. I could hear him and Corky cracking up.

Dog leaned out his window and scowled at John.

"Sorry, man!" John called, obviously not sorry in the slightest. "My foot slipped."

Dog mumbled something under his breath. Then the Beemer inched forward again and nudged the bus a little harder, spilling some of George's shake as Dog handed it over to him.

Dog yelled out the window, "Back off, Barney!"

"Hey hippies—suck this!" Corky thrust his hips into the air and grabbed his crotch.

Delightful.

John caught my eye and raised one shoulder, like *What can you do?*

Dog shook his head in disgust, handed me two fives, and said, "That cover it?"

"Yeah—wait, I'll get your change."

"Naw, you keep it. Take it eas—"

He was interrupted by a loud, prolonged honk as Corky leaned over and pressed his weight against John's horn. Dog swore under his breath and drove off with Virg hanging out the window, filming the street as it sped by beneath him.

John pulled forward and immediately started making excuses. "Don't be mad, Skater Girl. I try to keep him on a tight leash, but sometimes he gets away from me."

I was a little annoyed, but seeing John's aquamarine eyes lit up by the sun softened me a little. He really is movie star pretty, and even though I sort of hate myself for it, whenever he uses his nickname for me it makes me feel strangely glam.

"Don't worry about it."

Beside him, Corky cackled with glee for no apparent reason. Someone told me they call him Corky because once he chugged a whole bottle of wine and, prompted by his buddies, proceeded to eat the cork for five dollars. I could believe it; he really was that stupid.

"I hear you're quite a brainiac," John said to me. "Here's your quote for the day: 'Lord, what fools these mortals be.'"

"Shakespeare." I couldn't help gloating a little. "*A Midsummer Night's Dream.*"

"Very good! I'm impressed." He propped his sunglasses up

in his gelled hair and tilted his head in a not-so-subtle effort to see behind me. "Hero working?"

"Not today."

When he spotted Amber, he treated her to a smile that managed to be both lazy and smoldering. "Hey, Ginger."

Corky pulled the mirror down and examined a zit on his forehead. "I heard Hero's a total cock tease."

"She is not," I said.

"Where'd you hear that?" Amber asked.

Corky abandoned his zit-probing to look at her. "Around. She's the exact opposite of you, huh, Beezie?"

Amber arched an eyebrow. "Meaning . . . ?"

"Everyone knows you've given out more free blow jobs than anyone. And you're only a sophomore. You've got a shot at the—whatdoyoucallit—world record!"

Amber's hand tightened around the napkin dispenser and I thought for sure she was going to break his nose with it, but she just told him in a low, even tone, "Everyone's good at something, right?"

Corky howled with laughter. John just suppressed a grin and eyed her cleavage. I busied myself wiping down the espresso machine, hoping to stay out of it. If I were Amber I'd probably burst into tears, but that wasn't her style.

"What can I get you boys?" Amber asked.

"Coke," Corky bellowed. "You got a thirty-two-ouncer?"

"No," she said. "This isn't a mini-mart. Sorry."

"Whatever," he said.

"I'll take a macchiato," John said. "Be sure the foam is good and stiff."

"Oh, it'll be stiff," she told him. "Trust me."

Amber started making John's macchiato. I was about to hand Corky his Coke when she motioned me over. "Stand in front of me," she said. "And turn on the steam."

"Why?"

"Just do it," she said.

I did. As soon as the steam was on, emitting a high-pitched whistle, Amber angled herself behind me, snorted deeply, and hocked a huge loogie into the Coke. She snapped the lid into place and grinned.

"Voila," she said into my ear. "Coke con loogie."

"Oh, God," I said, closing my eyes.

"Here you go, boys," I heard her say at the window. I didn't dare turn around for fear that my face would give everything away. "On the house."

Corky said, "And I thought only the blow jobs were free!"

We heard an engine rev. It was Mr. Little, still not moving, just turning the engine over and revving the gas on his enormous yellow truck.

"You know that guy?" Corky asked.

"Mm-hm," Amber said. "My boyfriend. Very possessive. Carries a Glock in his glove compartment, just in case . . ."

John was already shifting into gear.

"Have a nice day!" we trilled sweetly as they gunned it out of the parking lot in a cloud of exhaust.

I'd just started to make myself an iced mocha when we got mobbed by more customers. The last in line were Uncle Leo and some guy I'd never seen before; they cruised up to the window in Leo's Merc.

"Hey there, Unc! What can I get you?"

"Couple iced coffees."

I got them their order and handed them over. "There you go. That's three dollars."

Leo handed me a ten. "Keep the change. Hey, heard from your old man lately?"

"He was here last weekend." *With the bimbophile,* I wanted to add, *and I only saw him for about five hours.* Instead, I said, "We had fun."

"Good, good. Geena, have you met Alistair Drake?" He motioned to the guy beside him. "He bought the place next door."

"Oh, no. Hi." *Alistair Drake, Alistair Drake. Where had I heard that name?* The guy had a dark, slicked-back ponytail, a hawklike nose, and his bare, muscled biceps were covered in the most intricate tattoos I'd ever seen. He was almost cute in a hard-edged, old-guy, Billy Bob Thornton sort of way.

"Nice to meet you." The Australian accent was unexpected. "Your uncle's giving me the tour."

I felt Amber behind me, and turned to see her staring, bug-eyed, like she'd just seen Kurt Cobain's ghost. I figured I'd better get rid of them and see what was up. She looked like she was about to have a seizure.

"Cool. Well, have fun," I told them. "Say hi to Hero."

As they drove off, Amber let her breath out in a gush, like she'd been holding it for an hour. "Oh my God. Oh my God," she said over and over.

"What? What is it?"

We went back and forth like this for what seemed like forever. Finally she said, "Do you have any idea who that was?"

"My uncle?"

"Not him, you idiot! The other guy. The one with the ink."

"Oh," I said, "him. Alistair Drake. Why are you making that face?"

She spoke slowly and deliberately, as if she were squeezing each word from a nearly depleted tube of toothpaste. "Alistair Drake. Floating World Tattoos? Am I getting through here, G?"

"Oh," I said, "yeah, I kind of remember now. You want to work there, right?"

She closed her eyes as if I were beyond moronic, and when they sprang open she said, "I have to meet him!"

"I'm sure Uncle Leo would introduce you."

Her eyes lit up. "You really think so?"

That's when I hesitated. I'd never considered what Uncle Leo would think of Amber—what he would or wouldn't do for her. Usually the preferences and opinions of adults don't concern me much, unless they actively interfere with my own. Suddenly it occurred to me that I couldn't picture Uncle Leo liking Amber. In fact, I couldn't even imagine him *talking* to her. I mean, she was . . . colorful. Obviously, Uncle Leo wasn't exactly a right-wing Republican—he'd made friends with Alistair Drake, after all—but in general, his tastes were decidedly refined. He liked Schubert, Sotheby's, stinky cheeses, and crème brulée. I wasn't sure what he'd make of Amber in her tube tops and her body glitter.

"Um, yeah. I think so. I mean, I don't see why not."

She sensed something. "Don't lie to me, Geena."

"What? I'm not lying," I lied.

"Parents hate me. Always have, always will."

"Be quiet!" I went back to my mochus interruptus, adding espresso to the chocolate milk at last.

"It's true. Story of my life." She sat down, pouting now, and flipped through her sketchbook. "The only ones who like me are the pervs."

"Ewww." I made a face.

"Well, it's true." She studied her pages, cocking her head at different angles to examine the drawings. She seemed to be speaking more to herself than to me when she said, "I'll just have to figure out a way . . ."

Monday, July 14
1:00 A.M.

Hero's lost it.

I once had a cousin. Now I have a blond vegetable.

Mom says everyone goes a little brain-dead the first time they fall in love. No doubt—look at her. Her brain went so mushy she agreed to become Joan Sloane for life. Joan Sloane! If that's not a perfect example of love's ability to cut your IQ in half, I don't know what is.

Hero's sleeping over tonight. At this very moment, she's curled up in a sleeping bag on my bedroom floor. She looks perfectly normal, aside from the way her jaw hangs open like an old man's. I have evidence that her normality is only an illusion, though.

Exhibit A: Inside that sleeping bag, clutched in her delicate fingers, is a picture of Claudio she took from her bedroom window two days ago. In the photo he's about half a centimeter tall—just a tiny black speck in a sea of grapevines. When I told her as much, she went on and on about how she knew it wasn't exactly a close-up, but somehow she'd captured the essence of him—his adorable lankiness, his innate intelligence and sensitivity as evidenced in his humble-yet-ready-for-anything posture. She made me look at it with her for an eternity. Finally, when I was so tired of squinting at it I could scream, I told her, "If his essence is an indistinguishable fleck of black, then you're right, you really captured it."

She didn't talk to me for an hour after that.

The girl's hopeless.

The problem with love is it totally ruins your ability to relate in a normal human fashion. For example: What do we do when we're together? Half the time we spend staring at a photograph of a speck in a field. The other half she tries to bribe, threaten, or otherwise coerce me into dating Ben Bettaglia. She says she can't possibly wait until her birthday party to see Claudio. The more she asks, the more determined I am to resist. Has it occurred to *anyone* that being cast as the virgin's bodyguard is not exactly flattering? Am I such a killjoy that everyone assumes no one can possibly get laid in my presence?

1:55 A.M.

I wonder if PJ told Ben Bettaglia about me being recruited as the sex police? Oh, God, now *everyone* thinks of me as the Abstinence Enforcer.

Saturday, July 19
10:20 A.M.

I am absolutely not getting out of bed today.

Just hung up with Dad. Amazing. Here we've got a grown man so gaga over his midlife crisis bombshell he can't even string a sentence together anymore.

Observe our conversation, ladies and gentlemen of the jury, and tell me if this man is fit to father:

ME: So, when are you coming up here next?
DAD: I, uh— Sure, baby, that looks fine.
ME: What?
DAD: Oh, nothing, I was talking to— The pink.
ME: The *pink*?
DAD: Jen. I was talking to Jen. Sorry. What was I saying?
ME: When are you going to visit?
DAD: *(Manic giggling. I ask you: Should a father, under any circumstances,* giggle?*)*
ME: Dad?
DAD: Sorry, just . . .
(He clears his throat in this weird, embarrassed way that makes me suspect there is something pseudo-sexual happening on his end, which is against the law or, at the very least, puke-inducing.)
Listen, Geena, maybe I should call you back. You going to be home for a while?
ME: I guess.

Hung up totally depressed and confused about the nature of existence. Tried yogic breathing, skimming the best scenes in *Wuthering Heights*, and inhaling four chocolate chip cookies, but am still lying in bed staring at the ceiling, wondering why we even bother.

10:40 A.M.

If love can make a grown man giggle uncontrollably and a girl-genius stare for hours at a photograph of a comma-sized boy, what might it do to a five-foot-two, chocolate-chip-cookie-addicted weakling like me?

11:15 A.M.

Why isn't Dad calling back?

What if he marries his midlife crisis?

I am not wearing lavender, pink, or any form of butt-bow to their wedding. I will wear black. I'll pierce my septum, my tongue, and maybe even my nipple. (Ouch. Maybe just the septum and tongue, then.) If they ask me to make a toast, I'll recite Sylvia Plath.

12:50 P.M.

Mom came home from teaching summer school and found me prostrate on my bed, flipping listlessly through a stack of old *Skateboarding* magazines.

"What's wrong?"

I snorted. "What *isn't* wrong?"

She came over and sat beside me. "Are you on your period, honey?"

If a girl between the ages of twelve and twenty has a crisis, everyone immediately cries, "Hormones!" Why is that? I was in the midst of an existential, soul-wrenching moment. The fact that I just got my period had absolutely nothing to do with it.

Luckily, just then the phone rang, allowing me to avoid her question.

It was Dad. We talked for twenty minutes. He had apparently managed to secure a bimbo-free zone, because his ability to combine subjects and predicates to form independent clauses had increased dramatically. He's visiting next month. So far, no mention of weddings or butt-bows, thank God.

"Feeling any better?" Mom was standing in the kitchen in her silk blouse and linen slacks, eating cut-up peaches and cottage cheese. I thought of Amber's mom with her boy toy, and of Aunt Kathy, who Hero can never see again for as long as she lives. I went over to Mom and put my arms around her neck.

"Whoa," she said, putting her bowl down and hugging me back. "What's this all about?"

I shrugged. "Nothing."

Mom raised an eyebrow. "You *are* on your period, aren't you?"

I laughed. "Shut up!"

5:55 P.M.

At Hero's house, Uncle Leo was there with a professional party planner, talking about decorations. The planner was in her mid-thirties and she was wearing chocolate brown suede pants with a white, sheer linen blouse over a tank top. She looked very chic in that calculated-to-look-casual way. You could tell she only moved to Sonoma after it got all shi-shi. Probably she's an L.A. import, the sort you see at farmer's markets buying armloads of lilies and thirty-dollar bottles of olive oil, talking about Sonoma like they've been here since the turn of the century. I think of them privately as the EUWWs (Ex-Urban Wine-Country Wannabes). I know it's sort of elitist to be so anti-outsiders, but come on, these people wrote the book on elitism; if I give them a taste of their own medicine within the confines of my own brain, is that a crime?

"Wow," she said when she saw me in my sweaty FUCT T-shirt carrying my board. "You can really ride that thing?" Her highlights ranged from chili-pepper red to pumpkin, and I wondered idly how much she'd paid for them.

"Yeah." I was bored, but not desperate enough to encourage conversation with a perky little EUWW.

"I would be terrified." She laughed, looking at Uncle Leo. "Although I used to roller-skate. Is it kind of the same thing?"

Her tone was saccharine and patronizing. She was one of those adults who think anyone under the legal drinking age is essentially an overgrown toddler. I wanted to say *Goo-goo ga-ga*, but instead I said, "Not really, no."

"Anyway." Uncle Leo cleared his throat. "Let's get Hero down here, since it's her party."

"Yes, of course," the EUWW replied, all smiles.

I was sent to fetch Hero. In my house, you can stand in any room, shout someone's name, and even if they're out in the yard they'll probably hear you. In Hero's house, you've got to hike about four miles before you find another human soul. I sometimes wonder if Uncle Leo gets lonely, sitting in his sleek, modern chairs, eating the dinners Elodie whips up. Everything in that house is incredibly tasteful and expensive, but nothing about it is cozy. Esperanza and Elodie keep it running like a four-star hotel, and still Uncle Leo often looks like he hasn't slept well for weeks.

As I wandered down the hall, delicate strains of Mozart told me Hero was in the music room; I found her playing the baby grand in a pink tank top and denim shorts. Sunlight was pouring through the huge picture windows; her hair was a blinding gold. She looked like an angel dressed for the beach.

"The EUWW's here," I said. "She wants to talk to you."

Her fingers froze and she looked up, startled. At first she seemed not to recognize me. Sometimes when Hero's playing piano, she slips into another world. "Who?"

"Party planner," I explained.

That was the magic word: *party*. She jumped up from the bench and twirled me around. "It's going to be so *fun*!"

"I'm sure it—"

"And Claudio's coming! Oh my *God*! What if I have gas that night?"

I faked a look of concern. "Let's cross that bridge when we get there."

After we'd trekked back to the living room, the party plans started in earnest. I sank into the cushy leather couch with a Rock Star soda and watched the show. Hero kept pushing for pink roses and baby's breath and swaths of lace, while Uncle Leo and the EUWW wanted big glass bowls of floating camellias and candles. Personally, I wanted them to rent a dilapidated warehouse, hire a punk band, and get a mosh pit going. It'd be like a Berlin squat circa 1970-something. Awesome. But I didn't want to make things more complicated than they already were, so I kept my mouth shut.

Just as I was getting so bored and caffeinated I thought I'd scream, Bronwyn breezed in, all smiles, home for the weekend. She was wearing a jade green sundress with a chunky turquoise choker and cute little sequined shoes. I thought she was lovely, but this was definitely a new look for her. She usually sported men's trousers from Goodwill and little T-shirts that said "Meat is Murder" or "Eat More Kale."

After about two minutes of listening to the EUWW go on about the virtues of pears as a decorating motif, Bronwyn jerked her head toward the kitchen and I extracted myself from the couch to join her there.

"So," she said, pouring herself an icy glass of lemonade and adding three spoonfuls of sugar, "I hear you're being recruited as a chaperone."

I grimaced. "Is that messed up or what?"

"I'm just glad it's you and not me. Dad knows I'd hand Hero a box of condoms and call it a day."

"Yeah, but what are *my* qualifications?"

She eyed me thoughtfully as she sipped from the frosty glass. "I guess he thinks you're suitably hostile toward the opposite sex."

"I'm not hostile."

She gave me her *Yeah, right* smile. "Then why not go out with this Ben guy?"

"No way!"

She nodded patiently; she was in full-on therapist mode.

"Does your father's relationship with a younger woman make you feel like men aren't trustworthy?"

"Have you been sniffing Wite-Out or something? What's that got to do with anything?"

Bronwyn put her glass down. "Here's what I'm seeing: Hero's finally starting to grow up, and now she finds you're not moving forward with her. Dating is an essential step, and whether you date Ben or someone else is beside the point. You just can't stay angry at your dad, that's all."

My jaw dropped. "Bronwyn, aren't you the one who said relationships stifle your individuality?"

"Maybe . . ." She sat on a stool at the marble counter and swiveled a couple times. "But that was before I met Richard."

Great, I thought. *Another one bites the dust.* "Who's Richard?"

She pressed her lips together, suppressing a giggle. "My poly sci professor."

"And you call him *Richard?*"

Her grin turned mischievous. "We have . . . chemistry."

I almost choked on my soda. "Are you doing him?"

She leaned toward me. "Shhh! You want Dad to hear?"

I was shocked. "So you are?"

"Well, that's not exactly the term I'd use, but yes, we're in a relationship, if that's what you're asking."

"No way!" I couldn't help it—I was horrified and fascinated at once. "How old is he?"

"Thirty-eight." She said it casually, like it was no big deal.

"Yuck!" Dad's only a few years older than that.

"Fine, we won't talk about it if you're going to be such a baby."

I was shamed into silence by that, as she knew I would be.

She took advantage of that and changed the subject. "Hero thinks I'm a bad influence on you."

"Hardly. *Normally* you're the only person over eighteen who makes any sense."

She smiled. "She says I've filled your head with feminist propaganda."

"I love your feminist propaganda!"

"That's sweet. But the point is, you and Hero both have to live your own lives, you know? You can't let my paradigm color your experiences. You've got to explore relationships in your own way, at your own pace. You get what I'm saying?"

I squinted at her. "You're saying I should go out with Ben Bettaglia?"

She shrugged. "I can't tell you what to do. But Hero says he's pretty cute."

A car honked outside. Bronwyn sprang from the stool and raced to the window like a cat suddenly drawn to the flutter of wings. Then she darted around the kitchen in a mad flurry, grabbing her leather clutch and rearranging her hair.

"How do I look?" she asked me.

"Great. Why?"

She shot me a sly grin. "Hot date," she muttered under her breath, and then yelled a vague "See you later!" to the house at large before escaping out the door.

"Where's she going?" Uncle Leo walked into the kitchen, looking tired. Hero and the EUWW trailed in after him.

"Don't ask me," I said.

He ran his hand over his face and blinked at Hero, who

was pointing at a catalog excitedly while the EUWW took notes. "Get lots of these vases, the silver glittery ones, maybe fifty? And I think the cake should be three-tier, at least, with one of these figurines at the top."

"That's a bride, hon. That's for wedding cakes." The EUWW's smile was strained.

Hero looked crestfallen, but then her face lit up. "I know! We'll paint her dress pink, with glitter—then she'll look like me."

I didn't think I could take much more of that, so I went outside and practiced my board flips. I needed a challenge right then. I was all worked up from the Rock Star soda, Bronwyn's crazy relationship counseling, and Hero's descent into Pink Glitterland.

After a good forty minutes of ankle-braking maneuvers, I was sweaty again and feeling better. When I went back inside, I found Uncle Leo in the kitchen with several wineglasses and five bottles set up in front of the EUWW. Leo's so into his wine, he'll make a taster out of anyone. He poured from a bottle of red and she sniffed it, then took a sip, swishing it around in her mouth.

"That's our old-vine Zin," Uncle Leo was saying.

"Mmm," she said, taking another sip. "I bet it would be wonderful with black truffles."

"You're going to love this," he told her, pouring her half a glass. "Much more complex."

She stuck her nose in the glass and said, "Plums and . . . tobacco?"

He clapped his hands together. "Exactly!"

The EUWW could talk the talk. Uncle Leo was in heaven.

Hero was nowhere in sight, and the scene here was starting to get to me. I suddenly felt disgusted with everything and everyone; even the thought of skating home depressed me. It occurred to me that Amber might have her mom's car. I could meet her halfway and we could go get cones at Baskin-Robbins, or maybe catch a movie. I grabbed the portable phone from the living room and headed out to the deck. When I pushed the button, though, I heard voices instead of a dial tone.

"I told you I'd take care of it, didn't I?" Hero was saying in a clipped, businesslike tone. I started to hang up, but then I heard the other voice and I nearly peed my pants from the shock.

"Yeah, but I want to know how." It was Amber! I covered the mouthpiece with my hand, holding my breath. "Alistair Drake is like famous, okay?"

"He's our neighbor. It'll be easy. Still, I'm only saying you'll meet him. I can't guarantee anything else."

"That's all I'm asking. But it has to be someplace where we can talk. I need time to work on him."

Hero sighed impatiently. "I know. I'll handle it. What I'm worried about is Geena. You really think she'll do it?"

"Oh, totally. Just do what I say when I say it, and she won't even know what—"

There were voices behind me then, Uncle Leo and the EUWW coming out onto the deck with big goblets of wine. Hero said, "Hello?" I hung up the phone, dropped it on a lawn chair, and grabbed my board.

"You going home?" Uncle Leo asked, surprised.

"Yeah, I forgot I have to—to . . ."—I looked around wildly, spotted a sculpture in the garden of a barefooted nymph—"trim my toenails!"

"If you wait ten minutes I'll give you a ride," he offered, but I was already skating down the drive, bombing Moon Mountain so fast I almost wiped out on the turn.

Sunday, July 20
4:00 P.M.

When I got to Triple Shot Betty's this afternoon for work, I was surprised to see Hero and Amber in there together. Usually they avoid the same shift. I thought of the conversation I overheard yesterday. Coincidence? I wondered . . .

I approached the back door slowly, trying to be quiet. I wasn't sure if they'd seen me skate into the parking lot. At first I thought they had, but neither of them waved, so maybe not. I wanted to see if I could glean more clues with a little detective work.

"The thing is," Amber was saying in a clear, loud voice, "Ben's crazy about her. He thinks she's totally sexy. But you know if we tell her, she'll only use it to humiliate him in front of everyone."

"I know." Hero sighed. "She's so anti-love. All she cares about is her skateboard and her GPA."

I was having absolutely no trouble hearing either one of them; they were talking at a volume that ensured the entire parking lot would catch their drift. *Gee, guys, thanks for being so discreet while stabbing me in the back.*

Amber half shouted, "I feel bad for Ben. He hasn't been

eating or sleeping at all. It's interfering with his training too. He might not even race this year . . ."

Hero said, "That's terrible. Do you think we should tell her? Maybe deep down she likes him. Don't you think he's cute?"

"Are you kidding? He's gorgeous! I'd totally go for him, but he's way strung out on Geena. It's all he can talk about."

"Let's tell her," Hero suggested again.

"No, we can't. She'll just twist the knife—you know her." I heard a car drive up to the window then, and Amber said, "Hi, what can I get you?"

I hung back and waited for a few minutes, thinking they might say more. They didn't talk about me again, though. I went inside and worked my shift, but the whole time my mind was abuzz with Ben Bettaglia. Was this really possible? Was he seriously into me? I put whipped cream in a lady's iced tea and lemon in someone's mocha. I was a mess.

After work I went into Safeway for the newest issue of *Skateboarding* magazine and ran smack into Ben in the frozen food aisle.

"Hey Sloane," he said. "How's it going?"

I just sort of stood there, feeling crazy inside. It was like running into Ashton Kutcher after watching his movies four times back to back. I'd been thinking about him so much all afternoon that actually seeing him was totally surreal.

"You okay?" he asked.

"Huh? Yeah, why?" I pulled at my braids self-consciously.

"You always have a smart-ass comeback. I've never seen you speechless." Just then his eyes moved from my face to my chest. I looked down too, and was horrified to discover that my nipples were totally erect under my thin white Triple Shot Betty tank top. I folded my arms quickly across the Uniboob, mortified.

"It's cold in here," I said.

"Yeah." He smirked at the shelves of Tater Tots and Lean Cuisines. "Well, it *is* the frozen food aisle."

"Profound observation. Have you always had such a firm grasp on the obvious?" Before he could answer, I added, "Wouldn't get near the butcher shop if I were you. I know the smell of blood makes you faint."

"There's the old Sloane. Had me worried there for a sec."

As I walked away I told him, "Don't worry about me, Ben. Snarky's still my middle name."

8:40 P.M.

Lying on my bed, staring at the ceiling, thinking about Ben Bettaglia. Why was I so mean to him at Safeway? Why did the Uniboob have to betray me?

Oh God, can it really be true? Does Ben like me?

Misery, thy name is Boy.

11:30 P.M.

I wonder if those Victoria's Secret bras with extra padding actually eliminate the bullet-nipple effect. Maybe they can do something about the Uniboob too.

Wednesday, July 23
2:40 P.M.

In my campaign to think about anything but Ben Bettaglia, I came up with a fantastic weight-loss idea this morning. Amber and I both noticed that, after yesterday's binge on chocolate chip cookie dough ice cream, our butts were looking noticeably larger.

"Hero's party is in ten days," I said. "No way around it. It's boot camp for the Bettys."

Hero sent out invitations two days ago, and I was relieved to discover that Amber was on the guest list. I still haven't figured out what they're up to exactly, but they seem more civil lately, less openly hostile.

"God," she groaned. "I don't care if my ass gets big as a house—I hate sweating."

Just then Mrs. Smeby, our high school guidance counselor, drove up in her bright red Beetle. She was flashing a huge, immovable smile that consumed the better part of her face.

"Good morning, girls." The grin was so stiff and unyielding, when she spoke I was reminded of a ventriloquist's dummy. "One triple low-fat caramel macchiato, please."

Mrs. Smeby wasn't a regular, and I wanted to make sure I'd heard her correctly. Despite our name, we don't get all that many triple shot requests. I leaned slightly toward her and said, "Did you say triple shot?"

Her smile faltered for a fraction of a second, but it was back in place so quickly, I couldn't swear it had moved at all. "Precisely." There was an edge to her voice. "Thanks so much, Beatrice."

I turned around and rolled my eyes at Amber. Mrs. Smeby had been my counselor for two whole years now, and in all that time, despite repeated reminders, she couldn't get it through her brain that nobody, not even my mother, ever called me by my real name.

"Beatrice," Amber said in a sickly sweet voice, "would you like me to steam the milk for that?"

I just nodded at her in an *I'll get you later* fashion, and went to work brewing Mrs. Smeby's triple shot. When she'd gone, Amber cracked up.

"Oh my God, why did she call you that?"

I thought about lying, but what was the point? It would be on my driver's license in a matter of months, anyway. "It's my first name. Geena's my middle name."

"Beatrice?" Amber looked incredulous. "You've got to be kidding. I thought you said your parents were hippies."

"Yeah, well, hippies with a love of Shakespeare."

"No biggie," she said. "I won't tell anyone. My real name's Margaret."

"Seriously?"

She stuck her tongue out. "Disgusting—total fat girl name. When we moved here, I reinvented myself. My mom still calls me Maggie. Don't tell anyone."

I shook my head. "Of course not."

"Wow, did you see Mrs. Smeby's *face*? She's got a serious case of perma-grin. Her jaw must be so sore at the end of the day."

That's when my brilliant idea hit me.

"Wait a minute. What if we could do that, but with our butts?"

Amber didn't immediately recognize the sheer genius of it. "Smile really fake with our asses?"

"Seriously—like a constant workout, without the sweat. We'll just walk around with our butts clenched all day. By the time we get off work, we should have buns of steel."

Amber paused to think this over. "You mean, we just tighten them, and walk around like that?"

"Yeah."

"We don't have to wiggle them or squat or anything?"

I shrugged. "Why should we? Isn't the point of exercise to flex the muscle? We'll use Mrs. Smeby's patented Constant Clench Technique. Did you see how hollowed out her cheeks were, by the way?"

"The cheeks in her face?" Amber asked.

"Shut up!" I said, slapping her arm playfully. "Come on, let's get started. Are you clenched?"

We spent the rest of the morning and the early part of the afternoon working on our CCT. I have to say, though, Amber really lacks discipline. I had to check her form every ten minutes by poking at her with a broom handle to see if she jiggled. Usually she did, but that was all she needed to activate CCT again. Some people just won't do what's good for them unless you make them.

After work, we were so proud of our success with CCT, we decided to get double scoops at Baskin-Robbins. Sitting there in the pink plastic chairs, I suddenly couldn't stand it another second. I had to ask her what she knew about Ben.

"Amber, how well do you know Ben Bettaglia?"

"I know him," she said. "Why?"

"I just . . . I heard somewhere—"

"That he likes you?" she interrupted.

I could feel myself blushing. "Yeah. Do you know anything about that?"

She considered me a moment, then sighed. "I promised him I wouldn't say anything. Everyone's afraid you'll just throw it back in his face."

"Do people really think I'm that mean?"

"Mean? Not exactly, just . . ." She trailed off.

"What?"

"Boy-hostile. You've got a reputation as a guy-basher."

"I'm not a guy-basher!" I pounded the table so hard my top scoop of chocolate peanut butter almost fell off. An old lady at a nearby table scowled at me. I lowered my voice. "I'm not. That's a vicious rumor."

She shrugged. "I guess there's only one way to prove everybody wrong."

"How?"

"Be nice to him. See what happens. Maybe you'll even gain a little *experience*." She licked her orange sherbet suggestively.

Saturday, July 26

1:10 A.M.

> To: cycletronic@gmail.com
> From: skatergirl@yahoo.com
> Subject: Hi there

Ben,
So, I know we've never really gotten along that well, mostly
because you're insanely competitive and I'm a peaceful
saint (who will, by the way, be valedictorian) but I just
wanted you to know that I am not "boy-hostile." Got it? I
don't know who started that rumor, but it's slander. Period.
I think boys may be hygiene-challenged and dismal at
biology (unless you count the hours they spend investigating
Internet porn) but none of these less-than-desirable qualities
inspire hostility on my part. Just pity.

Geena

Perhaps not precisely the tone of titillating receptivity I'm
after. Delete.

1:55 A.M.

To: cycletronic@gmail.com
From: skatergirl@yahoo.com
Subject: Lonely?

Ben,
Do you ever find yourself unable to sleep in the middle of
the night? If you answered yes, when you find yourself
unable to sleep, do you start to wonder if maybe you're
the only person left on the entire planet? Like you imagine
that some horribly lethal chemical has infiltrated everyone's
air conditioners and miraculously you're the only human
who's immune to it? Because it's just so quiet out and so . . .
lonely? And then do you start to think, what if there's one
other person who shares my chemical makeup or is some
kind of genetic mutant and they're out there right now too,
and what if that person is Ben (in your case, Geena)—

Whoa, whoa, whoa! What am I, Seductress from the Twilight Zone? Delete.

Why am I even writing him? This is ridiculous. Ben and I have coexisted since diaperhood, and we've never exchanged a single e-mail. Why should I start now? I'm turning off my computer and going to sleep, before I freak myself out any further.

3:20 A.M.

To: cycletronic@gmail.com
From: skatergirl@yahoo.com
Subject: After Hours Lexis

Hey Ben,
I can't sleep, so I'm studying SAT vocabulary words.
Here's my evening, in a nutshell:
Abed: adv. In bed; on a bed.
Bowdlerize: v. To expurgate in editing (a literary composition) by omitting words or passages.
Captious: adj. Hypercritical.
Pusillanimous: adj. Without spirit or bravery.
Recessive: adj. Having a tendency to go back.
Vicissitude: n. A change, especially a complete change, of condition or circumstances.
Bettaglified: adj. The inability to express oneself in any way that is not snarky, even when one wants to be nice.
This message has been brought to you by your local valedictorian-to-be.

Geena

7:10 A.M.

Still no response from Ben. Don't panic. Maybe he's one of those Luddites who only checks his e-mail once a day.

I can't believe I sent him such a random note. Bettaglified? What the hell was I thinking?

My new policy, from now until my death: Never, ever, send e-mails after three a.m.

6:05 P.M.

Today I tried to pretend everything was normal, despite my nerves about the absurd, nonsensical e-mail that will no doubt ruin my life. Hero and I worked the early shift, were stalked by the usual stalkers, and made a little under three dollars each in tips. Business as usual. Good thing we get free caffeine or we'd have to call Amnesty International.

Amber showed up just as we were getting off, yelping with glee behind the wheel of her mom's car. It's an old beat-up El Dorado with so many dents it looks like some nutcase went at it with a sledgehammer (I think one of her ex-boyfriends did, actually), but it's a convertible, so we were psyched. Amber looked divine driving it—like a fiery red-headed goddess at the helm of her sparkly gold chariot. Plus, with all those dents, her mom's never going to notice that she sideswiped a Dumpster on the way into the parking lot.

When she first showed up, Hero acted all unimpressed and aloof. I was caught in the middle, as usual. I wanted to go for a spin with Amber—her excitement was contagious. But I felt terrible, leaving Hero there, stranded in the parking lot waiting for her dad to come get her.

Luckily, Amber extended an invitation just in time. "Come on," she yelled. "Hop in, for Christ's sake." She looked pointedly at Hero. "Both of you."

I opened the passenger side, tossing my board in the back. Hero hesitated. "My dad's supposed to pick me up any minute," she said, anxiously looking at her watch.

"So call him!"

Turns out he was stuck in traffic outside Santa Rosa anyway, so he had to say yes (thank you, gods of 101). Hero climbed in back, looking kind of dazed at this turn of events, tucking her cell back into her miniature pink purse.

We had wheels and freedom and plenty of caffeine coursing through our veins, but we needed a mission. It was incredibly hot out, so I suggested a movie—not that there was anything good playing, but the AC sounded delish. Amber rejected that suggestion immediately. Too boring. That's when she got The Look. When Amber gets The Look, there's no telling what will happen next.

"I know who has a poo-ool," she sang.

Hero leaned forward against the front seat and looked from her to me and back again. "Who has a pool?"

"Amber," I said, my voice a low warning, "I hope you're not suggesting we just show up there uninvited."

Hero furrowed her brow. "Show up where?"

"Hello! I happen to know their folks left for Maui this morning." Amber sucked at her iced vanilla latte with a demonic little grin.

"How do you know that?" I asked.

"The Jamiesons?" Hero was catching on at last. "Are you talking about the Jamiesons?"

"Sarah Jennings told Lilly, who told Sam, who told Stacy, who told me. Duh."

"Look," I said, "even if their parents are gone, we can't just show up there. It's rude."

Amber scoffed. "Oh rude, shmude. Don't be such a stick-in-the-mud. Hero, you up for it? I bet Claudio's there . . ."

Just then Ben Bettaglia walked out of his dad's shop and started toward his bike. He was wearing cargo shorts, a lemon yellow T-shirt, and a backwards baseball cap. There were so many hot-boy pheromones coming off of him, I swear I could smell him from halfway across the parking lot.

Amber didn't even hesitate. She honked the horn, and when he looked up, she waved him over.

"Oh no," I moaned. "What are you doing?"

"Leave it to me," she said coolly. "I eat guys like Ben for breakfast."

Hero got the giggles. There I was, the alleged guy-basher hanging out with Goldilocks and Queen Beezie. I was doomed.

"Hey," Ben said, thrusting his chin out in that upside-down nod thing guys always do. "What's going on?"

"Nothing much. Hot as hell today, huh?" Amber's tone was casual and friendly. I couldn't understand how she managed. I was suddenly so nervous, I was sure I'd puke up the cereal, toast, biscotti, and two iced mochas I'd had that morning.

"Yeah, it's hot all right." He kept his eyes on Amber's face, but every now and then he'd sneak a look at me. Whenever he did, I felt myself go all gelatinous inside. All I could think was *Bettaglified*.

(!!!)

"What are you guys up to?" Ben asked.

Amber's eyes sparkled and I knew she was going in for the kill. "We're heading over to the Jamiesons', maybe go swimming. Hop in. We'll give you a ride."

This adorable little half smile crept over his face. He glanced back at his bike for a second, shrugged, and climbed into the backseat.

It was no longer a perfectly normal day.

On the way to John and PJ's house, Amber almost tore the door off an old lady's Chrysler, sent four yuppie tourists scampering for the sidewalk, and cruised through a red light, but somehow we survived the ten-minute drive. When we got there, PJ's blue truck was parked outside. As we climbed out of the car, Hero squeezed my hand so hard I thought my fingers might pop off. Somehow having Ben with us made showing up there seem a little less ridiculous; it gave Hero and me the courage to follow Amber right up the front steps so we could cower behind her as she rang the bell.

When the heavy oak door swung open, PJ was there with an Oakland Raiders towel wrapped around his waist. His dark shaggy hair was spiky-wet, and he was dripping all over the tile floor, oblivious to the puddle forming around his ankles.

"Hey man," he said, looking past Amber to Ben. "Never thought you'd deliver a carload full of babes."

"In case you didn't notice," Amber said, "the babes are delivering him."

I swear to God, Amber always says the thing I can't think

of until hours later, when I'm moping around in my room, regretting the stupid things I *actually* said.

"What's up?" Ben tried to act natural, like he got abducted by three Bettys in a convertible every other day, at least.

"Come in, you guys. This is great. The parents slip out one door, and the party comes in the other."

"That's us," Amber said. "Instant party."

The Jamiesons' house was sprawling and posh—a Mediterranean-style villa, with bougainvillea climbing up the peach stucco walls. Inside, it was all bright Mexican tiles and thick rugs, cozy twill couches and chairs in festive colors. The big bay windows looked out on a huge, kidney-shaped pool, a hot tub, and the valley below. I could see Amber looking around, impressed by the size and grandeur. Hero barely even noticed; to her, this was nothing.

On the drive there, all I could think was *Bettaglified—why? WHY?* But once we were out by the pool, I started to relax a little. The sun was beating down on the bright turquoise water and Claudio was leaning on his elbows at the pool's edge, half in and half out, smiling broadly. His hair, which usually hung down in his eyes, was wet and slicked back. He *was* cute. Hero deserved a little summer romance. Suddenly I couldn't remember why I'd been so opposed to the idea of double-dating, if that's what they really wanted.

There was an awkward pause as we all stood there, unsure of what to do next. It hit me all at once that we didn't have bathing suits. The water looked absolutely divine, and I wanted more than anything to plunge in, but there was no way in hell I was going to run around there butt-ass naked.

I did the old head-jerking, time-for-a-conference thing to Amber and Hero, corralling them as far from the guys as possible, until we were huddled together on a few lawn chairs in the far corner of the yard.

"How are we going to swim without suits?" I said.

Hero looked suddenly stricken. "Oh my God. I never even thought of that."

You see what I mean? The girl can conjugate Latin verbs in her sleep, but lately her grasp of the obvious is slipping.

Amber got all condescending. "*Please.* Don't tell me you've never been skinny-dipping."

"We have," I said defensively. "But not in broad daylight, with *guys.*"

"So, we'll leave our underwear on," Amber said, flipping her hair over one shoulder. "It's exactly the same as a bathing suit, if you think about it."

Hero's eyes were wide. "Maybe we should just drive to our houses and get our suits."

"If you're going to be babies about it, forget it—you can walk home."

I locked eyes with Hero. We did our cousins-trying-to-mind-meld-and-discover-some-way-to-avoid-showing-acres-of-flesh look, but it wasn't working.

I sighed. "Okay. You win," I told Amber. Then I peeked under my waistband and tank top to remind myself which underwear I had on. Turquoise hip-huggers below, regular old white cotton bra on top. It wasn't going to win me lasting fame in the history of lingerie fashion, but neither was it likely to shame me eternally in the eyes of Ben, Claudio, and PJ.

"Oh no," Hero said. "I'm wearing all white. They'll see right through it. I might as well be naked."

Amber smirked. "Wait till you see what I'm wearing."

We didn't have to wait long. She stood up, dropped her shorts, peeled off her tank top, and ran at top speed for the pool. From where we sat, we had a perfect view of her naked butt cheeks gleaming white in the sun. Amber was wearing a black lace thong.

She dove into the pool recklessly, abandoning grace for speed.

The boys all turned and stared. Ben looked flustered. PJ looked impressed. Claudio looked nonchalant. I guess chicks in Italy must run around in thongs all the time.

"Great," Hero grumbled. "They're looking. We're doomed."

"Let's just get this over with," I said. "Like ripping off a Band-Aid."

Hero looked uncertain. "We could walk to your house from here," she said. "It'd only take a couple hours."

"Think of it as Life Experience," I mumbled. "Isn't your dad always saying we need more of that?"

"I don't think prancing around PJ Jamieson's pool in our underwear is exactly what he had in mind."

She did have a point, but I could already feel my nerve slipping away, so I grabbed her hand and said, "Right now. I'll do it if you will."

Instead of answering, she stood up and pulled her T-shirt over her head.

Those three seconds spent dashing madly for the pool

were the longest three seconds of my life. Just before we sprang over the edge and into the water, I made the mistake of locking eyes with Ben. Something about the curve of his lips made goose bumps rise all over my body. I must have looked like a huge plucked chicken flying through the air.

I guess we kind of broke the ice when we took our clothes off; after that, things seemed less awkward. Ben borrowed some shorts from PJ, and the guys competed for the Most Explosive Cannonball title. PJ brought us beers and some towels when we got out, and we all lounged on the patio furniture, sipping cold Coronas and feeling kind of adult about it. Amber stayed in her underwear, looking like a slightly oversized but no less cocky Victoria's Secret model; Hero and I both draped our towels over us, mummy-style, claiming we were cold.

Everything was more or less dreamy. The fragrance of hot cement and chlorine was so summery. I thought the beer tasted sort of vile, but the bubbles filled my head with a pleasant effervescence, carbonating my brain. Ben was sitting in a chair near my feet and I was stretched out on a cushioned chaise, soaking up the sun. I had to squint to see him, but each time I did, it was worth it. He was eating chips, and once he dropped one on my leg. When he reached to pick it up, his fingers brushed my shin, and the goose bumps spread all over again, making me glad that most of my body was buried under PJ's *Free Willy* towel.

"What's up, kiddies?" The second that John sauntered through the French doors, the relaxed atmosphere went all tense and wonky again.

"Hey, John." Amber peeked over her sunglasses at him,

then made her way in his direction. She had enough modesty to drape her towel around herself sarong-style as she stood up, though her black push-up bra was on full display.

"Looking good, Ginger." John gave her a slow once-over, then looked past her to Hero and me. "Hi, Blondie. Skater Girl."

We just waved and pulled our towels around us more tightly.

John and Amber were too far away for me to hear their conversation clearly, but every few minutes she'd fling her damp hair over her shoulder and laugh like he was the funniest guy alive. He stood close to her and spoke in low, intimate tones, but I noticed that he kept sneaking glances at Hero over Amber's shoulder.

After drinking half a bottle of beer, I needed to pee, so I tucked the towel around me and went inside to look for a bathroom. As I wandered down the hall, I passed what must have been PJ's room. I couldn't resist the urge to check out a boy's natural habitat. The floor was covered with clothes. The bed was a tangle of sheets and blankets. There was a massive stereo system, a huge collection of CDs and records, and some bookshelves with a ragged assortment of paperbacks leaning haphazardly against one another. The walls were plastered with posters of rap stars. Above the bed was a blown-up, slightly blurry photo of PJ shaking hands with Ice-T.

The bathroom was right there, but I couldn't help being intrigued by the door left a few inches ajar at the very end of the hallway. I tiptoed across the tile floor and listened for a long moment before pushing the door open gently, poised to dart for the bathroom if anyone was in there. It was all shadows, the blinds closed against the dazzling afternoon sunlight. The walls were filled with pen-and-ink drawings of faces, and even though the light was dim, I could see they had an almost photographic precision. There were also quite a few framed pictures of John—headshots, I guess, and some stills from his commercials. There was a long series of dance photos side by side, and in each one he had his arm wrapped protectively around a different pretty, slender girl with shiny hair. They were all from Sonoma Valley High, though I didn't know any of them very well. There were a couple of costumes laid out at the foot of the bed—a velvet cape, leather pants, a couple of wigs. No doubt it was all stuff for Sonoma Shakespeare's summer show; I'd heard he had a leading role, as usual.

Over in the corner was a stainless steel desk with a sleek new laptop open on it. The screensaver seemed to be a slideshow of John's photos. I couldn't stop myself; the images were yanking firmly at my inner Nancy Drew. Above the desk, his bedroom window was cracked open and I could just make out the low rumble of John's voice, interrupted once in a while by Amber's coquettish peals of laughter. I inched closer.

The first few photos weren't that interesting—just John and his muscle-bound buddies doing guy things: fishing, snowboarding, toasting the camera with Heinekens at the beach. Each picture had a different caption, like *"Corky, Brad, Ansley, and me kicking it at the coast."* I was about to leave, disappointed at my bland discoveries, when a picture of Amber popped up. She was wearing a soft pink sweater, looking

straight at the camera with an expression of such pure adoration and straight-up love, it took my breath away.

Then I saw the caption: *"Blowjob Beezie just before she drops to
her knees."*

A sick feeling swirled with slow-motion oiliness in the pit
of my stomach.

The next image made my mouth go dry. It was of Hero.
He'd probably gotten it from her MySpace account; she was
in a pretty white sundress, laughing, her nose splayed with
freckles. She looked about thirteen. The bold-faced type
beneath her read: *"The cock tease must be tamed."*

"'Abandon all hope, ye who enter here.'"

I must have jumped halfway to the ceiling when I heard
those words. I turned to see John filling the doorway, his pale
blue eyes fixed on my face.

I gaped at him idiotically. "Sorry, I just—" What? How
could I explain what I was doing there? "Just—had to pee."

"This isn't the bathroom. Don't know if you noticed."
He peered through the shadows at me. His voice seemed to
teeter between teasing and deadly serious.

"Yeah, I—took a wrong turn, I guess." A nervous giggle
escaped my lips. Inside, I was a messy jumble of embarrassment and anger. What the hell was he doing, writing that
misogynist crap about my best girls? I thought he was supposed to be *smart*.

He was still blocking the only way out. I longed to just
push past him, out to the pool and the sunshine and Coronas
and laughter, but I didn't dare.

"Anyway, you know who that is?" he asked.

"Who who is?"

"'Abandon all hope, ye who enter here.'"

For a second I couldn't think straight. Finally I said, "Dante?"

"Bingo. Wow, you really are a brainiac."

"Just a lucky guess."

"I doubt that." Something about the way he was studying me gave me the creeps. "I'm glad you girls came over. I've been wanting to get to know you and Hero. Your cousin is such . . ."—he searched the ceiling for the right word—"an enigma."

Don't you mean a cock tease?

"Yeah, she sure is." I clapped my hands together, hoping to signal the end of our conversation. "Okay, well, I'm going to run to the bathroom now."

His blue eyes flashed in the gloom. "You don't like me, do you?"

"Of course I do! I just have to pee, is all."

"Hero doesn't like me either. Wonder if I'm losing my touch." He smiled in a way that had nothing to do with happiness. He still didn't move.

"I'm sure you're not. Excuse me." I managed to squeeze past him. He smelled of cologne and mints. I walked quickly down the hall to the bathroom, not daring to look back, and locked the bathroom door, as if he might actually try to follow.

○ ● ● ○ ● ○

While I was peeing, I kept seeing the sketches of all those faces on John's wall. There was something that tied them together, though they had different hair, different expressions. Then it hit me: They all looked like John.

Whoa. That was weird.

I thought about the girls with shiny hair in the dance pictures. If the rumors were even remotely true, they'd all had sex with him—Amber too. I tried to imagine kissing him, but now the eerie, wolflike blue of his eyes was more creepy than sexy. I was sitting there on the pot, considering all of this, when I noticed that through the small, screened window above the toilet I could hear what was being said out by the pool.

"So what's up, man? Are you going to make a move?" PJ was asking.

I heard Ben say, "I don't know. I'm still having a hard time believing you guys."

Amber said, "We're her best friends, okay? We should know. She's totally into you. I'm scared to think what she might do if you don't like her."

"What do you mean?" Ben sounded concerned.

"She'd die," Hero piped in. "Really. She'd kill herself."

"To be honest, before you guys told me all this, I thought she hated me."

Amber laughed. "She acts tough, but deep down she's just a girly girl in love."

Wait a minute, why are they saying I like him? I thought he was supposed to have a crush on me.

Slowly at first, then more rapidly, the wheels started turning in my brain: the strange phone call I overheard at Hero's house; the loud, oddly theatrical conversation at TSB. Amber needed an introduction to Alistair Drake. Hero needed a chaperone. PJ wanted to get Claudio and Hero hooked up so he could have some peace. All they had to do for everyone to get what they wanted was hook me up with Ben. Suddenly, the unexpected truce between the virgin and the whore made sense.

That e-mail. Oh, God. Me and my stupid vocabulary.

I jumped up from the toilet, forgetting to flush. I could feel all the blood in my body rushing to my face. I looked in the mirror and was horrified by what I saw: a beet red girl with two long, stringy, wet braids. How could I have been so stupid? Ben never liked me—it was all a practical joke. I'd been too idiotic to recognize that the good old virgin-whore crew had set me up.

I washed my hands in a hurry and considered my next move. I couldn't cower in there forever, but I couldn't face them either. It was at least two miles to my house, and even if I could sneak my board from Amber's car without anyone noticing, I'd feel pretty weird skating all that way wearing nothing but a *Free Willy* towel over damp underwear. I'd have to just go out there, put my clothes on, and leave. If they thought it was weird, so be it. I wasn't going to speak to any of them for as long as I lived anyway, so if it was awkward now, that was just too bad.

I marched outside, looking straight ahead. I think they must have sensed something was wrong immediately, because their laughter and chatter died away as soon as they saw me. I made my way mechanically to the pile of clothes we'd left in the far corner of the yard, yanked on my shorts, and pulled my tank top over my head. I could still feel my face burning, but I didn't care. There was no point in keeping up appearances, since I'd already been completely and utterly humiliated.

"Hey," Amber said quietly as she sauntered up to me. "What's up?"

"I'm going." I bent down to tie my shoes. "See you."

"Hold on—why?"

"Not my scene." I finished tying my shoes and stood up straight. "Later." I started for the back gate, but she grabbed my arm.

"Whoa, Geena, slow down. What's wrong?"

I looked her in the eye. "Why did you do it?"

"Do what?"

"Set me up." We were speaking in low voices now, but the others were so quiet over by the pool, they might have been able to hear. I glanced at them over Amber's shoulder and saw that PJ, Claudio, and Ben were all trying to be cool, like they weren't listening, but Hero was trotting toward us in her Coca-Cola towel, her face scrunched into a scowl of concern.

"What are you talking about?" Amber asked. "Nobody set you—"

"I *heard* you, okay? He never even liked me. It's all just a joke."

Hero reached us just then, pink and upset. "What's wrong?"

I shook my head. "You guys just stay here, have fun, talk about me all you want. I've been knifed in the back before. I can handle it."

Amber made an impatient sound, but Hero's eyes immediately brimmed with tears. "Geebs, we did it out of love. Really."

Amber glared at her.

I laughed, but it was a hard, unfriendly sound. "If this is what it means to be loved, I can do without, thanks."

With that I turned on my heel and made for the gate.

○ ● ● ○ ● ○

I think I'd been skating for about five minutes when I heard someone running up behind me. The sun was scorching, and I knew I was getting so sunburned I'd peel like an egg later. I was hot and humiliated and in no mood for company. I figured it was probably Hero—Amber wouldn't run if there was a pack of rabid dogs on her heels. I spun around, ready to tell my traitorous cuz that I was a big girl and didn't need an escort, thanks, when I found myself face-to-face with Ben Bettaglia.

He was glazed in sweat, breathing hard. The sight of him brought back the sting of my embarrassment, and I planted my fists on my hips. "What are you doing?" My tone was ice cold.

"Can we talk?" He bent over slightly, hands on his knees, still panting, and looked up at me with those big brown eyes.

"I don't know. Are you capable? You seem to be having trouble *breathing*."

He chuckled, still a little breathless. "I cycle seven days a week, but running kills me. I should do it more often." When he recovered, I kicked my board into my hands and he fell into step beside me. We walked in silence for a long moment, the sun in our eyes. Finally, he said, "Looks like our friends played a little joke on us."

"More like *my* friends played a joke on *me*," I said pointedly.

"Not exactly. After you left, I got them to fess up. They were all in on it together. Claudio and PJ agreed to tell me you were—you know, into me—while Amber and Hero worked on you." He spread his palms out. "We were both had, I guess."

I snorted. "Some friends."

"Yeah, I know. They suck."

We plodded along for another minute. A cyclist whizzed past, and Ben followed him with his eyes. "Nice toe clips," he mumbled.

"Sorry?"

"Oh, nothing, I just . . ." He trailed off. When he spoke again, his words came out all in a rush; it reminded me of that time in English when we had to recite sonnets, and Ben raced through his so quickly it sounded like one extremely long word. "What-are-you-doing-next-Saturday?"

"Saturday? It's Hero's party." I started chewing on the tip of my braid. It's a disgusting habit, I know, but when I get nervous, it calms me down.

"Oh, yeah, I got an invitation. It sounds . . . fancy."

I nodded. "She's going a little crazy with it."

He didn't say anything for a while. "Are-you-going-with-anyone?" he blurted at last.

"No."

"You want to go?"

I tried to get a good look at his eyes, to see what he was up to, but he was staring fixedly at the sidewalk. I stopped walking. "Is this another trick? 'Cause you know, fool me once—"

He spun around to face me and his expression was so

surprised, so sincere, it stopped me mid-sentence. His hair was sticking up all funny from the pool and his bony knees were poking out of his wrinkled, baggy shorts, and suddenly I knew he wasn't playing me. He wanted me to go with him to Hero's party, and even if everything up until then had been a complete joke, nothing could change the look on his face right now.

"Okay," I said. "I'll go with you. Or, you know, meet you there, anyway. If you pick me up, Mom'll whip out the baby pictures."

He looked relieved. "Sure. That's cool. We can meet there."

I fiddled with my board, picking at the SANTA CRUZ sticker. "Did you, um . . .get my e-mail?"

"Yeah." He smiled with just his eyes. "Bettaglified. Interesting. I wonder if I'm Sloanified."

Before I could think too hard about that one, a distraction appeared. Monty Styles, a senior who had supposedly gotten not one but three girls pregnant, chose that moment to drive by in his souped-up Honda Civic. The car was packed with barely pubescent girls sporting big hair, and hip-hop was blasting from the windows. They all screamed at us for no apparent reason, their hoots rolling across the perfectly manicured lawns. We both just sort of grinned at them, unsure of what else to do.

When the bass was no longer rattling inside our ribs, Ben did something bizarre. He grabbed my shoulders, pulled me to him, and kissed me. The bright world of summer disappeared, and I was dragged headfirst into a vortex of lips and (ohmygod!) tongues. It reminded me of this time when I got pummeled by a wave in Santa Cruz; one minute it was just me and the pelicans and the blue sky, the next I was being yanked by the hair this way and that, lost in a world of frenzied bubbles and saltwater swirling in all directions.

When we finally came up for air, I could hardly believe we were still surrounded by perfect green squares of emerald lawn and bland, expensive houses. I half expected us to find ourselves on another planet.

Ben was staring at me intently, asking me questions with his eyes I couldn't quite translate, let alone answer. I shivered a little, even though it was 100 degrees out.

"Are you cold?" he asked in a whisper, running his hand lightly along my arm.

I looked down and saw a long trail of goose bumps stretching from my shoulder to my wrist. Worse, my nipples were standing at attention, just like they had in the frozen food aisle. My body is so disloyal. "I guess I am. Probably 'cause my underwear's all wet."

The second it was out of my mouth, I cringed.

"You know—from the pool," I amended, but it was too late.

"Yeah," he smirked. "Sure, Sloane. From the pool. That's what they all say."

I turned around and started skating away from him.

"I'll see you Saturday," he called after me.

I just raised my hand in a wave without turning around and veered right. There was a hill there just waiting for me to bomb. My whole body was buzzing; thoughts tumbled crazily around inside my brain. I needed to feel the force of gravity, to tuck into a low crouch and listen to the air whistling past my ears; otherwise, I might just float off into the cloudless sky with pure, buoyant joy.

Sunday, July 27
10:20 A.M.

Hero and Amber called all last night and this morning. My mom keeps asking, "What is it, babe? Why won't you talk?" I just told her it was personal and sequestered myself in my room.

I don't know what to think. My cousin and my best friend totally lied to me.

Ben Bettaglia, my rival since the fifth grade, kissed me.

Sometimes, a girl just has to dive under the duvet and regroup.

8:30 P.M.

After hiding in my room most of the day, I heard a knock on my door—a delicate tapping sound that somehow penetrated the folds of my bedspread. Fifty bucks said those were Hero's tiny, French-manicured fingers out there.

"Yeah?" I called from under the covers.

Sure enough, Hero said, "Let me in, Geebs."

I flung the comforter off of me and bellowed, "Go away, Judas!"

"Please?"

"Traitor!"

There was a pause. It lasted so long I almost wondered if she'd retreated on tiptoe, but then her small, clear voice said, "I'm coming in."

"No, you're not."

"Yes, I am."

I yanked the comforter back over my head. There was no lock on my door—my mother, who unfortunately models herself after Mussolini on issues of personal privacy, won't allow it. I pressed my face flat against the sheets and listened as Hero entered my room. Boy, she had some nerve. I felt her weight (what there was of it) pressing into my side of the bed. I rolled away.

"Geena, I'm sorry. Really, I am." She paused, but I didn't respond. "It was selfish and wrong, but I didn't think you'd get hurt."

I threw the duvet off so suddenly, she shrank away from me, looking terrified. "Oh, really? You didn't think it would hurt, discovering that my best friend and my *cousin* tricked me into believing a boy actually likes me?"

Hero grabbed my hand with a pleading look. "We thought you'd be cute together. All you needed was a little nudge."

"A nudge? This is not a nudge. This is tactical warfare."

I heard Mom talking to someone in the hallway, their voices low. Then there was another knock at my bedroom door. I clutched my forehead. "Who is it?"

"It's me," Amber said.

"Come on in," I called, "we're just reviewing Operation Disgrace Geena Sloane."

Amber closed the door behind her and leaned against it. "Wow," she said. "You look terrible."

"Thanks," I replied. "You look like the girl who sold me down the river."

She crossed the room and flounced onto the bed. "Don't be so melodramatic," she said. "There's no damage done."

"Says you."

Amber took out her lip gloss and applied a thick coat. "Geena, you know perfectly well that our plan worked. You like Ben, Ben likes you, we all live happily ever after."

"And I suppose you were only thinking of me, huh? Not of Alistair Drake, for example." I let that statement hang there, watching them squirm.

"How'd you know about that?" Hero asked.

Amber shot her a hostile look. "Ever try *denying* an accusation, Hero?"

"I have my ways," I said, hoping to sound mysterious and knowing.

"The end result," Amber said, "is the best of all worlds. You get Ben, Hero gets Claudio, and I get an introduction to Alistair. Is that really so awful? It's win-win-win."

I considered this a moment. "How can I ever trust you, though?"

"Trust is overrated. Trust too much, you're just naïve. Valuable lesson in the ways of the world." Seeing I wasn't completely convinced, she tried another angle. Grabbing Hero's hand, she added, "Bonus points: Conspiring has made us friends. Isn't that what you wanted?"

Hero looked at her hand in Amber's like she wasn't sure how it had gotten there, but then she pasted on an unconvincing After-School-Special look of sisterly affection.

I shook my head. "You guys are too much, you know that?"

Amber leaned toward me with a Cheshire cat grin. "You know you love us."

Thursday, July 31
2:05 P.M.

All morning at TSB, I had to endure Hero obsessing about how to wear her hair on Saturday. She had this magazine filled with nothing but hairstyles, most of which looked painfully absurd. Also, Hero's hair is so baby fine and straight, there really isn't much she *can* do with it. I mean, it's beautiful, but it doesn't respond well to an onslaught of products. Unfortunately, this brand of logic has not yet penetrated the thick, pink atmosphere of Planet Hero.

"Do you like this one?" She pointed at a picture of a girl with masses of springy black ringlets piled high on her head.

"It's okay." How she was going to manage that one was beyond me, but I knew it was pointless to say so.

"What about this?"

"I don't know, Cuz. You really think cornrows are your style?"

She looked unsure. "Maybe not."

Thank God someone drove up right then. I was about to run screaming from Hero's Wonderful World of Hair. Unfortunately, the person who happened to appear when I looked out the window was John Jamieson. His cold, reptilian smile greeted me as I slid the window open. Ever since Saturday, when I snooped in his room, I've had a sick feeling about John; I just haven't known what to do about it.

"Okay, Skater Girl, here's your quote for the day: 'A man cannot be too careful in the choice of his enemies.'"

"Oscar Wilde," I said.

He slapped the steering wheel in delight. "Very good! Amazing."

"You always have a quote for the day?"

"Not always. Just when I'm feeling pretentious."

"Would you like some caffeine with that pretension?"

He threw back his head and laughed. It's a sound that's slightly famous at Sonoma Valley High; you'd hear it at pep rallies and football games and everyone would turn around and search for its source. It's one of those harsh, hard laughs that sounds more like heavy artillery than happiness. When he was done laughing, he made a little gun with his left hand and pointed it at me. "You're a card, Skater Girl. I'll have a macchiato."

"With stiff foam," I said, remembering his order from before.

"Exactly." I went to make his drink and I heard him saying, "Oh, look, it's the lovely Hero."

Hero waved. "How's it going?"

"Wonderful, wonderful. I hear you and my Italian brother Claudio are . . . *friendly.*"

"I'm not sure what you mean."

"Nothing at all. Anyway, I'm happy for you. He's infatuated, of course." He lowered his voice a little, but I turned off the steamer just in time to hear him add, "I can see why."

I brought him his macchiato. "Anything else?"

"Oh, yeah," he said, taking his drink. "I'm having a party

tomorrow night. Parents are out of town. I know it's last-minute, but carpe diem and all that."

Hero started to say, "But—"

I stepped on her toe. "Great. Is it at your dad's?"

"Yeah—should start around nine or ten."

"Okay, cool. That'll be two dollars."

He paid me, tipped a dollar, and revved his engine. "Oh, almost forgot! It's got a theme—pimps and hos."

"Really?" I said. "Like costumes?"

He smiled. "Sure, you know, get a little trashy—have some fun. Just to mix it up." He looked at Hero with a suggestive smirk. "It's a chance to express that bad girl inside that's just dying to come out and play."

The guy was really outdoing himself on the slime-o-meter with that one.

When he was gone, Hero whined, "But my party's Saturday. Everyone will be exhausted and hungover now."

"You really think John Jamieson is going to cancel his shindig because you said so? If you complained, he'd probably move his to Saturday, just to see what would happen."

Her pale, delicate forehead wrinkled with confusion. "I doubt he'd do that."

I shook my head. "I don't trust him."

"You think he's throwing this party specifically to mess mine up?"

I thought about it. "I don't know. But he's got something up his sleeve. I can feel it."

"Amber's so into him."

I pulled a face. "I know, but why?"

She looked surprised. "Wait a minute! When he asked me out last month you acted like I was crazy to say no."

"Yeah, because—I don't know—everyone wants to go out with him."

"So why's it weird if Amber likes him?"

"Because she dated him already and he doesn't—you know—respect her." I felt flustered. A part of me wanted to tell her about the photos, but I didn't want to freak her out. Who knows? Maybe someone else had written those stupid captions—Corky, maybe. I wouldn't put it past a guy like him. Still, if John wasn't a total scumbag, why hadn't he deleted them?

"Amber went out with John?" Hero asked.

"Yeah. For a little while. It didn't work out, though. I just worry she's going to get hurt. Something about John seems sketchy . . ."

Hero shook her head and adopted a condescending tone. "You should really examine that hostility of yours."

I frowned at her. "What's that supposed to mean?"

"You know what Bronwyn would say—it's your chronic distrust of men flaring up again."

That pushed my buttons. "Hello! Can you not see this? Don't you think he seems slightly two-faced?"

She sized me up. "You've got to get over this, Geena. It's not healthy."

I threw a rag in the sink. "Fine! Don't listen to me. But John Jamieson is not to be trusted. That's all I'm going to say."

Friday, August 1

10:15 A.M.

Less than twelve hours until John's party and still the ho-muses have failed to inspire. I hate shopping. I mean yes, when you find the right sweatshirt or the perfect pair of Pumas, and the wallet holders cough up the funds without too much hassle, that moment when you slip into your purchase can be magical—a new lease on life via retail rebirthing. But those moments are rare. Usually, shopping is a torturous activity involving fluorescent overhead lights exposing way too many quivering bulges. I'd rather kick it in a burlap sack than follow my mom into Macy's, where she'll inevitably press a *Little House on the Prairie* floral sundress to my body and sigh wistfully before my death stare forces her to put the hideous thing back on the rack with a pouty, "If only you'd wear something *pretty.*"

It took me two weeks to find something halfway decent for Hero's party. Now, in less than twelve hours, I'm expected to transform myself into a glittering specimen in full bootie-licious regalia.

Oh my God! BB just sent me a text message. *RU going 2night?*

Got to think of a clever response, without seeming like I'm trying too hard. Something simple yet funny, memorable, charming, titillating but not raunchy. Brevity is key. I must leave him wanting more.

Oh, for God's sake.

Yes.

Hitting SEND . . . there. Let him chew on that for a while.

1:45 P.M.

Hero called this morning. "Amber's coming over," she said. "You want to come?"

"Wait wait wait. Amber's going to be at your *house*?"

"Yeah." Her tone was annoyingly nonchalant. "So?"

Let's review, shall we?

June: Hero and Amber declare themselves mortal enemies.

July: Secret pact forms between them, thus avoiding actual scratching out of eyes and/or ritual scalping.

August: "Amber's coming over. You want to come?"

I'm all for peace, love, and understanding, long live the sisterhood, blah, blah, blah, but this is ridiculous.

"Geebs? You there?" Again, Hero's tone implied nothing out of the ordinary was happening.

"Yeah." I swallowed hard and tried to get a grip. We were sixteen, not six. I should be able to share a friend with my cousin. That *was* the whole point of introducing them, right?

It's just that it would have been totally different if Hero had invited me first. The idea that I'm the afterthought really gets to me.

"Are you mad or something?" Hero sounded impatient.

"No. Not at all. What time should I come over?"

"Whenever. I'll be here."

I paused, chewing on the end of one braid. "When is Amber coming over?"

"Any minute now."

"Right," I said. "See you soon."

I made record time skating to Hero's. She lives about three miles outside of town, and her road, Moon Mountain Drive, is a nightmare grade you can't possibly skate up, though it's heaven coming down. Usually I make Hero pick me up at the bottom of the hill in her dad's golf cart, but today I just went ahead and ran all the way up, carrying my board. I was determined to get there before Amber did. When I arrived all sweaty and panting, I realized immediately that my mission had failed. There was the gold El Dorado in all its dented glory, soaking up the sun. It was parked right in between Uncle Leo's gleaming Mercedes, his antique Jag, and Bronwyn's red Jeep. The four cars side by side looked a little perplexed, like they couldn't quite figure out how they'd come to occupy the same patch of real estate.

I walked in without knocking; cousins have certain birthrights, don't we? I wasn't sure what to expect. It was hard to picture Amber as her usual brassy self in the midst of Uncle Leo's marble sculptures, linen drapes, and crystal bowls filled with Asian apple-pears. There was just something unnatural about the whole idea.

When I walked in, though, there they were, spread out on the huge leather sectional couch. All four of them were laughing their heads off. Amber was wearing a humongous pair of garish plaid pants, a polo shirt, a stiff white visor, and enormous mirrored sunglasses. The whole outfit was clearly Uncle Leo's. She was standing on the couch with no shoes on, gripping a golf club and pretending to prepare for a swing. Bronwyn and Hero were both collapsed against the couch, immobilized by giggles. Uncle Leo sat on a nearby ottoman, his belly shaking as he wiped away tears.

I was speechless. I just stood there, surveying the scene, unsure of how to proceed.

It was Amber who noticed me at last. "Hey, G," she said. "How do I look?"

This prompted another wave of hysterics from her fans.

"I get it," I said. "You're Uncle Leo, right?"

"Close." Amber winked. "I'm actually his evil twin."

Hero laughed so hard at that, I thought she might hyperventilate. Was it me, or was this just not as funny as they all seemed to think? I mean yeah, whatever, Amber looked mildly amusing in a clownish sort of way, but was she really entertaining enough to warrant such violent hysterics?

"Cool," I said, and headed to the kitchen for a soda.

What was happening? Why did I feel suddenly like the kid who gets picked last for dodgeball?

Bronwyn came into the kitchen while I was in there gulping down my Rock Star. She was wearing a little white miniskirt and a polka-dotted halter top. It seemed like she was drifting further from her rebel-chick roots every day. "You should try these kumquats I got at the farmer's market," she said. "They're amazing." She held out a bag of what looked like baby oranges.

"Thanks," I said. "I just ate."

She shrugged, and popped one into her mouth.

"You sure are home a lot this summer," I said. "Why aren't you in Berkeley?"

She pursed her lips in an *I've got a secret* smirk and kept chewing.

"What's that look for?" I asked, leaning in a little closer.

When she'd finally swallowed, she said, "I've got my reasons."

"Like . . . ?"

"Richard has a summer home in Glen Ellen." There was a gleam in her eye that was slightly manic.

"But couldn't you guys hang out just as easily in Berkeley?"

The gleam went dull and she shook her head. "Not exactly."

"Why not?" I was starting to get a slightly queasy feeling about all this.

She mouthed the word *married* just as Amber and Hero came running into the kitchen. I kept my eyes on Bronwyn, reeling with this new information, but she turned and slipped out the door.

Meanwhile, Amber and Hero were all pink-cheeked and excited. "Let's go to Goodwill," Hero said to me, grabbing my hand.

"No better place for whoring clothes," Amber added.

I was so relieved to be included in their circle again, I made up my mind to go along with whatever it was they wanted. "Okay, but I'm not going to squeeze the Uniboob into a bustier, okay? Let's just get that straight right now."

"Oh, come on!" Amber teased. "Your rack would look awesome in a bustier."

"No way."

"Yes! You're always hiding them under baggy T-shirts." Hero laughed. "Let them be free!"

"You mean, let *it* be free. That's why it's called the Uniboob, okay?"

Amber and Hero were laughing hysterically when Uncle

Leo walked in. "Okay, okay," he said. "Stop that, or I'll be forced to drug test you."

"We're not on drugs," Amber told him. "We're just high off July!"

"Why do you need to go to Goodwill? Is this some kind of costume party?"

"Pimps and hos!" Hero cried. "We're going to dress like cheap tarts and drink beer like normal teenagers."

Uncle Leo didn't look too happy about that. I did my best to intervene. "Come on, Leo, it's just a healthy expression of intense hormonal activity. Besides, I'm going to be there, so how much trouble can we get into?"

He looked skeptical, but he patted my shoulder and said, "I hope you mean that, Geena. I really do."

4:30 P.M.

John's party begins in approximately 330 minutes. Oh my God.

I'll probably have a nervous breakdown right here on my bed just thinking about it.

Is Ben Bettaglia going to kiss me again?

4:50 P.M.

I'm not wearing this hideous vinyl bustier. I don't care what they say—I'm just not doing it.

7:00 P.M.

I've got on the bustier. Oh. My. God.

Amber and I are at Hero's. They totally gave me a hard

time when I tried to pair my regular old Sector Nine T-shirt with the too-tight red miniskirt I got at Goodwill. Eventually, I caved and tried on the bustier they insisted on buying for me, "Just in case." I feel like a sausage spilling out of my casing. I can't breathe. My voice sounds like I'm on helium.

Although, I have to admit, it does sort of separate the Uniboob into distinct entities.

En-titties. Har-har.

I think the lack of oxygen is getting to me.

7:35 P.M.

I can't believe it. Ben Bettaglia called me. On my cell. He called *me*.

I was way too nervous to talk, so Amber relayed the message: He'll be there tonight.

Please, God, don't let him laugh at my newly cleaved Uniboob.

9:10 P.M.

As we were huddled before the mirror in Hero's bathroom getting ready, Hero had a mini-meltdown. She suddenly tossed her comb onto the counter and said in a petulant voice, "I don't know how to be sexy. I look ridiculous."

"You look fabulous," I said, retrieving the comb and running it through her baby-fine bob. I wasn't just saying it either—she really did. She'd chosen to go with a *Matrix*-esque, sleek, Catwoman-of-the-future motif, and it was working for her. Frustrated by the lack of choices at Goodwill, she'd opted to shell out the cash for proper fetish wear at the mall. She had on a black catsuit and a dark leather jacket. But the thing you noticed most about her outfit was the pair of thigh-high lace-up patent leather boots that would make any dominatrix proud.

"I can't go like this," Hero complained. "Everyone will laugh their asses off."

Amber was leaning close to the bathroom mirror, concentrating on applying a pair of gold, glittery false eyelashes. She was wearing leopard-print bellbottoms and a sequined tube top that left most of her midriff exposed. "Are you joking?" she asked, glancing at Hero over her shoulder.

"No." Hero was still pouting.

"Then you're blind," Amber said.

"Hero," I said, "you look amazing."

She shook her head. "Bronwyn's the sexy one. All I can hope for is runner-up."

I put my arm around her. "That's so not true."

Amber was focused on her false eyelashes again. I kicked her gently. "Is it?" I prompted.

"Ow!" She turned to look at Hero. One false eyelash was only partway on, and it dangled precariously as she blinked. "Chica, you're obviously a lot hotter than you realize. Hello! You've been in town like two minutes and you've already got guys banging down your door."

Hero allowed herself a bashful half smile. "I do not."

"Come on, cut the false modesty, okay? You've totally got it; you just need to work it a little." Amber turned back to the mirror. "Man, I'm about to shove this stupid eyelash kit up Maybelline's ass!"

Touching scene of female bonding officially over.

9:45 P.M.

We'll leave in about fifteen minutes. Amber says getting there any earlier is the social kiss of death. To kill time before we go, Amber and Hero are messing around on Hero's laptop. They found John Jamieson's Web site; he's got all these headshots and resumes on there, like for casting directors, I guess, or in case Lindsay Lohan suddenly needs him as a costar.

"Oh, my God," Amber said. "Why does he have to be so cute?"

"He's not that cute—ouch!" I was experimenting with a curling iron at Hero's dressing table, with rather painful results.

They both looked at me like I was crazy.

"What? He's not."

"So if he asked you out, you'd turn him down?" Amber challenged.

I didn't even hesitate. "Absolutely. Hero did."

Amber turned to Hero. "He asked you out?"

"Um, sort of. It wasn't a big deal." She looked uncomfortable.

"It was too! He tried to get her out on that yacht his friend owns."

Amber sucked her breath in. "And you said no?"

"Of course she said no. She's into Claudio. Anyway, John's totally overrated."

Amber looked at me. "What do you have against John all of a sudden?"

"I just don't trust him." I was thinking of those creepy

photos I saw on his computer, but I pretended to be too en-
grossed in my hair-curling to say more than that.

"You definitely shouldn't trust him," Amber said, "but he's
still sexy."

I eyed Amber. "You're not still into him, are you?"

Amber turned back to the screen. "No. Of course not. I
mean, not seriously. "

Hero and I exchanged a look when she printed the page
with his photo on it. "Then why are you printing that page?"
I asked.

She picked it up off the printer. "None of your business."

When Amber's retorts are that lame, you know something's up.

Saturday, August 2
2:30 A.M.

I'm so exhausted . . . don't even know if I can write. I better
get it all down now, though, before it gets too muddled inside
my brain.

Disaster #1: Pimps and hos party?

Can anyone say *John Jamieson sucks?*

We got there with our false eyelashes, our catsuits, our
thigh-high boots, glittery blue eye shadow, and, in one
unfortunate case, a medically unsound bustier, only to find
that everyone else was wearing jeans and T-shirts.

I was ready to donate my body to science.

If it weren't for Amber, we probably would have turned
on our four-inch heels and marched back out. While Hero

and I were blushing furiously, shooting each other morti-fied looks, Amber assessed the situation quickly, named the culprit, and strutted over to him, her green eyes flash-ing fire.

"So, I guess you think this is funny?" She stuck one hip out and crossed her arms in front of her chest.

John was standing in the midst of four toothpick-thin freshmen girls, all of them sporting overly processed hair and faces so caked with makeup they looked like underfed mannequins. He was apparently regaling them with stories of his latest commercial, a Cheez Whiz ad that aired last week, while pouring them shots from a bottle of Jack Daniel's. When Amber approached, he gripped the bottle in front of him like it might protect him from her wrath. "Misunderstanding, I guess," he said, his sculpted shoulders rising toward his ears before dropping again.

Corky, who was lurking just outside the ring of emaciated John fans, emitted a braying sound that vaguely resembled laughter, and the rest of the people crowding the living room tittered in response. Amber shot Corky a look so withering, his laughter stuck in his throat.

Amber's face took on a hard, determined edge as she turned back to John. "Fine. Misunderstanding, then. But don't think for a second you can ruin our night." She grabbed a shot glass from the nearest anorexic and downed its con-tents in one gulp. Without hesitation, she went over to PJ, who was set up behind his turntables, and flipped through his LPs until she found one she approved of. As he replaced P. Diddy with vintage Prince, Amber jumped up onto the coffee table, her bright white boots scattering magazines every which way. "Ladies and gentlemen . . ." Her voice was confident, loud enough to silence the whole room. "May I present to you, the Ho Brigade!" Then PJ pumped the volume up until "Erotic City" was so loud you could feel it in your throat. Amber waved Hero and me over. We glanced at each other—a split-second cousin consultation—before crossing the room and leaping up onto the coffee table beside her.

We danced on that table for at least an hour, shaking our butts like we were confident, campy chicks out for a good time, and not the victims of a practical joke. The bizarre thing was we actually pulled it off. Some of the little freshmen toothpick girls who lived in mortal fear of doing anything remotely energetic were even copying us; I caught them imitating our hoochie-mama dance grooves like they'd just seen them on MTV.

"Hey—Hero! Over here!" John was snapping pictures with his cell while we danced. Hero was soaking up the attention, striking silly poses with a joy and abandon I'd never seen her display in public.

Amber kept trying to crowd into each shot, doing more and more outrageous moves just so John would notice her, but all he seemed to care about was aiming the lens at Hero. Amber wasn't happy about that. Each time John ignored her, her expression hardened just a little bit more. Finally she turned to me and said, "I need a drink." Then she jumped off the table abruptly and made a beeline for the kitchen.

I spotted Ben across the room just then. He looked kind of puzzled at first, and I was seized for a moment with a debilitating self-consciousness, like those nightmares where you suddenly realize you're naked in civics. I tugged at the straps of my bustier, horrified that he was seeing me like this. But then our eyes locked and a slow smile spread across his face—that look he gets, like *Jesus, what will she do next?*—and my confidence went from running-on-fumes to spilling-over-full, just like that.

Ah, the mystery of me.

Disaster #2: The virgin-ho gets drunk.

Well, one of the virgin-hos, anyway. This one can't stand the taste of Jack Daniel's, which is all they had since the keg fell through. Evidently, the keg company wouldn't take Corky's fake ID, even though he's had to shave since the sixth grade and now looks approximately forty. Being resourceful, the Jamieson brothers conned Jana Clark into snagging six cases of Jack from her parents' liquor store. I tried half a shot and felt like I was going to yuke, which was just as well because believe me, my co-hos needed babysitting in the worst way.

As soon as Hero and I stepped down from our coffee table dance floor, John came over and wrapped his arm around her like a jovial uncle after too many cups of eggnog. I stood there feeling distinctly chopped liver–ish. It's not like I was dying for John to drape his big, meaty arm over *my* shoulders, but let's face it, being the odd ho out really sucks.

"Hero, baby," he said. "I know you're mad, but seriously, I'd never set you up. It was an honest mistake. We changed our minds about the pimps and hos thing, but I lost your number, so I couldn't let you know. Anyway, it all turned out fine, didn't it? You're the life of the party and every girl here wishes *she'd* thought of wearing blue eye shadow and"—his eyes fell on me—"a vinyl bustier." He squeezed his lips together, trying not to laugh. I just crossed my arms and ignored him.

"You set us up and you know it," Hero said. "You totally suck. End of story."

I did a double take. Was this the boots talking? Hero suddenly had an attitude.

"Ohh, feisty," John growled. "I love a girl who's not afraid to bite." A lascivious smile spread unpleasantly across his eraser pink face.

"Come on, Geebs." Hero swiveled out of his embrace and pulled me toward the kitchen. "Let's get a drink."

I trailed after her, inwardly cursing my too-tight skirt. Between that and the bustier, it felt like I was wearing a boa constrictor. I snuck a peek at John over my shoulder, wondering how he'd take being openly dissed. He didn't look upset; his eyes were glued to Hero's butt like it was a priceless piece of art he had to have.

Claudio came up to us in his striped T-shirt and pressed chinos. He said something to Hero in Italian. She shrugged, answered him in a surprisingly terse tone, and flounced off. I hurried after her.

"What was that all about?" I asked.

She looked annoyed. "Some guys can be so possessive. I guess he didn't like the way I danced. Whatevs."

Whatevs? Since when did Hero use *whatevs?* She sure was on a tear tonight.

As we turned the corner into the kitchen, we collided with Ben Bettaglia. Unfortunately, he was carrying a glass, and as we smacked into him liquid erupted from it, showering all three of us.

"Oh my God, I'm s-so sorry," I stammered.

"No biggie," he said. "Just water."

"My hair." Hero fussed with her now damp do. When she saw me standing there, staring up at Ben, she smirked knowingly and kept going without me.

"Oh," he said, peering carefully at my face. "You've got a drop right"—he rubbed his thumb along my cheekbone— warm, gentle, lingering pressure that made my throat feel thick—"there."

"Thanks." It came out barely a whisper. I wondered if the Max Factor mascara Amber had applied in thick coats had found its way under my eyes, transforming me from goddess to linebacker. "So, you having fun? I guess you're not drinking." I nodded at the now empty glass.

"Yes—I mean no," he said. "I mean, yes, I'm having fun, but no, I'm not drinking."

"How come?"

He thought about it for a second. "One, I'm in training. Two, I think that stuff"—he nodded at a tray of shot glasses floating past— "tastes like lighter fluid. Not that I've ever, you know, tasted lighter fluid, but . . ."

"Right, no, I totally know what you mean," I said. "The stuff's fetid."

He grinned. "Fetid. Good word."

"From the SAT list." I laughed.

A loud cheer went up from the kitchen, and I peered around

Ben to see Hero tossing back a jumbo-sized shot of Jack. She almost choked on it, but John patted her on the back a few times, and once she'd caught her breath, she flashed a wobbly grin. The crowd around her cheered again.

Claudio sauntered over to us. "Hero is so . . . how do you say? A party dog?"

I smiled. "Party animal, you mean?"

"Yes. I'm sorry—my English."

"No," I said. "I get you. And actually she's not usually. She's never had more than a couple glasses of her dad's wine. I guess she's just . . . experimenting."

Claudio nodded, his brow furrowed. "She may be sick."

"Don't worry," I said. "Hero's pretty smart. She won't do anything *too* stupid."

Just then Hero bounced a quarter into a shot glass at the center of the kitchen table. John was there at her side, egging her on. Her thin, pale arms shot straight into the air, fists clenched, and she squealed at the top of her lungs. She didn't even resemble her old self tonight. Usually she wears a tiny bit of mascara, tops. But after Amber's makeover her face was so plastered with blue eye shadow, blusher, and candy apple red lipstick, she was difficult to recognize. The body-hugging catsuit left very little to the imagination, especially now that she'd discarded the leather jacket.

"She look . . . different," Claudio observed. He kept sneaking glances at her, trying to be subtle. His worried little frown made me feel sorry for him. I wanted to go over there, seize her delicate little pink ear, drag her over to Claudio, and make her talk to him in a normal, decent, intelligent fashion—not in squeals and giggles, which seemed to be her language of choice at the moment. Here she was, barely six feet from the guy she supposedly couldn't live without, and instead of hanging out with him she was playing quarters with the pompous prick who'd done everything he could to humiliate us.

"John told us it was a costume party," I said to them, smiling weakly. "Pimps and hos."

Ben said, "A-ha," looking mildly relieved, like maybe those straitjackets wouldn't be required after all.

"It was kind of messed up," I said. "John's idea of a practical joke. But, whatever. We're trying not to let it ruin our night." I felt ridiculous again, in spite of myself—silly and exposed. I looked around for Amber. She was never self-conscious. When we'd climbed up onto the coffee table, her relentless confidence had spilled over onto me, making me feel like a glamorous guest star instead of a stupid chick who'd been had. Now her spell was wearing off, and my bustier was digging into my ribs.

"Want to go outside?" Ben's voice snapped me out of my morbid shame spiral. "It's kind of . . . smoky in here." I followed his gaze and saw that the Sandalwood Sisters were stinking up the kitchen, passing a huge joint back and forth. They were also, I noticed, laughing through pursed lips at my outfit. Like they had any right to judge my fashion choices. Rasta wiggers are supposed to be all about peace, love, and THC, but they can be petty as anyone, I guess.

"Sure," I said. "Okay."

Ben looked at Claudio. "You want to come?"

Even though I sort of wanted to be alone with Ben, I

liked that he didn't just ditch his friend like most guys would.

Claudio shook his head and glanced uneasily at Hero. "Maybe I'll just . . . how do you say? Keep an eye on."

I smiled. "Yeah, that's a good idea. If the hos start table dancing again, call me in for backup."

He nodded, but I don't think he was really listening.

Once we were outside by the pool with the cool air on our faces, I felt instantly more at ease. The night smelled like chlorine and freshly cut grass. We could hear music pulsing through the walls of the house, but all at once the party seemed distant—like something that was happening to someone else. Out here, it was just Ben Bettaglia and me. I could feel my hands tingling and my heart pounding. Sitting there with him was flooding my body with a dangerous, heady drug.

"Are you having a good time?" In the dark, his eyes looked black.

"Yeah, I guess so. I mean, it's sort of embarrassing"—I gestured vaguely at my outfit—"but I probably shouldn't care what people think."

He said, "It's human."

"I guess."

We were sitting on separate lawn chairs, facing each other, and our legs were about six inches apart. I stared at the shape his knees made inside his jeans, and then the wind shifted and I caught a whiff of him. It was a great smell, like laundry detergent, toothpaste, and something else that had no name. That part was him, I guess—his skin or whatever—and just thinking about that made me feel a little light-headed. I remembered Mr. Patel, our biology teacher, saying that smell is really tiny, evaporated particles floating through the air, so when you smell cut grass, it's actually invisible bits of grass going up your nose. Now I had Ben Bettaglia molecules floating inside me. It was a little overwhelming.

"How's Auggie doggie?" He was grinning at me; I could see the sarcastic curve of his lips in the moonlight.

"None of your business," I said, trying to sound offended, but ruining it by laughing out loud.

"You really are the weirdest girl I ever met," he said, shaking his head.

"Thanks a lot!" I wasn't pretending to be offended this time. I seriously was.

"Don't be mad," he said. "It's what I like best about you. You're not like anyone else."

He scooted his chair closer to mine, so that our knees touched. Then he leaned toward me, and even though I was still a little stung by his comment, I found myself tilting my head toward his, savoring the warmth of his breath on my lips. Our faces were only inches apart now, but he didn't kiss me. The tension was unbearable.

"So you've got a thing for freaks, huh?" My voice was so low and husky, I barely recognized it.

"Sure do. Especially cute freaks in cheap vinyl."

I pulled back slightly. "Don't even start on the bustier, man, or I swear I'll—"

He covered my mouth with his, and my mind went blank, killing any desire to finish my sentence. We kissed for a long time, and it was different from when he'd kissed me last week. That time—the first time—it was like falling. This was more like floating. Before, we were rushed, disoriented, pushing blindly into foreign territory. This time we explored each other's mouths quietly, patiently, like travelers tasting an exotic fruit for the first time.

"Sloanified," he murmured after a while. "Adjective: Unable to stop kissing a certain salutatorian (e.g., 'Dude, I'm so Sloanified')."

"Close," I whispered. "Except I'm sure you mean valedictorian."

   ° •   •   ° •   °

"Oh my Gawwwwd!"

I pulled away from Ben just in time to see a drunk, exhilarated Hero plunging, fully clothed, into the kidney-shaped pool. She disappeared for a moment, and I had visions of myself dragging her lifeless body from the depths, but luckily she re-emerged quickly, sputtering with laughter.

Claudio stood at the edge of the pool. "You're crazy!"

"Look out!" John came running through the French doors and launched into a cannonball that splashed everyone on the patio. Of course, monkey see, monkey do: Corky followed suit, and soon half the kids at the party were bobbing, fully clothed, in the deep end.

I looked around for Amber, but didn't spot her. Ben and I retreated into the shadows, staking out another lawn chair that was a little farther from the fray. This time I sat on his lap, and when we started kissing again, I wondered if it was lust or lack of oxygen that was making me feel so lightheaded.

We didn't pay any attention to our surroundings until I heard Hero's voice raised in protest. "I said no!"

I searched the crowd and spotted John cornering Hero at the far end of the pool. They were still in the water, and John had his shirt off. The broad expanse of his muscular back blocked my view of Hero, mostly, but I could see the top of her head and hear the tone in her voice. "I mean it."

"Come on," he was saying. "Stop torturing me."

She shoved him back. "Get away from me!"

Claudio, Ben, and I reached them at the same time. Claudio was going off in warp-speed Italian, endeavoring to pull Hero from the pool. She obviously wanted to get away from John, but having her shoulder half wrenched from its socket wasn't helping much.

"Claudio, ease up," I said, pulling his hand from her arm. "Hero, just get out of the pool, okay?"

She obeyed, managing to pull herself onto the deck, albeit without much grace. Claudio and I both helped her to her feet. She was dripping wet, of course, and mascara ran in inky black rivulets down her face.

"Geena was right," Hero spat at John, who remained treading water. "You're a total slime! I can't believe you're actually popular."

Okay, now he hates us both. Great.

John's face was distorted with sheer contempt. "Whatever, cock tease."

"Don't you ever touch me again!" Unfortunately, Hero's righteous little speech was cut short as she bent over and puked all over the deck.

"Uh, Cuz." I had to mouth-breathe to avoid following her lead. "Maybe we should head out. What do you say?"

She wiped her mouth with the back of her hand, a delicate

little gesture in a distinctly indelicate situation. "Geebs, I don't feel so good."

"No kidding. Come on, let's go." I turned to Ben. "You think we could catch a ride?"

He nodded. "Sure, no problem."

As Hero, Claudio, Ben, and I headed into the house, I hazarded one last glance back at John. He and Corky were sitting at the edge of the pool, watching our every move. This time, though, John wasn't staring at Hero with his usual lust. The look I saw in his eyes now sent cold shivers all the way up my spine.

o • • o • o

We found Amber sitting on the front steps, smoking a cigarette. "We're going to go," I said. "You ready?"

She shrugged. "Naw. I'll find my own ride."

"Where've you been?" I asked.

"Nowhere. Who cares? Nobody missed me."

"Amber"—I made her look me in the eye—"that's not true. And I've already got one bad attitude on my hands, okay, so be a pal."

She stood, wobbling slightly, and spit into the Jamiesons' lush garden. I think she was a little tipsy, though she could definitely handle her liquor better than Hero. "Who puked?"

I nodded at Hero. She was leaning against Claudio, rattling off a monologue in Italian that sounded maudlin and self-pitying. Claudio kept nodding and mumbling to her in reassuring tones. Her boots were completely splattered with vomit, and every time she took a step they secreted water with a squishing sound. Amber snickered, and I ignored her.

"We should really get those boots off before she gets in

the Volvo." I looked at Ben. "Unless you don't mind your car reeking of vomit."

"That would be fetid," Ben said, smirking. "But won't her dad be suspicious if she comes home barefoot?"

I considered this. "It's better than trailing puddles through the house and smelling like puke."

It took all four of us to unlace them and yank them off while Hero giggled hysterically on the lawn, but eventually we left the incriminating hoochie-boots behind. When Hero realized they weren't coming with her, she protested.

"My Barbarella boots," she whined. "I need them."

"Here," I said. "Look, I'll stash them in the bushes. If you still want them tomorrow, we can come back and get them."

"Someone will steal them. Amber, take care of my Barbar-boots!"

Amber answered with a noncommittal, "Yeah, okay."

"Good night," Claudio said, looking sadly at his drunk angel as she blew kisses from the backseat.

Just before we drove off, I rolled down the window and called to Amber, "You sure you don't want a ride?"

"I'm fine." She was standing in the shadow of a bougainvillea vine, her face dappled with delicate shapes, and somehow the sight of her there in her leopard-print bell bottoms and sequined tube top made me sad. A cool breeze kicked up; she hugged herself, shivering slightly. She didn't wave as we pulled away from the curb and off into the night.

○ ● ● ○ ● ○

When we got to Monte Luna, Ben actually got out and opened my door for me. I didn't want to leave the cozy, suntan-oil-and-damp-dog smell of his Volvo, but I knew it wouldn't do to linger in the drive, since Hero might toss her cookies again any second.

"Thanks for the ride." I rested my hand against his chest for a moment, just to feel the warmth of his skin beneath his T-shirt.

"Thank *you*."

I smiled. "For what?"

"For wearing that God-awful top—or whatever. It looks great on you, by the way."

"Get a good look," I said, "because I'll have to remove a rib if I want to wear it again."

"Va-va-va-voom-dee-ay," Hero sang as she clambered out of the backseat, "they took my boots away, I said I do not care, they took my underwear!"

"Shhh!" I glanced nervously at the living room window, where a light was still burning brightly. Getting Hero into the house, up the stairs, beyond the inquisitive eyes of Uncle Leo had to happen fast or we'd be busted.

"Duty calls." I quickly rose up onto my toes and planted a good-night kiss on Ben's smiling mouth. It felt so good to be alive right then, I wanted to scream.

As Ben drove away, I turned to my wasted cousin. "Whatever happens, keep walking. Don't actually *talk* to your dad, okay?"

"I can talk! I'm a good talker. *Je parle français. Parlo italiano.* Iway eakspay igpay atinlay!" She cracked up.

I addressed her in a dead-serious voice. "Hero, do you want to go to your birthday party tomorrow?"

"Yeah!"

"Then you're going to do whatever I tell you, and nothing else. Do you understand?"

She kicked at the gravel, a petulant child. "Okay. Jeez, you're mean."

I took her elbow and we started toward the house. As we neared the front door, I got a last-minute idea. "I know—if he tries to talk to you, act like you're really upset."

"Why?"

"You know how Leo is about tears; he won't want to deal."

She was distracted by a couple moths flitting around the porch light. "Ooh—butterflies," she cooed.

"Hero, are you listening?"

"Mm-hm."

"What did I just say?"

She looked at me, her face blank.

"Focus: If he tries to engage you in conversation, just act like you're crying. That's all you have to remember."

She started moaning histrionically; she sounded like a heifer in heat.

"Okay, let's take that down a notch," I coached. "Actually, take it down about seven notches."

Hero obeyed, whimpering softly.

"Good," I said. "But only do it when I say, all right? Otherwise, don't make a peep."

"You're not the boss of me," Hero whined.

I said, "Fine, you want your party canceled, go right ahead."

Now she was whimpering for real.

"Just follow orders." I took a deep breath and opened the door. "Let's do this."

We slipped through the foyer without incident. Unfortunately, we had to go through the living room to reach the marble staircase that led to Hero's room. As we tiptoed over the thick wool rugs into the dreaded light, we spotted Leo fast asleep on the couch, the latest issue of *Imbibe* open on his chest, a half-empty goblet of wine and his spectacles beside him on the coffee table.

We were a mere ten feet from the staircase when Hero somehow managed to knock a fern from its plant stand. It landed with a resounding crash on the hardwood floor, spilling dirt and shards of pottery. Leo jerked awake. We walked faster, but it was no use.

"What was that?" Leo demanded.

"Sorry," I said. "I knocked a plant over. I'll clean it up in the morning, 'kay?"

"Oh—right." He sounded groggy. "Esperanza will get it. You girls have a good time?"

"Yeah," I said over my shoulder, still headed for the stairs. "We had a blast."

"I thought you'd call for a ride."

"Sorry about that." I turned slightly toward him. "Ben drove us. He doesn't drink—he's in training."

"Good. Fine. Did people like your . . . costumes?"

"Yeah. We were quite a hit."

Hero looked like she was about to comment; I steered her toward the stairs again and said, "We're so tired." I threw in a huge, theatrical yawn. "We just want to hit the hay. 'Night, Leo."

"Oh, okay. Well, good night."

I thought we were finally home free as we started up the stairs, but then Leo called out, "Hero, honey, what happened to your shoes?"

Oh, God. That was it. Hero started to giggle.

"Hero?" Leo repeated. "Did you hear me?"

"Cry!" I commanded under my breath.

Hero's giggles became fairly convincing if slightly-over-the-top sobs.

"What is it, sweetheart? You okay?"

The strained confusion in my uncle's voice almost made me confess all. Instead, I left Hero there, leaning against the banister, and went to him. "She's okay. She's just—you know—it's been a long night."

"Did something happen?"

I leaned toward him, lowering my voice to a conspiratorial whisper. "It's just that time of the month. You know how we get."

His expression immediately went from alarmed to embarrassed. "I see. Well, do what you can."

Presto! Note for future use: "That time of the month" is every girl's get-out-of-jail-free card.

12:10 P.M.

Went home briefly to get my halter dress for Hero's party, and Mom was waiting for me at the kitchen table. Either she's psychic, or she totally reads my journal, because I haven't said a word about Ben, but somehow she knows something's up.

She was sitting there with a tray of peanut butter crackers, milk, and about twenty pamphlets on STDs she got from her friend Connie, a nurse at Kaiser. When she started showing me pictures of genital warts, I put down my cracker and said, "Mom, is this really necessary?"

She said, "Honey, I just want you to understand the risks."

"Yeah, thanks. Now I'm so traumatized I won't have sex until I'm a senior citizen."

She smiled. "Great. I guess I've done my job then. Do you want a sandwich?"

No wonder everyone thinks I'm a guy-basher. My mother's conditioned me to believe they're hideous vectors out to infect me with life-threatening diseases.

2:30 P.M.

Hero's face is still vaguely chartreuse, and her mood is black as coffee. The girl's a mess. She looks like something out of *Creature from the Black Lagoon* (namely, the creature). I'd feel sorry for her, if it weren't sort of funny. Whenever I turn on the stereo she covers her face with a pillow and moans theatrically.

Having overdone it on vino himself a time or two, Uncle Leo will definitely recognize the signs of a hangover, so we're keeping Hero sequestered in her room until she looks a little less creature-like. Elodie's been cool enough to bring us aspirin, snacks, cold washcloths, and cucumbers for Hero's puffy eyes. I think by early evening she should be ready to emerge from her faux menstrual hut.

7:10 P.M.

Hero's party starts in less than an hour, and we still haven't heard from Amber. It's making me nervous. Why would she just disappear? She was supposed to be here by six at the

latest so we could get ready together. I've called her cell like
twenty times, but all I get is voice mail.

On the semi-bright side, Uncle Leo's been so involved with
the party planner, he hasn't noticed that his daughter is still
Bride-of-Frankenstein pale. I think there might be something
going on there, but I'm not going to speculate. The horrors of
middle-aged sex are too nasty to consider. When they start
to flirt, I go outside and skate around the fountain until the
urge to upchuck passes.

The house and yard look amazing, albeit rather pink.
The party planner managed to take Hero's sugar-spun fantasy and turn it into a palatable party scene. There are
fairy lights strung around the garden that twinkle brightly
amidst the foliage. A gauzy, pale tent filled with appetizer-
laden tables takes up one corner of the yard. Huge bun-
dles of pink roses and white lilies adorn every surface, and
masses of cream-colored candles sparkle from inside delicate glass lanterns. The upper deck has been transformed
into a dance floor, and the huge disco ball suspended from
invisible wires looks like it's just floating there magically.
The hot tub's frothy with mounds of pale pink suds, and a
couple machines placed strategically out of sight are filling
the air with thousands of tiny bubbles. The overall effect
is sort of *Tinker Bell gets her groove on*, which is pretty appro-
priate for Hero.

Uncle Leo hired PJ to do the music. I'm stoked about
that. And since my outfit is about four thousand times more
comfortable than last night's ho ensemble, I should be way
more prepared to dance, though I think I'll avoid tables this
time. I've got on this totally hot olive green halter dress

with a bright red hem and matching red sandals (no ankle-breakers, tonight, thank God). It's pretty unusual for me to splash out on two super-femme outfits in a row, but what the hell.

More later . . .

Sunday, August 3
5:50 A.M.

The party got out of hand all at once. One minute there was just a handful of guests milling around awkwardly, most of them sporting pocket protectors and fanny packs. The next thing I knew there were two hundred kids swarming Hero's yard, many of whom I'd never seen in my life. In fact, some of them looked more like twenty- and even thirtysomethings with full-on facial hair, body-piercings, and tattoos. Uncle Leo was ready to have a seizure.

The appetizers were instantly demolished. The hot tub was so full, it looked like cannibal stew. I suspect most of the people in there were in the skinny, but luckily the pink bubbles camouflaged whatever lurked in the depths.

Hero was obviously confused, but she tried to keep up appearances. She floated around in her sparkly pink dress, attempting to greet everyone, forever the polite hostess. Meanwhile, a mosh pit formed under the disco ball. Since PJ was MIA, a guy with purple hair and a pierced septum commandeered Uncle Leo's stereo system, playing music that honestly sounded like airplane engines amplified to ear-splitting volume with occasional shrieking vocals thrown in. I mean, I like a little distortion, but this was just obnoxious.

Uncle Leo and the EUWW stopped asking for invitations and started drinking Petite Syrah straight from the bottle.

Still there was no sign of Ben, Amber, or Claudio. I wandered around in search of them, feeling nervous and abandoned. Ben finally showed up around ten with PJ, Claudio, John, and Corky. He apologized when he found me.

"What took you so long?" I was hurt, but trying not to make a big deal about it. The last thing I needed was to morph into the clingy girlfriend.

He shook his head like it was a long story. "My Volvo blew a gasket, so I had to get a ride with PJ. Those guys took forever, and when they finally showed, they were all . . ." He trailed off.

"All what? Drunk?"

"They'd been drinking some, but it was more than that."

"What?" I was mystified by the whole situation.

He hesitated. "You haven't seen it yet, have you?"

"Seen what?"

"The MySpace thing. You haven't heard about it?"

"No. What MySpace thing?" All at once I felt sweaty and clammy. I took off my sweater, revealing my completely un-Geena dress. He did a slight double take, as if seeing me for the first time.

"Wow. Geena. You look . . ."

"What? I look what?" I couldn't keep the irritation out of my voice.

"Hot." He ran a hand through his hair. "Incredibly hot."

"Um . . . thanks," I mumbled. "So do you."

He seriously did. There was nothing particularly original about his outfit—khakis, a white tank top, white button-down shirt over that, untucked and hanging open—but the end result was making my pulse race dangerously.

"Anyway," I said, shaking my head a little. "What's up with MySpace?"

Ben licked his lips. "I really don't want to get involved. It's so stupid."

"What's stupid?"

He took a step closer and, placing one finger under my chin, tilted my face toward his. "Whatever happens, I just want you to know I had nothing to do with it."

Despite the butterflies in my stomach, I found myself closing my eyes, absorbed in the delicious little landmarks of kissing: warm hand on small of back, full length of body coming closer, making contact, lips hovering, honing in . . .

Just as the eagle was about to land, my damn cell phone rang.

"Hold on," I said. "I have to get this." It was Amber's special ring tone, so I retrieved it from my bag. "What's up? Where are you?"

"I have to talk to you." I could tell right away she was crying.

"What's happening? Why aren't you here?"

"I couldn't come."

"Yeah, but why? Where are you?"

More tears on her end. "I can't tell you on the phone. I'll explain tomorrow. I just wanted to make sure you were at the party."

"Of course I am. Hero's only been planning this since we were ten. We miss you, though." I surveyed the scene: screams from the hot tub as a fat guy in his underwear did a cannonball; Uncle Leo trying to dissuade a scantily clad couple from having sex on the lawn; Hero politely shaking the hand of a tall biker dude in leather chaps. It would be nice if Amber were here. She'd know how to handle this.

"Just watch Hero's back, okay?" Her voice was choked with emotion.

"Why? What do you mean?"

But she was gone. I stashed my cell back in my bag and looked at Ben. "Something's weird," I told him. "I don't know what exactly, but something's not right."

"I know. That's what I'm trying to tell you."

Just then an ear-splitting screech of feedback pierced the air. *Oh God*, I thought, *someone's found the mike.* The party planner thought it would be cute to have one for toasts, like at weddings. Everyone could tell funny stories about Hero growing up, that sort of thing. I thought it sounded stupid, but Hero went along with it. I think she secretly thought of this party as a dress rehearsal for her wedding, only this time she wouldn't have to share the attention with the groom.

"Yo, PJ's in the house. What's up y'all?"

Ben and I looked at each other. We were on the upper deck, and we hurried now to the railing to watch the scene below. PJ was standing there with the mike in the middle of the crowd, Claudio at his side. Somebody in the hot tub screamed, "Turn that shit off, man!" PJ turned to Purple Hair Guy and slid a finger across his throat. That put an end to the airplane jets coming through the speakers.

"Hey everyone, I'm the dude that's supposed to be spinning tonight. Unfortunately, I couldn't get here in time to set up on account of my homie Claudio needed a friend, like we all do sometimes." He paused. PJ was amazing with a mike. It wasn't what he said so much as *how* he said it—so comfortable and smooth, like he owned everyone there. "Anyway, I'm told this mike is for toasts, so I'd like to make one." He raised a plastic cup, and others (there had to be 250 people there now) raised theirs with him. Ben grabbed my fingers and held them.

"To Hero," PJ said.

Hero was standing near the living room window, and the light from inside illuminated her like an actress waiting for her close-up. She looked so fragile and pretty in her pink strapless dress with her mother's diamond choker sparkling at her throat.

PJ looked at her, cup in hand. "God only knows what they taught you at that boarding school, Hero. Back when I knew you in junior high, no one could say a word against you. But now that you've destroyed my man Claudio, I got to say I'm disappointed." He paused. "More than disappointed. Honestly, you make me sick. To see you smile so sweetly, no one would suspect you played all innocent to win this guy's heart"—PJ clapped a hand on Claudio's shoulder—"then took off your clothes for some sleaze with a camera, like a B-list porn star." A bunch of people hooted, some laughed, and PJ raised his drink into the air. "To Hero, the ho." Then he and Claudio knocked their plastic cups together and drank.

Things came a little unglued after that. People were laughing, shouting, calling out names. I saw Uncle Leo turn from pink to white, and watched as Hero dropped to the ground in a dead faint. Purple Hair turned on some old school punk—

maybe the Sex Pistols. I felt dizzy, standing there on the upper deck watching it all.

"I've got to go down there," I said to Ben. "Hero needs me. What is this, anyway?"

"Someone posted pictures—it's all over MySpace." Ben looked as miserable as I felt.

"Pictures of Hero? Doing what?"

"Just, you know, posing, I guess."

"Naked?" My head was spinning.

"Sort of, yeah."

None of this made any sense. "This is bullshit. I've got to go." I turned toward the stairs, but he grabbed my elbow.

"Geena, what can I do? I want to help."

I stared at him, speechless. Could I even trust him? His *homeboys* had just shredded my cousin's reputation. Having bogus pictures on MySpace was bad enough, but to have the crown prince of Sonoma denounce her in front of everyone was even worse! Now everyone would think it really was her, even though it couldn't be. Suddenly, all boys were suspect again.

I looked Ben in the eye. "Make PJ and Claudio regret this, or I will."

"What, like take them on?"

"No, read them poetry," I said, my voice thick with sarcasm. "Come on! Make them sorry. What else do guys understand but in-your-face threats?"

"I can't do that! They're my friends."

"Fine." I felt my chin quiver, but I forced myself to maintain control. "Then you're no friend of mine."

I ran down the stairs, ignoring him as he called my name.

The living room and yard were thick with bodies and I had to push my way through them, like wading through a forest of torsos and limbs. Hero was nowhere in sight. I asked everyone if they'd seen her. Corky told me, "Her dad dragged her down the hall. Man, if that was my daughter, I'd slap the bitch."

That was it; I couldn't take anymore. I pushed him back so hard, he fell against a table and his hand landed in the guacamole bowl. Everyone around us scattered and then circled in, ready for a fight. Corky was built like a Mac truck, and when I saw him staring at me crazy-eyed, his hand covered in green goo, I wondered briefly what I'd done, but the adrenaline coursing through my veins was so intense, I couldn't stop.

"You say another word about my cousin, you'll have me to answer to."

Corky laughed. "I never hit a girl before, but I could start."

I felt a hand on my arm, and whipped around to see PJ staring at me. Beside him was Claudio; his eyes were lined with dark circles and looked puffy, as if he'd been crying.

"Come on, Geena, this has nothing to do with you," PJ said. "I just had to tell the truth for my man here. We got no quarrel with you."

"The hell you don't!" I said. "You can't spread lies like this."

"Pictures don't lie," he said.

"Oh come on," I scoffed. "Hero posing nude? Please!"

PJ and Claudio just shook their heads like I was crazy.

"You're going to be sorry," I told them. "Trust me." Then I ran into the house, looking for Hero.

I found her hiding in her bedroom, crying into her pillows like she'd never stop. Dark rivulets of mascara stained her pale cheeks, and her lips looked swollen, like that time when she had an allergic reaction to rhubarb pie. I couldn't get her to talk, so I just rubbed her back and stroked her hair while she sobbed. When she calmed down a little, I moved back and forth between her bed and the balcony, giving her frequent updates.

First Uncle Leo got on the mike and told everyone to go home. When that didn't work, he told them he was calling the cops. That got about half the crowd to clear out, but the other half still lingered, congregating on the lawn mostly, smoking cigarettes, laughing and gossiping at top volume. That's when the party planner suggested Leo try the sprinklers. I guess she earned her fee with that one. The stragglers dispersed within minutes, cursing and climbing into their cars, shaking themselves like wet dogs.

When the commotion died down and everyone seemed to be gone, Uncle Leo came into Hero's room. I'd never seen him look so dead tired; his wrinkles were deeper than usual, his mouth set in a scary frown. He leaned against Hero's dresser while she sat up on her bed, hugging a pillow to her. I sat beside her, holding her hand.

"What's this about, Hero?"

"Uncle Leo," I said, "it's a misunderstanding."

He shot me a look of warning and I shut up. He turned his attention back to Hero and said, "Don't you dare lie to me."

Just then the party planner knocked lightly and stuck her

head in. "Leo, I—don't know what to say. I'm sorry things got so . . ." She trailed off, glancing at us, then back at him.

He didn't look at her. "It's okay—it's not your fault."

She lingered in the doorway. "There are three boys still in the hot tub. I thought you'd like to know. The clean-up crew will be here first thing—"

"Yes, fine," he said curtly. "Thanks."

"Good night, then." She disappeared.

Uncle Leo pounded a fist on top of the dresser and left the room. I snuck back out onto Hero's balcony and spied three heads in the hot tub: one bleach blond, one shaved bald, and the third in a Rasta beanie. I knew them right away. It was Dog Berry, Virg Pickett, and George Sabato—aka the stofers. They were passing a fattie around as they relaxed in the hot tub. The water level was only about waist-high, but they looked perfectly content.

"Psst!" I whispered. "Dog, up here. You guys have gotta go! Uncle Leo's pissed."

"Hey, Geena," Dog drawled in a lazy, totally baked voice. "It's cool. We got something to tell your uncle."

"Go on," I urged them. "Get out now, before he—"

But it was too late. Uncle Leo burst out onto the deck. "If you kids aren't out of here in ten seconds, I'm calling the cops."

"Man, you gotta chill. We got something to tell you," Dog said.

I crouched down, trying to hide in the shadows on the balcony, hoping Uncle Leo hadn't spotted me.

"Are you smoking pot? Goddammit, get out of here!"

Dog motioned for Virg to put the joint out. He obliged

by dipping the tip into the water, laughing as it sizzled. Dog shoved him and he shut up. "Listen, Mr. Hero's Dad, we got to tell you something, okay? Are you going to listen quietly, or do we got to shout?"

"What is it?"

"First I got to tell you, man, I love your wine. Seriously. It's like *tasty*. I mean, I'm not a wine guy, you know, I like Corona, little lime, maybe shot of tequila sans worm, but one time I tried yours and it was like—wow. Man. That was some gourmand shit. You got that down."

"I'm glad you like it." Uncle Leo's demeanor softened for half a second, but then he remembered himself. He folded his hands in front of him and said, "I need you boys to leave. You understand that, right?"

"The dude set Hero up." This from Virg, the bald one.

Dog glared at him. "I'm getting to that. See, what my friend's saying in his own loquacious way is that we got information you're going to need."

"I'm listening," Uncle Leo said, though I could tell he was losing his patience.

"It's the Cheez Whiz guy, man. He's behind this mess. We heard him talking to his muscle-buddy." Dog looked pleased with himself. "That's what we're trying to tell you."

Uncle Leo nodded very slowly, like he was taking this all in. "The 'Cheez Whiz guy,' you say?"

"That's right," George said. "That's the real deal."

"We couldn't leave without telling you. It was our civil duty. Hey man, how do you make your wine, anyway? It's *hella* tasty." Dog was licking his lips, looking like he could go for a sip of Cab right about now.

"Listen, guys, I'm going to tell you one more time: You need to go."

Dog nodded. "Oh, yeah, that's cool. Just wanted to give you the four-one-one, man. Come on, kooks, let's hit the road. Later. Keep up the good vintnering, huh?"

They got out of the hot tub and dripped across the patio to their bus, climbed in still soaking wet. Those guys. It was frightening to think they'd soon be of age to vote.

When Uncle Leo got back to Hero's room, he started the interrogation where he'd left off. This time he had a glass of wine to fortify him. "All right," he said. "Explain what happened last night, and remember, not telling is the same as lying."

Hero took a deep breath. "I got drunk. I don't remember everything, but I'm sure I didn't do what PJ—" Her voice broke. She tried again. "I'm sorry. Don't be mad. I can't take it if you're mad at me."

Uncle Leo ran a hand over his face. "Hero, a girl's reputation is very important."

"I know."

"These are serious accusations. You say you got drunk. What have I told you about drinking?"

Hero looked confused. "Um . . . not to do it?"

"In moderation, a little alcohol's okay, but if you get carried away, you lose your sense, boys take advantage. My God . . . I'm disappointed."

I couldn't keep my mouth shut another second. "Uncle Leo, it's a lie! She didn't pose nude for anyone—I was there."

"But she was too drunk to remember!" He was shouting. He'd never shouted at me before, and it made my blood run cold.

"She had a few drinks, yes, but I didn't. I saw what happened. Your daughter's no porn star, if that's what you're so worried about." I was yelling back! I couldn't believe it. I was raising my voice to my uncle.

His hands were shaking as he lifted his glass of wine to his lips. He drank, swallowed, and looked at the ceiling. "It's been a long night. We're all tired. Let's just get some sleep, okay?"

Hero and I both nodded.

When he was gone and the lights were out I heard Hero crying. I left the fold-out sofa bed and crawled under the pink satin bedspread with her. "It's okay," I whispered. "We're going to fix this."

"Claudio hates me," she whimpered. "What did I do?"

"It's a crazy misunderstanding. Something about MySpace. We'll deal with it tomorrow."

She sat up on one elbow. "What do you mean? What about MySpace?"

"I guess someone posted some nudie pictures that looked like you."

She made a tight, squeaky sound in her throat, then mumbled, "Oh, God. Come on—we have to look."

"You think? Won't it just upset you?"

She scoffed. "Like I'm not upset already?"

"Okay, I'll go get your laptop." I tiptoed across the room and returned with her Mac. We booted up and searched MySpace until we found what we were looking for. It didn't take long. The photos had spread to just about every under-twenty MySpace account in Sonoma County and beyond.

The caption read "Monte Luna princess gets down and dirty." There were a couple shots of Hero at the party in her thigh-high boots, fully clothed, dancing on the coffee table. There was one of her leaping into the pool. And then there were two pictures of a girl who looked exactly like Hero; at least, she had Hero's face. She was wearing a lace thong and cami in one shot, but she was sans-cami in the next. In both pictures she wore Hero's thigh-high boots.

"Shit," I said. "Where did these come from?"

Hero just sat there, tears streaming down her face. "It does look like me," she said. "But it's not."

"Of course it's not." I squinted at the screen. It looked to me like someone who really knew their Photoshop had pulled an all-nighter for this mean little trick. They'd done a good job, unfortunately. Most of the postings also had announcements about Hero's "sweet sixteen" bash; that explained why every derelict within a hundred-mile radius had shown up.

"Amber," Hero said.

As soon as it was out of her mouth, I knew she was right, but I didn't want her to be. "Let's not jump to conclusions."

"Oh my God. Last night—she stayed at the party, put on my boots, and had a little photo shoot. That *bitch*."

"Okay, maybe. But I'm sure she didn't think anyone would see—"

Hero blinked at me, incredulous. "Are you going to defend her? My life is ruined, and you're making excuses for *Amber*?"

"Your life isn't ruined, Hero. I'm just saying"—I glanced at the screen, had to look away—"there might be an explanation."

All of a sudden, Hero bolted for her bathroom. I could hear her retching into the toilet. She flushed, and came back, looking paler than ever. "I don't think I can talk about this anymore."

"Of course not," I said, shutting her laptop down. "And by tomorrow I'm sure the MySpace guys will delete these. They can't post stuff like this. If they're not gone by the morning, I'll keep reporting it until they do something."

"You think John took the pictures?" Hero climbed back into bed.

"Definitely." I got in beside her. "Don't worry. He'll pay. So will PJ—and Claudio."

"Oh, but not *Amber*?!" She was really irritated. I could see why, but I still wasn't ready to assume the worst.

"Let's just wait to hear what she says."

After a long pause, Hero whispered, "Maybe this is stupid, but I don't want Claudio to pay. I want him to like me again."

I sighed. "We'll see what we can do."

I don't think either of us slept much; I know I didn't. It was the worst night I can remember since Aunt Kathy died. We tossed and turned and once, when I finally drifted off, I woke to the sound of Hero sobbing in her sleep. An hour later, when the sunrise started to color the windows a pale, delicate blue, I got up and wrote all this down. I feel like I could sleep for a week. Life sucks. To top it all off, I have to work today. My God, what's happening to my summer?

1:50 P.M.

Sunday: the horror, the horror.

Operating on zero sleep. Caffeine props me up and moves me around, but underneath it all I can feel my innards, heavy and slimy and sleep deprived.

Everyone around town is talking about Hero, the perfect little boarding school princess who is now a confirmed skank. I could murder someone, I really could. I just haven't decided who.

Clearly, PJ and Claudio totally blow. Even if they didn't post any photos, they fell for it and publicly humiliated her, which is almost as bad.

I keep thinking about the stofers telling Uncle Leo, "It's the Cheez Whiz guy." Obviously they were talking about John. It's not like he was stupid enough to post the photos to his own account, but a suspicious number of his friends had them on their pages. Now, like I predicted, they've all been yanked, but it hardly matters; the damage is already done.

Hero's summer is totally screwed. Claudio won't return her text messages or e-mails. Uncle Leo grounded her for two weeks. Thank God he never actually saw the photos; luckily, he's computer-illiterate, and since MySpace is mostly the domain of non-geriatrics, none of his friends saw them either. Still, he's gleaned enough information to understand that his baby was drunk at a party, where she behaved somewhat badly, resulting in scandalous photos appearing on a mysterious Web site he keeps calling YourSpace.

She's allowed to work at TSB two more weeks, but then it's back to boarding school for her. He's being way harsh, in my opinion. I mean really, what evidence does he have against her? Everyone's so quick to believe the guys and disregard the girls. Um, excuse me, but does having a penis make you inherently more honest? This is so *Scarlet Letter*, man. Okay, so we wear skinny jeans instead of hoop skirts and camis instead of corsets, but the basic idea is exactly the same.

Case in point: This morning at TSB Jana Clark and Sarah Williams drove up in Jana's black Honda Prelude. Hero and I were on shift. Amber was supposed to work, but called in sick. I haven't gotten to talk to her since her phone call last night. Anyway, here come Jana and Sarah with their scary fingernails and their motionless hair.

Jana's like, "Two grande Frappuccinos, please."

"Quick reminder," I said, "this isn't Starbucks. We don't carry Frappuccinos. But I can get you a Betty Blitz." I was very polite about it, even though I could tell from their smirking, highly glossed lips that they were looking for trouble.

"How many calories are in those? Oh, never mind," Jana said. "Hi, Hero!"

Hero smiled weakly and waved with just the tips of her fingers. Jana, Sarah, Hero, and I all started out in kindergarten together, but somewhere around sixth grade they'd become foundation-caked she-devils with hairspray abuse problems.

"Sorry we couldn't make it to your birthday," Sarah said, flashing her enormous choppers. "We had backstage passes for This Is My Fist. It was wild."

"Yeah," Jana put in, "but we heard about it."

"*Allll* about it."

Their satanic laughter seemed to linger in the humid air long after they'd driven away.

I put a hand on Hero's shoulder. "It'll blow over."

She spun around and pinned me with an accusing glare. "Dad made me clean out the hot tub. You want to know what I found?"

I cringed. "What?"

"A pair of tighty whities, a pipe, and a ribbed condom." Her lip curled in disgust. "Happy birthday to me."

"Hey," I said brightly, "at least it was a rager. Wouldn't it be worse if no one showed?"

"I doubt *anything* could be worse than this."

"Look, it got out of hand. I'll admit that, okay? But we can't turn on each other. The thing now is to figure out who's responsible and make them sorry."

"I know who's responsible: Amber."

I held up a hand. "Innocent until proven guilty, remember?"

"She never showed, didn't come to work. Here I am, getting taunted by Jana Clark, and she's holed up at home, knowing she ruined my life."

"Hero, don't be so melodramatic. I really don't think Amber planned on hurting you."

"Oh, no?" She was gathering steam now; her mouth took on a righteous, tight-lipped meanness. "Then where is she? I bet this whole thing was her idea. She never liked me. You know that. She was jealous of me. All she wanted from the start was to see me humiliated." Her neck was getting all splotchy, a sure sign she was fighting tears.

"Amber wouldn't do that."

She shook her head. "You've got no idea who she is, do you?"

"Oh yeah, who *am* I?" We both spun around and there was Amber in the doorway. Her face was puffy and her hair looked like it hadn't been washed in days. "Go on. I'm dying to hear this."

"Amber!" I ran to her and gave her a big hug, but she felt stiff in my arms. She smelled like cigarette smoke.

Hero kept her distance. "This is all your fault."

"Oh, is that right?" She looked fierce standing there. She was dirty and retaining water, but she drew herself up to her full height and suddenly she looked like an Amazon. "I'm to blame, huh? What did I do, Hero? Okay, so I made some stupid decisions. But after that, I didn't choose what happened." Her voice trembled slightly. "None of it."

"See?" I said to Hero. "She didn't do it."

Hero looked at me, amazed. "You just take her word for it?"

"I was used," Amber told her, "just like you."

"Yeah, well you're not the one sitting in here while the whole town drops by to have a good laugh."

"Hero," I said, "she didn't do—"

Amber interrupted me. "And you weren't the one stupid enough to fall for some guy's bullshit, okay? I was. *I* was. And for that, I'm really sorry." Her voice cracked and her whole face was tense with pain. I wrapped an arm around her shoulder. She just stood there, unmoving, her eyes distant. Then she shook my arm off and ran out the door.

"I've got to go," I said. "Cover for me?"

"So what, she's saying she was tricked?"

"I'm going to find out." I ran out after Amber then. She was revving the engine of her mom's El Dorado. "Amber!" I yelled. "Wait up!"

But she didn't hear me, or she pretended not to. The El Dorado jerked out of the parking space in a fast, arcing reverse and I had to jump out of the way to avoid getting hit.

"Amber!" I screamed, but she was already tearing out into the street, narrowly missing a Mini Cooper. Oh God. It wasn't just any Mini, it was Lane's, and he was headed right for TSB.

I dashed back to work and slipped in while Hero was taking Lane's order—a double cappuccino, as usual.

"I'll make it," I said, taking his to-go mug from him.

Hero looked relieved when she saw me. She still hadn't perfected the mounds of creamy foam Lane likes best.

When Lane was gone, I looked at my cousin and saw that the red splotches on her neck had become bright pink continents. She wouldn't look me in the eye.

"Don't worry, Hero. I'm going to get to the bottom of this. And when I do, we'll clear your name, I swear."

She studied her fingernails with a frown. "Good luck."

6:10 P.M.

After work, I decided to skate to the Springs in search of Amber. I wasn't exactly sure where she lived, I only knew the general vicinity. I never really go to that area—I mean, I pass by there on my way to Moon Mountain, but I've never explored the neighborhoods. It was like visiting a third-world country. There were dismembered cars rotting on brown lawns, smashed windows, scary dogs frothing behind insubstantial fences. I passed a decrepit trailer rotting behind a veil of weeds. A toddler stood alone in the yard, staring up at me, her diaper sagging. At a street corner, a man with a leathery, wizened face sat on the hood of a yellow Mustang, his glassy eyes staring vacantly at the can of Bud in his hand. I sped up.

I was about to give up when I spotted the gold El Dorado. It was parked in front of a mint green house. I navigated a tangle of plastic chairs and milk crates strewn about the yard and stepped into the shade offered by the small covered porch. I hadn't even knocked when the door flew open.

"What are you doing here?" Amber looked mad.

I took half a step back. "I want to talk to you."

She widened her eyes in exasperation, but said, "Get in the car. Don't make any noise."

I tiptoed down the porch steps, made my way through the cluttered yard again, and let myself into the El Dorado. I tried to shut the door without making any sound, but it wasn't really closed, so I tried again and it slammed loudly.

Just then Amber flew out the front door, took all three porch steps in one leap, and ran for the car, keys clenched in her fist. I'd never seen her move so fast. Then I saw long, skinny brown legs push through the door, and there was her mom. She stood on the porch, her fried bangs teased into an '80s plume, her hip cocked to one side.

"Where the hell you going, Maggie? Don't take my car— you're not taking my car!"

Amber swung herself into the driver's side, turned the engine over and gunned it. At first we lurched forward, almost slamming into the truck parked in front of us, but then she managed to wrench it into reverse, and we backed up enough to clear the truck. I threw a nervous glance back at the house. Amber's mom was still there, her face enraged but exhausted. A guy with long hair, who looked a little like Bono, staggered out the door with a cigarette; he was wearing nothing but plaid boxers.

When we were on Napa Street headed toward town Amber said, "I hate her."

"I've got an idea. Want to go to Geevana?"

She looked at me like I was crazy. "There's a pack of smokes in the glove," she said. "Get 'em."

I opened the glove compartment, fished through a bunch of receipts, a McDonald's bag with one squished fry still in there, several lipsticks, half a Butterfinger, until at last I found the slightly creased pack of Camels. I fished one out and started to hand it to her, but hesitated.

"What's your problem?" she snarled.

"They're harder to kick than heroin, you know."

She snatched the cigarette from me. "There should be matches," she said, feeling around on the seat. She looked down for too long and almost rear-ended a tourist bus.

"I'll get them," I snapped, and sifted through the collection of Coke cans littering the floor until I produced a book of matches from Motel 6.

She lit her cigarette without incident. Tossing her hair over her shoulder, she coughed a little, trying not to. "What's Geevana, anyway?"

"Turn right at the next light," I said. "I'll show you."

○ ● ● ○ ● ○

From Geevana Ridge, you can see all of Sonoma Valley spread out below you like a huge green and gold quilt. The hills look soft as lion fur from a distance, though up close the tall, dry grass is scratchy and full of stickers. Today the sky was bright blue, with only a few puffs of whipped cream clouds floating near the horizon. The vineyards form big emerald squares cut into blond hills. This time of year the vines get heavy as the grapes turn swollen and juicy. You can smell them from Geevana—that ripe, dusty odor that will always make me think of home.

Amber and I sat on the lowest branch of my favorite old oak, Albert, her puffing away on her second cigarette, me worrying that bringing her there was a mistake. She'd maintained a sullen silence since we'd gotten out of the car. I'd never taken anyone there, not even Hero, and I wondered why this had seemed like a good idea.

"I've been worried about you," I told her.

"Well, don't be."

"I left like a million messages on your cell." I ran my hands through Albert's moss, comforted by his texture. "You missed work."

"I know."

"What's going on?"

She stubbed her cigarette out, grinding it into the bark. I cringed. She was hurting Albert. I know it's babyish, but I really do feel close to him. It, I mean.

Amber tossed the butt onto the acorn-strewn ground, and I told myself I'd come back later to pick it up. She said, "I can't believe I fell for his shit again."

"John's?"

"Yeah."

I turned to her. "What did he do? I knew he was behind this."

She kind of smiled, but it was more of a grimace. "I must've inherited my mom's vile taste in men. Did you see her latest? He's a tweaker, just like my dad."

"That guy on the porch?"

She nodded. "He's brand-new. She picked him up hitch-hiking. They'll last two weeks, I bet."

I'll admit I was intrigued by the story of the hitchhiking Bono, but my curiosity about what had happened with John won out. "What were you saying about John, though?"

Her jaw flexed at the sound of his name. "He must think I'm incredibly stupid."

"Why? What happened?"

She picked at a scab on her wrist. "I think his first plan was to get Hero wasted and have sex with her at the party. He can't stand it when a girl isn't into him. When that didn't work, he moved to plan B."

"Which was?"

"He started working on me as soon as you guys left. I was drunk and lonely and . . . I don't know, needy, I guess."

"You still like him, huh?"

She looked at me, then away, then back again. "I never really got over him. He's the first person I met here. I felt like he was some sort of—this is so lame!"

"What? Go on."

"Like he was a sign, you know? An omen. I was so stoked about leaving Lake County, getting away from my mom's old boyfriend, starting fresh. John fed me all this shit about how beautiful I was, how even when he goes off to college I could visit him all the time—he was so convincing." She stared at the ground, her eyes glazed and far away, remembering.

"And then what happened?"

"He just turned on me, you know? Like he became this completely different person. He spread all those rumors about me, made fun of me in front of his friends. I've never been so humiliated."

"So, Friday," I began, then hesitated. "I mean, what about the pictures?"

"It's like, when I'm alone with John, he makes me feel like the sexiest girl in the whole world." She tugged a bit of moss from the branch. "He got me to put on those stupid boots, and he started taking pictures. He kept saying, 'Come on, Ginger, don't you trust me? When I'm at Yale, I want to remember you just like this.' After that, the whole night's sort of a blur."

I sighed. "I can't believe him."

"What a joke. When I saw what he'd done on MySpace, I was so irate. I wanted to kill him. And at the same time, I wanted him. God, it's so messed up."

I watched a couple vultures circling in the distance, swooping lower, barely flapping. "The guy's evil."

Amber nodded. "And now Hero totally hates me."

I touched Amber's hand. "She won't when she hears what happened."

"Yeah, she will."

"No, she won't! You didn't do anything wrong. I mean, okay, so you took some sexy snaps for a guy you like—that's not a crime! And you never would have done it if he'd told you what he had planned."

Amber chewed her bottom lip. "It doesn't matter."

"She'll be mad at John, not you."

She jumped to the ground and tugged her skirt down. "People like her don't listen to people like me."

"That's ridiculous."

"No, Geena, it's not. You don't know, okay? You have no idea."

"Amber—"

She walked toward the car. "Let's go."

I hopped down off the branch and started after her. "Just because Hero's rich doesn't mean she's stupid. She'll know you're telling the truth."

She glanced over her shoulder. "It's not that simple. We're from different planets."

"What about me? I believe you."

"What do you want, a medal?" She opened the car door, got inside, slammed it shut, and started the engine.

When I slipped into the passenger's seat beside her, she was scowling out the windshield. "You've got no idea what it was like, moving here. This town is totally locked down. Everyone knows each other and you're all rich—"

"I'm not rich."

"Everyone—the emo-kids and the wangsters and the hicks—you all have money! Only you don't see it. It's like everyone's living this wine country fantasy."

I thought about the little girl with the sagging diaper by the trailer. "I'm sorry," I whispered.

"I don't want your pity!"

"I don't mean—it's not pity. I'm sorry for not seeing how hard it is for you. It's just that you act so strong all the time."

She stared at her lap. "'Act' being the operative word."

"But we're friends, right? That's not an act."

She leaned against the steering wheel, her forehead against the rubber, and then she turned her head so her cheek was against it instead. Her green eyes took me in for a long moment before she said, "Yes. We're friends."

"Good."

She turned off the car. "I really wanted to go to Hero's birthday party."

"We wanted you there. You should have come."

"I couldn't," she mumbled.

"We missed you."

When she turned to me again, her face was wet with tears. "I missed you too."

Monday, August 4

4:00 A.M.

Can't sleep. Keep tossing and turning, trying to find a way to untie this knot of lies. Finally, got up and sent a text message to Amber: *We have 2 tell H.*

To my surprise, my cell phone rang three minutes later. It was Amber. I guess I'm not the only one losing sleep over this.

"So what are you saying? It's okay for me to look like a slut, but not Hero?"

I stared at the wavy pattern on my bedspread, feeling dizzy. "Everyone needs to know the truth—not just Hero, but PJ and Claudio too. Everyone."

"Oh yeah? What's the truth, Geena?"

Her tone was so unfriendly. "The truth? You were tricked by John into posing for him."

"You're so naïve," she said, disdainful now.

"What? That's what happened."

"Okay, first, you know what the gossip hounds will turn

that into? 'Amber's an aspiring porn star nymphomaniac.' Second, no one will believe us. Even if Hero does, PJ and Claudio will assume we're making it up to save Hero's reputation. They saw what they saw."

I thought about that. I was used to assuming people would believe me if I told the truth. Obviously Amber had a different take on things. She had a point, though. PJ and Claudio might not believe us, especially with John in their camp, spinning his web of lies.

"I see what you mean," I said, feeling suddenly exhausted.

Her tone didn't soften. "But I'm glad to know you wanted to sacrifice my reputation for Hero's."

That stumped me. "What reputation, exactly?"

She hung up on me.

I sat there, staring at the small circle of light cast by my bedside lamp, puzzling. Amber was the power slut of Sonoma Valley High, the nasty little bombshell who wasn't bound by virginal expectations. Why was she suddenly worrying about protecting her reputation, when there was nothing left to protect?

I called her back. "It's me. Don't hang up. I thought you were proud of being . . . you know . . . promiscuous."

She sighed. "When you get boobs in the fifth grade, people talk. Pretty soon you realize you can't stop them, so you act like you're proud of it."

"You mean, you've been pretending?"

"I wanted to be normal, Geena. When I moved here, I thought I could start over, but that lasted like five minutes. You want to know the truth? I never even had sex with John. He made all that shit up."

"Why would he do that?" I asked, frustrated.

"Why? Umm, maybe because we *almost* did it, except he *couldn't.*"

"You mean like . . . ?"

"Tiny little thing, couldn't get it up."

I giggled. "Are you serious?"

"Yeah. And the next day, guess what? I'm suddenly the ho. Haven't you noticed that all the girls he goes out with end up on the official skank list?"

I thought about the girls in those dance photos on his walls: Marcy, Lexa, Nikki, Kim. It's true; I never thought about it before, but after they dated John, their respectability suddenly plummeted. They got kicked off cheerleading squads and debate teams for sketchy, ambiguous reasons. One by one, each of them became persona non grata in the cafeteria. The guy was a one-man demolition crew, destroying girls' reputations like they were disposable. All the while, he was the one jumping from girl to girl, yet he remained the golden boy, untouchable; *he* was the slut, if anyone was. And not even a very good slut at that.

"This guy is going down," I said.

"No, he doesn't do that," Amber teased. "He's squeamish about actual body parts."

"You know what I'm saying. He's got to pay."

"Come on, Geena. Dude's slippery as hell. He could talk his way out of a blow job in the Oval Office."

"Those days are over," I said. "He's met his match."

"And what's your plan exactly, Miss Vengeance?"

"I've got to think about it more," I said, "but I know there's a way. Are you in?"

She hesitated. "Let me sleep on it," she said.

"Amber! He used you. He used all those girls. We can't let him get away with it."

There was silence on her end.

"Come on," I urged, "in the name of slandered beezies everywhere."

She said, "I was in love with him, Geena."

"Okay," I whispered. "Think about it. Call me when you decide."

2:00 P.M.

Amber still hasn't called. I've tried her cell ten times. Working with Hero today, it was hell keeping my mouth shut, but what could I do? My hands are tied until Amber gives me the green light. She doesn't want me breathing a word to anyone until we've got some sort of plan.

It's official: Boys suck.

Haven't talked to BB since the party. Obviously he's firmly entrenched in the enemy camp. Fine. He looked funny when he kissed, anyway. I opened my eyes once and his were kind of cross-eyed, like a Siamese cat.

2:40 P.M.

Dad was supposed to visit next weekend. We were planning on going movie-hopping, like we used to on scorching Saturdays when he lived here. Half an hour ago he phoned to say he wasn't coming.

"Are you serious? But *Blood Moon* opens next Friday. I really want to see it." I hated how whiny and immature I sounded, but lately I was losing patience with his habit of eleventh-hour ditching. Besides, this movie was a huge deal—*Snakes on a Plane* and *The Blair Witch Project* were child's play next to the hype surrounding *Blood Moon*, and nobody could beat Dad when it came to savoring a good horror flick.

"Honey, I'm sorry, but Jen's mother is sick right now, and she needs me to help out."

That was it. Something inside me gave way—a mudslide of messy emotions. "*She* needs you? Dad, did it ever occur to you that *I* need you?" There was a lump in my throat, but I kept talking. "Did you ever think about that?"

There was a long pause on his end. Finally, he said, "Sweetie, I see how hard this is for you."

"Do you?" I snapped. "Because lately I get the feeling you don't see *anything* but your little arm charm."

His voice hardened. "Young lady, you're out of line."

"No, I'm just mad, okay? I'm pissed, and I'm not afraid to say it. If you want to be a part of my life, you better start showing up." I hung up the phone. Then I stood there and stared at it, my heart pounding.

Mom came into the kitchen, taking off her gardening gloves. I could tell by the look on her face that she'd heard at least part of our conversation. "You okay?"

I shrugged. Then I burst into tears.

She held me, stroking my hair and whispering, "Shhhh."

Sometimes, that's all there is to say.

6:10 P.M.

Amber called me at last. Of course, I was with Hero, comforting her while she cried for hours in her room, watching Claudio in the vineyards with binoculars every ten minutes just to torture herself. She's so strung out on him. Is love an STD? From what I've seen, it's harder to cure than herpes.

"Okay," Amber said, "I've decided I'm in. But your plan better be good, or this is all going to blow up in our faces."

"Oh, hi there, *Mom*," I said, trying to sound casual. "Yeah, I'm at *Hero's*."

"Don't tell her anything," Amber warned.

I said, "I know, I know. I'll be home in an hour."

"And whatever you do," Amber whispered, "don't tell Ben Bettaglia, okay? If the guy grapevine hears about this, we're dead in the water."

"Sure, okay, I'll pick up some cat litter. Anything else?"

"Watch your back, G." Then she hung up.

Hero paused in her sobbing to look at me quizzically. "Why does your mom want cat litter? You guys don't even have a cat."

"She uses it for . . ." I searched my brain madly, but all I could come up with was "teaching."

"She uses cat litter to teach English?"

I nodded. "She's kind of unconventional in her methods."

Hero frowned. "But *how* does she use it?"

The girl was relentless when she fixated on something. "Um, when their papers are really bad, she gives them a little bag of cat litter. It's her way of telling them their writing is crap." I laughed. "She's kooky."

Hero collapsed against her pink velvet pillows again. "The world's gone insane."

I exhaled with relief. "Pretty much."

Tuesday, August 5

5:05 A.M.

Great, now I have to formulate a plan. I've sworn to bring down John Jamieson, and I've no idea how I'm going to do it. I feel like a tiny gnat plotting the demise of Godzilla.

Evidence—that's what we need. Witnesses. Like in a court of law.

The stofers! We've got to find them. They know something, I'm sure of it.

9:45 A.M.

Saw BB when I skated down to KFC for my morning BM. OMG, he tried to IM me last night, but I LOL'ed. I mean, WTF? As far as I'm concerned, he's totally FUBAR.

11:30 P.M.

I asked Amber if she knew where to find the stofers. She said she'd seen them a couple times at some weird little mini-mart on West Napa. I told her we're going there after work. When she asked why, I said, "We need witnesses." Then I filled her in on everything I'd overheard that night on Hero's balcony, when the stofers were waxing poetic about the Cheez Whiz guy. She agreed that tracking them down was worth a shot, since so far we had exactly nothing in the way of evidence, witnesses, or even a plan.

When we got there, Virg was behind the counter, filming

the cigarette racks. George was standing by the magazines, flipping through a copy of *Penthouse*. Dog was playing a video game, twitching before the screen. Bingo.

"Hey, Dog," I said, positioning myself near him as he white-knuckled the steering wheel and worked the gas pedal. "How's it going?"

"You see that? I got serious air, man! That was hella cutty." His eyes were glazed and bloodshot. I could see the colored lights of the game reflected there.

"Listen," Amber said, leaning one hip against the machine. "Forget *The Fast and the Furious* a minute, okay? We need your help."

His eyes darted from the screen to Amber's cleavage, artfully revealed beneath the plunging neckline of her halter top. An exploding sound blasted from the speakers and the neon green Ferrari went up in flames.

He slapped the controls. "Damn," he said. "I almost got high score."

Amber smiled without parting her lips. "Sorry." She didn't sound sorry at all. "We need to talk to you about Hero's party. What you saw."

He looked from her to me and back again, blinking. "What did I see?"

"You know," I said. "The thing you were going to tell Uncle Leo when you were in the hot tub."

He squinted as if thinking hard, then shook his head. "Nope, sorry, don't remember."

"Come on! Try," I said. "It's really important."

Amber drummed her fingers on the game console. "Chicks everywhere will thank you profusely."

Dog looked at her with a mixture of lust and concentration. I thought he might pull a muscle in his brain. "I remember the hot tub . . ." he said, ". . . bubbles. Pink bubbles."

"That's right," I prodded.

"She had *pink bubbles?*" Amber sneered.

"Go on," I told Dog, ignoring Amber. "Pink bubbles. What else do you remember?"

"Virg had this *kind* sticky from Mendo. We were stoked." His expression went all dreamy as he remembered. "There was a dude there looked like Carrot Top. Or wait, maybe that was the other party . . ."

"Okay, try to focus," I urged, masking my dwindling patience with an encouraging pat on the shoulder. "Think hard: Hero's party. Last Saturday. There was something you wanted to tell Uncle Leo about the Cheez Whiz guy."

"The Cheez Whiz guy!" Virg cried, suddenly tearing his camera away from his face. "I got him right here." He tapped his camera, excited.

Amber and I turned to the counter. "You've got John Jamieson on film?" I asked.

"Big deal," Amber said. "He probably just taped one of his commercials."

Virg looked offended. "No, man. I got top secret footage. When he makes it big, it's going to be worth buku bucks. I'm going to sell it to *People* magazine."

"Why, what's he doing in this 'top secret footage'?" Amber was still skeptical.

Virg laughed. "He's taking a leak."

"Great. Real crack team, here, Chief," she told me under her breath.

"Can I see? Do you have it with you?" I asked.

Virg puffed up a little. "Yeah, man. I've got like seventeen hours of footage in here. You want to see George taking a dump on Mrs. Smeby's car?"

George looked up from *Penthouse.* "Come on, dude. That's personal." He looked more proud than embarrassed.

Amber said, "Oh, Jesus."

"That's okay," I told Virg. "All we want is whatever you've got on John Jamieson."

"Oh, yeah! That's right." Virg was having a brain wave; I could see distinct activity stirring in his bloodshot eyes. He looked at Dog. "Remember, kook? We were gonna tell Hero's dad about how Cheez Whiz set her up."

"Ding-ding-ding-ding!" I cried, running over to the counter. "What did you hear him say?"

"Look, listen, and learn." Virg pressed some buttons, watching the viewfinder, until he had it cued up. We leaned our elbows onto the counter and he turned the camera toward us so we could see. Then he pressed PLAY, and we were watching John Jamieson peeing into the fountain in front of Hero's house.

"Gross," I said. "I skate around that fountain."

Then we heard John saying, "You see the look on Blondie's face when PJ made that toast? That was so tight."

Corky's distinct braying laughter was heard, and then he too stepped into view, whipped out his manhood, and peed into the fountain. "You think she faked that faint?"

John wagged the drops off and tucked himself into his pants. "No. She's the real thing—purebred pussy. I'd totally hit that."

Corky was still peeing. "You the Man!"

John was looking at the house now, considering. "You think anyone suspects?"

"What?"

"That we set it up. You know, getting those shots of Ginger, making it look like Hero—you think anyone knows?"

Corky finished peeing at last and said, "Naw. I mean, maybe Beezie, but who's going to believe her?"

"Yeah," John said. "I guess you're right. By the way, you get a piece of her yet?"

Corky shook his head. "I tried at your party, but she left before anything got started. Total blue balls."

"Too bad," John said. "Once you get her going, she's the bomb. Best blow job in town."

I glanced at Amber, who was riveted to the screen. She looked both furious and fascinated.

"You would know."

They laughed then, Corky's horsy braying blending with John's heavy artillery. It was a creepy sound.

Virg pushed STOP. "See? Cheez Whiz guy and Corky, peeing and plotting."

"Oh my God." I couldn't believe it. Not only did we have witnesses, we had evidence. "How did you get this without them seeing you?"

Virg used a deep baritone, like some sort of Rasta sage. "I be one wit de trees and de bushes—de eye in de sky."

I looked at Amber. "We've got it."

For a second I thought she might cry, but then she burst into maniacal laughter. "You're right." She leaned across the counter and kissed Virg on the cheek. "You're so beautiful! I can't believe this. We're going to nail John Jamieson."

Virg was in shock. He touched his cheek. Then he registered what she'd just said. "We tried, but Mr. Vino didn't listen."

"Ohhh, yeah . . ." Dog was a little slow on the uptake. "Now I remember. Monte Luna Dude—his wine is hella tasty!"

I beamed at them. "This is going to change everything for Hero."

"Who's Hero?" Dog ran his hand through his hair, making it stick up even more than usual; his forehead scrunched into ridges of confusion.

"Wipeout" suddenly started playing, and Dog punched the ANSWER button on his cell. "Dog here," he said. "Really? Right now? . . . Yeah, yeah, yeah. Sweet! Thanks for the four-one-one, man."

George put the *Penthouse* away. "What is it? Double overhead?"

"Better. Fight at Taco Bell!"

I got a bad feeling, all of a sudden. "Who?"

"Ben Bettaglia's taking on that Italian dude—you know, the one who hangs with PJ?"

Amber said, "Oh, *mierda*."

"No kidding," I said. "We've got to get over there and stop them."

George looked at me like I was crazy. "Stop them? There hasn't been blood at Taco Bell in, what? Three days?"

I turned back to Virg. "Can we borrow your camera? We really need that evidence."

Virg clutched it to his chest possessively. "No way. Nobody gets Baby."

"Please," Amber begged. "We'll love you forever!"

Dog was already halfway out the door. "We got to get there, man! It's going to be over."

A little kid with glasses walked in. The chime sounded as his light-up sneakers crossed the threshold, and he made a beeline for the video games. Virg watched him walk in, looked at the surveillance cameras, then back at the kid. "Hey, grom!" he called. "Want a job?"

The kid turned and stared, his face blank.

"I'll give you ten bucks worth of tokens if you'll man the counter for twenty minutes."

The kid ran over and took his place at the register. His chin barely cleared the cash drawer. Virg jumped over the counter, still clutching his camera. "Ladies," he said, linking arms with Amber and me, "let's nail this prick."

○ ● ● ○ ● ○

When we arrived at Taco Bell, there was already a crowd gathering in the parking lot. The text message tree had evidently alerted every kid within a ten-mile radius, and there was a good chance more were coming. I just hoped we could intervene before the bloodlust in that parking lot reached its boiling point. I cringed, thinking of all the broken noses and dislocated jaws that had graced that square of asphalt.

As Amber and I pushed our way to the front, the stofer trio trailing in our wake, we spotted the nucleus of violence. Ben had Claudio up against PJ's truck, a fistful of his striped shirt clenched in one hand. I was surprised at the little jolt of electricity that raced through my system. I heard my own words ringing in my head: *Make them re-*

gret this, or I will. Now Ben yanked harder on Claudio's shirt and slammed him against the closed door of the truck so his head bounced against the window. Ben was at least four inches shorter than Claudio, and there he was, defending my cousin's honor. It filled me with an unexpected surge of adrenaline. Either I was totally crushing on this guy, or there was so much testosterone in the air it was starting to affect my physiology.

"Don't hurt the truck," PJ was saying, alarmed.

Ben looked over his shoulder at PJ. "You're next, buddy."

PJ looked shocked. "Ben, what's up with you, man? What do you care about Hero?"

I stepped forward. "He cares because she's innocent."

Everyone looked at me, and I felt my heart rise into my throat as my eyes locked with Ben's. "He cares because what you guys did was wrong."

"Oh, man," PJ said, "are you still stuck on that, Sloane?"

"Excuse me!" I told him, getting in his face now. I felt the crowd's interest quicken as I jabbed at his chest with two fingers. "It might be nothing to you, but Hero's totally getting shit on."

"We see her photos," Claudio said. "She's a hoochie!"

Great. The guy barely speaks English, and what's the word he commits to memory? *Hoochie.*

"It was me in the photos," Amber said, stepping forward. The crowd reacted with a collective gasp crossed with murmurs. Some guy called out, "Beezie!" Amber looked around at the ring of faces, her cheeks flushed. "I was totally tricked. We were all tricked."

"Pretty elaborate," PJ said. "You sure looked like Hero."

"Photoshop," I told him. "John was behind the whole thing."

PJ laughed. "You're telling me John went to all that trouble just to make Amber look like Hero? That's insane."

"It's insane but true, dude." Virg came forward, brandishing his camera. "You were set up, and we got proof."

The crowd was starting to lose interest. I could feel the tide of animal desire ebbing. There was too much conversation, not enough action. Somebody yelled, "Kick some ass, man!" but exactly who was supposed to fight whom was getting murkier by the second, and I could see the relief in Ben's eyes as he backed away from Claudio.

"Check it out," Virg said, holding the camera up. Ben, Claudio, and PJ gathered around. "Exhibit A."

A few people lingered, craning their necks to see the small display screen, but most of them wandered off, disappointed. The process of clearing someone's name wasn't half as interesting as witnessing a cracked skull. They were getting in their cars when a cell phone rang, and seconds later someone yelled, "Fight at Jack in the Box!" Suddenly engines roared to life and the air was blue with exhaust. Soon it was only Amber, Virg, PJ, Claudio, Ben, and me. Even Dog and George had abandoned us for the promise of a little brutality with a side of fries.

I watched the boys' expressions as they stared at the screen on Virg's camera. PJ's face went from skeptical to angry, Ben's went from relieved to disgusted. Claudio just looked confused.

"I don't understand," he complained. "What is this, 'blow job'?"

"I'll draw a picture for you later." PJ turned to Amber and me. "Sloane, Amber, I'm so sorry. Seriously, I had no idea. I feel like a complete idiot."

Ben was speaking into Claudio's ear, explaining, and suddenly Claudio cried out, "No . . . no!" before dissolving into Italian.

Virg said to PJ, "I got to get back to work, man. Can I get a ride?"

"Sure." PJ seemed grateful for such an easy exit. As Claudio and Virg piled into his truck, Claudio still spewing anguished Italian, PJ looked at Amber and me again. "We'll fix this, okay? I'm going to do what I can."

"John's got to burn," I said. "Simple as that."

PJ seemed uneasy. "He's psycho when he's pissed. We've got to be chill about it."

"I don't care what it takes," I said. "I want him to know how Hero feels."

As they drove off I turned around and there was Ben, watching me with his dark, liquid eyes.

Amber sensed a moment coming on, and said, "I'm going inside for a Coke. You want anything, G?"

"No," I told her. "I'll be there in a minute."

When she'd gone inside, I turned back to Ben. The air was stifling and scented with grease. It was late afternoon, but still the sun was harsh. I stepped into the shade of the building, and he followed.

"Thanks," I said.

He kicked the pavement. "For what?"

"You know . . ."

"Oh—what? That?" He gestured vaguely at the parking lot.

"Yeah. Standing up for Hero."

"Naw, he just ate my bean burrito."

I raised an eyebrow and we both laughed. Then his hands disappeared into his baggy pockets and he shrugged. "I figured if I didn't do something you'd slash my tires."

I nodded. "I am pretty handy with a switchblade."

He took a step closer. "How's Auggie doggie handling all this?"

"He's hanging tough."

"Glad to hear it."

I leaned over and kissed his smirking lips. I felt like I could stand in the shade of that Taco Bell for years, tasting his mouth, breathing in the heady perfume of grease, sun-baked asphalt, and Ben Bettaglia.

Pretty soon Amber came out with her Coke, calling, "Hey, playa! Can we get a ride back to my car?"

Ben blushed. "Sure."

We climbed into his decrepit Volvo. As he drove us back to the mini-mart, Amber leaned forward from the backseat and said, "Were you really going to hit him? I mean, don't take this the wrong way, but he's got some size on you."

Ben cracked a smile and glanced at me. "I figured Sloane here had my back."

"Yeah, but come on," Amber persisted. "I mean, my God, you shave your legs."

"Hey! I'm a cyclist. That's what we do."

Amber looked from him to me and back again. "You guys are good together. Couple of freaks. I'm glad we tricked you into getting it on."

Normally, I'd be mortified, but I was too elated to scold

her. I leaned back in my seat and enjoyed the ride, sneaking occasional sideways glances at Ben and watching his arm muscles rearrange themselves every time he shifted gears.

○ ● ● ○ ● ○

It was time to fill Hero in on the whole sordid business. As soon as Ben dropped us off, Amber and I got in her car and headed for Moon Mountain.

"You think she'll forgive Claudio?" Amber narrowly avoided sideswiping the ice cream man, then ran a stop sign. She didn't miss a beat. "I don't think I would."

"Amber," I said, clinging to my seat belt. "You're aware that you nearly killed us just now? Twice?"

"Relax."

"Where did you learn to drive, anyway?"

She looked at me. "Funny. That's exactly what the guy at the DMV asked."

"What did you tell him?"

Her thick hair was flying in her eyes. "Hold on," she said, "safety maneuver. You steer."

I reached over and took hold of the wheel while Amber searched the trash-thick floorboards and the seats for something to hold her hair back. After swerving to avoid a cat, I yanked the elastic from one of my braids and handed it to her. "Here," I said, "just keep us alive, will you?"

Once her hair was secured in a ponytail she said, "Yeah, the guy who gave me the driver's test said, 'Where'd you learn to drive, a third-world country?' I told him, 'Buddy, if you don't pass me I'm telling your boss you tried to feel me up.'"

"You did not!" I said.

She found a pack of gum buried between the seat cushions and popped a stick in her mouth. "I don't skate, G. I don't even walk if I can avoid it. I had to get around somehow."

"Yeah, but threatening the DMV guy with a false accusation of sexual harassment—"

"Who said anything about false? He *did* try to feel me up."

"Oh," I said. "Well, that's okay then, I guess."

∘ ● ● ∘ ● ∘

The maid, Esperanza, opened the door and broke into animated Spanish when she saw us. At first I thought she was excited to see me, though we'd passed each other in the halls at least four times a week throughout the summer and she'd never been particularly effusive before. Then I saw it was Amber she was doting on. She even pinched her cheeks, exclaiming over her like she was a long-lost daughter. Amber smiled sweetly and produced a few Spanish phrases in response.

"What was that about?" I asked, after she'd let us in and we were making our way toward the kitchen.

"My mom used to work with her," Amber said. "At Sonoma Mission Inn."

"Really? Doing what?"

Amber undid her ponytail, handed the elastic to me, and finger-combed her hair back into place. "Housekeeping. I used to help out, before I started as a Betty."

"Does your mom still work there?"

Amber made a sound of disdain. "She never works anywhere longer than she has to."

We entered the kitchen, where Hero was piling fruit into a blender. When she saw us she put a half-peeled banana down and stared. "What's she doing here?" she asked me, nodding at Amber.

Amber put her hands up. "See? I told you."

"Whoa, whoa, whoa," I said. "Back up. Hero, you've got to chill, okay? We have amazing news, but if you're rude we're not going to tell you."

"I'm being rude? What do you call what she did to me?"

Amber started to turn toward the door, but I grabbed hold of her arm, holding her in place while I told Hero, "I'm serious. She's totally innocent. All you have to do is listen."

She sighed, thought for a moment. Finally she said in a sullen voice, "Anyone want one of these?"

We told her everything over smoothies out on the deck: how John promised the photos would be kept secret, how the stofers found out, Virg's footage, Taco Bell. Amber even told her about her history with John, and his history with every alleged slut in Sonoma. As she listened, Hero's face went through various permutations of surprise, relief, and disgust. When we stopped talking at last, she rested her elbows on her knees and said, "Oh God, I'm so sorry. I totally assumed the worst."

"No biggie," Amber said. "I'm used to it."

"But that's what makes it so awful," she said. "John picked you because he knew no one would believe you if you tried to rat him out."

I recalled Corky's words on tape: *Maybe Beezie, but who's going to believe her?* Hero was right. They chose Amber because nobody took her seriously.

"Wow, you're right," I said. "That is so messed up."

"You guys are just now getting this?" Amber stood up and

walked to the edge of the deck. She sounded annoyed. "I mean come on, story of my life."

Hero went over and leaned against the railing beside her. "I'm really sorry. I should have given you the benefit of the doubt."

"You didn't like me." Amber's tone was cool, but it warmed a bit when she added, "But then, I haven't exactly been likeable."

"I didn't give you a chance," Hero told her. "And I was wrong."

There was an awkward, loaded pause and I thought, *Is it really happening? Are they actually calling a truce?* It was like watching a pair of novice tightrope walkers—one misstep and all would be lost.

"I know we've had kind of a rough start," Hero said, "and we don't have all that much in common. But maybe you could—forgive me?"

Amber took her time before answering. "Actually," she said, a slow smile spreading across her face, "we have more in common than you think."

"Really?" Hero let out a nervous giggle and I thought, *Don't screw it up now, Cuz.* "Like what?"

"A common enemy."

Saturday, August 9
11:40 P.M.

Dad called tonight and said he's taking me to New York for my birthday; we'll fly there Labor Day weekend, just the two of us. It doesn't exactly make up for all the times he's flaked on me over the past year, but it's a step in the right direction. Maybe I should have told him off sooner.

Something I realized this morning: With Mom, I know I'm mad at her the second she does something lame. With Dad, it sometimes takes months to admit just how pissed off I am.

Weird. I'll have to ask Bronwyn about it sometime—see if anyone's come up with a theory about that one. Hopefully it won't have anything to do with that creepy Electra chick.

Tuesday, August 12
11:00 P.M.

PJ and Claudio finally got their shit together. Amazingly, it's taken them this long to organize an apology befitting their crime. Claudio's called; he even stopped by yesterday after work, though Uncle Leo told him Hero wasn't home. Hero watched from her bedroom window, apoplectic with the conflicting desire to see him and to make him pay. Her advisers (Uncle Leo, Amber, Bronwyn, and I) have all assured her that accepting his apology too readily will teach him nothing. He should suffer a little for what he's done.

"But he was tricked," she kept saying tonight. "He thought I was an underground porn star."

Amber and I exchanged a quick *Not this again* look. The three of us were painting our toenails in Hero's room. It was precisely the sort of girly bonding I'd imagined back in June. Sure, it took me a couple months to get here, but I've arrived in the promised land of shared pedicures at last.

"Hero, even if that was you in those photos, why is that his business? It's not like you were engaged," Amber said.

Hero squinted at her toes, three of which were cotton-candy pink. "He felt betrayed. I understand that."

"Have you even kissed the guy?"

Hero hedged. "What's that got to do with anything?"

"It's essential," Amber told her decisively. "First exchange of bodily fluids."

"You make it sound like a lab experiment."

Amber rolled her eyes at me, then turned back to Hero. "Answer the question, princess."

"Well, no. We haven't kissed. Not exactly."

"There's no *exactly* here, okay? Either you have or you haven't." Amber can be a stickler for accuracy.

Hero sighed impatiently. "What I mean is, he blew me a kiss. It was very romantic."

Amber made her lips disappear in an effort to keep from laughing. I was less successful. I giggle-snorted, then tried to fob it off as a cough.

Bronwyn burst through the door and we all turned. She looked awful—well, as awful as you can look when you've got terrific bone structure, amazing skin, and an eight-digit trust fund. Her cute little heart-shaped face was streaked with black tire marks of mascara and her eyes were puffy from crying. "I want you all to take a good look," she instructed us, flinging her arms out to her sides like a mascara-streaked Jesus. "I am now officially a dumped mistress."

Hero mumbled, "Ever hear of knocking?"

I led Bronwyn to a chair. "What happened?"

"He deep-sixed me." She dug a handkerchief from the pocket of her leather jacket and blew her nose. "I was his summer fling! I thought we were in love."

"I'm so sorry," I said.

Bronwyn closed her eyes like someone enduring a terrible pain. "I can't believe I was that dumb. Stupid, stupid, stupid!"

"Men," Amber said.

Bronwyn's eyes popped open. "Yes," she said, as if Amber had just revealed the cure for cancer. "Exactly. *Men.*"

"Well . . ." My tone was tentative. "He *is* married."

"He's married! Precisely my point," Bronwyn said. "I mean really, what was I thinking? Can you believe he almost talked me into changing my major?"

"But you love psych," I said.

"Not that part. Women's studies. I was going to change from psych and women's studies to psych and poly sci. All because he convinced me that women's studies is for bull dykes with hairy armpits."

"Shhh," Hero said. "What's that?" We all got quiet then. The strains of an acoustic guitar floated through the open French doors. Then we heard a guy's voice singing in Italian. It sounded a little like Uncle Leo's opera CDs, except you can tell those guys are fat. This singer sounded skinny, and frankly, a little off-key. There was only one skinny, off-key Italian it could possibly be.

We crowded onto the balcony to investigate, forcing Hero to stay hidden. It was all part of Operation Make Him Suffer—he wasn't to see her until he'd proven himself worthy. Outside, twilight had taken hold; the sky was a haunting blue, with just a few stars twinkling bravely. The air smelled like dust and grapes and night-blooming jasmine. There was a crescent moon dangling near the horizon, and little wisps of fog nestled in the cracks between the hills. Down on the patio, Claudio was strumming a guitar, serenading us. His voice wasn't exactly melodious, but his usually shaggy hair was slicked back and his face was so sweet and sincere, the flat notes hardly grated on your nerves at all.

"What's he singing?" I asked Bronwyn.

She tilted her head, listening. "He's saying, 'My eyes are the windows of my soul, which is grieving, and my heart is as full as . . . an ashtray?"

"His heart's as full as an ashtray?" Amber said. "Huh, that's pretty good."

Hero was flattened against the wall, hidden from sight. "His heart's as full as the moon!" she corrected.

"I liked ashtray," Amber grumbled.

The song ended, and out of the shadows came a deep, rumbling bass beat. We leaned over the balcony railing and spotted PJ with a miniature version of his usual gear set up under the awning. He grabbed the mike and stepped back a little farther, keeping himself hidden. When PJ started to rap, Claudio moved his mouth; the result was a poorly dubbed martial arts flick, hip-hop style. We laughed so hard tears streamed down our faces.

"Listen to my tale of woe,
I got a matter of minutes to go,
Before my heart turns into a stone,
I'm so tired of being alone.
I saw your picture on MySpace
Your golden hair and your angel's face
But wait, that girl wasn't you,
I'm so confused—what can I do?

I was tricked by the slimy bro
And that's my tale of woe.
So baby, if you've got a heart
Tell me girl, can we start
Over and over and over
Crimson and clover . . ."

Here PJ sampled a couple bars from "Crimson and Clover"
while we laughed on the balcony, clapping and cheering.
Hero was peeking through the blinds looking happier than
I'd seen her all summer.

"Hold up." It was Uncle Leo, striding out onto the patio in
his Armani suit. He'd been at some sort of board meeting and
he looked very intimidating. "Turn that off."

PJ immediately obliged. The driving hip-hop beat and
the eighties sample cut out abruptly, leaving only crickets.
"Mr. Sloane," PJ said. "Please don't be mad. We wanted to
apologize."

"By sneaking into my yard and playing that—that rap
crap?"

"Sir, we—Claudio and I—we just wanted to show you
how much we regret all the misunderstandings."

Uncle Leo drew himself up to his full height, which is well
over six feet, and looked down his nose at PJ. "Misunderstandings? I've sent Hero back to Connecticut two weeks
early because of these so-called 'misunderstandings,' did you
know that?"

"No. I—I'm sorry to hear that, sir," PJ stammered.

"I won't have her subjected to these absurd rumors. I just
won't do it."

"Like I said, we're really sorry, sir." PJ shoved his hands into the pockets of his jeans and they nearly fell off, they were so baggy. "Claudio and I both messed up. And if there's anything we can do to make it up to you . . ."

"There is something. I want you to take Geena and Amber out this Friday." He glanced up at us. "They've been through a lot lately."

PJ was definitely thrown by the proposition; so was I. "Um, okay. No problem."

Claudio stepped forward, his hand outstretched. "Sir, yes, we take them to dinner, because I am so sorry Hero was a hoochie."

From behind the curtains, Hero let out a squeaking sound.

PJ stepped in front of his friend, saying, "He means he's sorry she was *called* such terrible names and he wants to make it up to you."

"Fine." Uncle Leo's tone was brusque, but I knew him well enough to detect a note of suppressed laughter. "The two of you get here by six on Friday. Bring Ben Bettaglia. You'll treat them to a fine meal, then take them to a movie and be home by one."

Beside me, Amber dug an elbow into my ribs.

"Yes, sir," PJ said.

After a pointed look, Claudio echoed PJ. "Yes, sir. Thank you."

"Now get your gear out of here, and if you ever spread rumors about my daughter again, I will personally remove your testicles and display them in the plaza with your names on them."

Whoa. Go, Uncle Leo.

When we heard PJ's truck start up, we all ran downstairs and found Uncle Leo on the couch, flipping through *Wine Spectator.*

Hero flung herself onto the cushions beside him. "Dad, what was that about?"

He continued to study the magazine. "It takes more than a little guitar and a turntable to make up for their stupidity."

"That was *sweet,*" Amber said. "I love that testicle bit. Man, where'd you get that, an Al Pacino flick?"

Leo's eyes glittered. "Your generation didn't invent the art of invective, you know."

Bronwyn sat on the other side of her father and slipped an arm around his shoulders. "Brilliant performance, Pop. Really." She seemed to have recovered some from her jilted-mistress meltdown.

"But now I'm supposed to be in Connecticut!" Hero complained. "And I want to go to dinner too."

Uncle Leo put the magazine down. You could tell he was enjoying all the attention. He took off his spectacles and polished them with a handkerchief. For a moment, his face and the smell of his aftershave reminded me of my father's. I felt a thickness in my throat, but I swallowed hard and the moment passed. "If he thinks he's really lost you, he might appreciate you more."

"But I get to go too, right?" Hero asked.

"Of course. Until then, just let him worry about how badly he messed up."

Hero got all hyper then. "I'm going out with Claudio!"

"Friday, right? We have to check out *Blood Moon*. It's opening Friday at midnight," I said.

Amber high-fived me. "Right on! That's so perfect."

"All right then, you can stay out until two. At which point, fearing for his testicles, Claudio will return you safely to my doorstep."

"Two?" Hero whined. "Don't you think that's a little harsh if the movie doesn't start until midnight?"

He put his glasses back on. "Not at all."

"I think two thirty is a lot more realistic," Amber said.

He glared at her.

I nodded. "Two thirty would be extremely generous."

He picked up his magazine again. "Two fifteen. That's my final offer."

We all squealed and hugged him and jumped up and down on the couch until he yelled, "If you don't leave me in peace, I'll make it midnight!"

Wednesday, August 13
3:40 P.M.

Hero can't work her final week at TSB, so Amber and I are covering for her. We don't want word to get out that she's not in Connecticut at all, but is actually serving up lattes and mochas at Sonoma's finest coffee establishment. It's okay with Hero; she's got plenty to keep her busy between now and then. Since Bronwyn needs something to take her mind off "Professor Prick," she's made Hero her little improvement project. Every day Bronwyn piles her sister into her Jeep (making sure Claudio doesn't spot them from the vineyards) and whisks her off to a different spa, shopping center, or salon. She's even convinced Hero to redecorate her room; it seems Little Miss Arrested Development has finally agreed that the pink ruffles she once adored have grown stale.

I asked Bronwyn if all this retail therapy and spa touring wasn't a tad bourgeois for someone who spearheaded the "Fashion Kills" awareness week. She just shrugged and said, "People change, Geena. Get over it."

I thought about that as I watched Amber walk through the door of TSB sporting a brand-new look. She was wearing her Betty tank top, but instead of her usual Daisy Dukes or distressed-denim mini, she'd paired it with a pale pink knee-length skirt, matching ballet flats, and a pure white cardigan.

"Wow," I said. "Look at you."

She propped her cat-eye sunglasses on top of her head. "What?" Her tone dared me to mock her.

"Nothing, just . . ." I touched the sweater, confirming my suspicions: cashmere. "You look good."

She bit her lip. "You think so?"

"Yeah, totally. Different, though. Are those new clothes?"

She nodded. "Hero was getting rid of some stuff."

"Oh, right." I was tempted to feel jealous for a moment—*why wasn't I offered first dibs?* Then I remembered the last time Hero tried to give me her hand-me-downs. I told her, "No offense, Cuz, but if I wanted to look like an Ice Capades contestant, I wouldn't wear cutoff Dickies, now would I?"

"You think I look dumb?" Amber asked.

"No. It's just a big change for you, that's all."

She started making herself a vanilla latte. It was foggy out, and she made it hot this time. "You know, the truth is, I want to cultivate a new image. I'm sick of living with this white-trash ho-bag persona. I want a little respect."

"People respect you," I said.

She wasn't buying it. "Come on, Geena. The only respect I get is for my alleged blow job record, and that's not even factual."

"But you have . . . ?" I hesitated.

"Had sex?" she supplied.

"I mean, I know not with John, because he couldn't—get it up, or whatever—but with someone else . . . ?" I wasn't trying to pry, but I'd been wondering, and it seemed like the right moment to ask.

"If you ever tell anyone this, I'll kill you, okay?"

I nodded. "I won't tell anyone."

She leaned closer and whispered, "Technically, I'm a virgin."

My jaw dropped. *"You?"*

"I would have with John." She made a face. "Though now I'm glad I didn't."

"You're not a virgin," I said, amazed.

"Swear to God."

"But you're so not like that. I mean—you know what I mean."

She shrugged. "I figured it was better to embrace my skank status than to fight it. I didn't want to be Marcy Adams."

Marcy Adams is a junior who looks and acts like a PTA mom, but is rumored to have hosted several orgies in the basement of her parents' mansion. Also, she supposedly poses on a regular basis for an Internet porn site called Lolita's Lair and frequently exchanges sexual favors for crack.

She wears Peter Pan collars and floral skirts, but the rumors spread like wildfire anyway. She went out with John for a little while last year.

Amber looked down at her outfit, suddenly horrified. "Oh, God. I'm turning into Marcy Adams, aren't I?"

"Amber, what if Marcy Adams is as innocent as you?"

She looked at me like I was totally slow. "Well, yeah, I bet she is. But what does that matter? John is king around here, and he's told everyone we're beer sluts." She looked depressed now. "This isn't going to work. I'll just be a skank in pink chiffon."

"But John will be at Yale soon," I said. "You'll have a new lease on life."

She shook her head. "Doesn't matter. There are so many little John Jamieson acolytes at school, the rep will stick. And if I manage to shake it, he'll still be home for holidays. He can do more damage in a week than most people manage in a decade."

"You're right," I said. "The only solution is to publicly humiliate him with such force that he'll lose all credibility forever."

Amber blew her hair out of her eyes and sipped her latte. "Good luck. The guy's got Satan on his side."

Just then—speak of the devil—John drove up in his Beemer. As usual, Corky was riding shotgun, looking like a muscle with hair. Jay-Z was blaring from the stereo. I went to the window and waited until he turned it down to a bearable level.

"How's it going?" My tone was polite, even friendly, but inside I was seething. My reasons for pandering to him now were different than they were a week ago. Before, I was afraid of him. Now I was scheming. A plan was starting to formulate in the dark workshop at the back of my brain, and I didn't want my enemy to be even remotely aware of my diabolical intentions.

"I'm okay. What about you, Skater Girl?"

Right then, even though I hated him, I could totally see why so many girls had fallen under his spell. The blond hair, those high cheekbones, the little dimple that showed up in his right cheek when he grinned—it was all too perfect. But his sex appeal went way beyond that. He was like a bright golden box with a dark, bitter secret inside. Who could resist the sinister intelligence that blazed behind his ice blue eyes?

I forced myself to sound nonchalant. "I'm good. Hi, Corky."

Corky was applying oil to his enormous biceps. He looked at me and said, "You got a thirty-two-ouncer?"

Déjà vu. God, that guy's a loser. "Nope, sorry, just eighteen. You want a Coke?"

He nodded, and turned his powers of concentration back to oiling his muscles.

"What can I get you?" I asked John.

"The usual—macchiato, stiff foam."

"Coming right up," I said.

As I got busy with their order, Amber hung back, trying to make herself invisible in the shadows. John spotted her, though, and treated us to his machine-gun laugh. Corky joined in, and soon everyone within twenty yards of us was turning to see what the big deal was.

Amber marched over to the window. "You got a problem?"

John shook his head. "No, Ginger. I think it's great."

She fell for it. "You think what's great, exactly?"

He held his palms up. "The new look."

Corky laughed so hard, he could barely get the words out. "Is this the Blowjob Barbie ensemble?"

That was it. Screw keeping a low profile; these bastards needed some instant karma. I reached up to the top shelf where we keep the extra-super-hot habanero sauce. Amber keeps it stashed there to go with the mircowave burritos she usually brings in for lunch. I squirted a healthy shot into each paper cup, then poured espresso and steamed milk into John's, Coke with ice into Corky's. A couple of lids and voila! Volcanic caffeine, coming right up.

I went to the window and handed them over. My hands were shaking slightly, but they were laughing too hard to notice. John reached for his wallet. "Those are on the house," I said. "I hope the foam's stiff enough."

"Thanks, Skater Girl." The schmuck actually winked at me. "I'm sure it's plenty stiff."

I giggled coquettishly. Amber was looking at me like I was a total traitor. I shot her a look that said, *Just wait.* "Enjoy," I told them.

That's when they both took their first sips. John's face turned red as a radish. Corky started choking. John leaned over and spit macchiato con habanero all over the side of his spotless car. His glazed eyes found mine. "You," he wheezed.

"Is there a problem?" I gave them my concerned customer-service face.

Corky was hyperventilating. Amber bit her lip, trying not to laugh.

John narrowed his eyes at me into scary little slits. The effect was slightly marred, though, by the tears streaming down his cheeks. "You'll pay!"

"Actually," I said, my voice still sweet as sugar, "you're the one who's going to pay."

He chucked what was left of his coffee in our general direction, but luckily I slammed the window shut quickly enough to avoid major splatter. They tore out of the parking lot, tires squealing.

Amber threw her arms around my neck. "Oh my God," she said. "No one's ever done anything like that for me."

"It was nothing," I said. "Really."

Suddenly she pulled back, her eyes scared. "He'll come after you, G. You'll be his next victim."

"Not if we get to him first," I said.

"But how?"

"We need to get phone numbers for all the girls John's dated, okay?"

"What? Why?"

I got out the phone book. "Safety in numbers."

"You're not making sense," she said.

"Trust me," I told her. "I've got a plan."

"But what do we say when we call them?"

I thought for second. "Ask them if they'd like to be charter members of the BAM Committee."

"BAM? What's that?"

"What else?" I grinned. "Bettys Against the Man."

Amber took the phone book from me. "This," she said, "is getting good."

Thursday, August 14

9:40 A.M.

Operation Redwood Terror is scheduled to begin twenty minutes from now. Please, Bettys throughout the ages, hear my battle cry!

We will be avenged!!!

1:20 P.M.

The trap is set. Hero called John this morning. All the BAMs were there in her room, sipping our TSB drinks and clamping our hands over each other's mouths whenever a giggle would threaten to erupt.

"Hi, is this John?" Hero employed her sweetest, most sex-kittenish tone. We had him on speaker phone, which was admittedly dangerous, yet irresistible.

"Yeah. Who's this?"

"It's Hero. What's up?"

"Uh, nothing much. Wow. Didn't expect to hear from *you.*"

His surprise wasn't exactly surprising. I mean, the last time she'd seen him she'd called him a "total slime" and puked all over his deck. She looked a little panicked, though, and I hurriedly scribbled on a piece of paper *DON'T PANIC!!!*

"Well, tell you the truth, John, I owe you an apology."

We all nodded encouragement at her.

"I just got so wasted at your party—I totally didn't know what I was saying! I don't even remember it, but I hear I wasn't very nice to you."

"It happens." John still sounded a little cagey; we needed more ammo. Amber grabbed the Sharpie from my hand and scrawled, *C DMPED YR ASS. B SAD!!!*

Hero nodded, then started in with some muffled sobs. "And now Claudio thinks I'm a slut because of this whole MySpace thing—what a disaster. I just can't believe he'd be so shallow. He's not the person I thought he was at all."

"Hey, you sound upset . . ."

"God, you've been so nice to me all summer, John. I had it all wrong! I thought Claudio was so great. Now I see he was just a decoy, distracting me from what I really felt all along."

John lowered his voice to an intimate, throaty growl. "And what do you really feel?"

"Oh, John. I feel so much. For you."

Insert finger down throat! Hero was transforming before our eyes into a full-on soap opera goddess! I was a little shocked, and slightly worried it might be too much for John to swallow.

"Hero, I've been waiting all summer to hear you say that."

Never fear; evidently John speaks fluent cheese.

"Will you pick me up tonight at eight? My dad will be out." She lowered her voice to a near whisper, and Marcy had to practically tackle Kim, she was giggling so convulsively. "I'm dying to see you."

"Uh, yeah. Sure. I can rearrange my schedule."

All six of us BAMs silently danced around like a pack of mimes on E.

"Great. See you then."

Excellent! The unsuspecting swine is right where we want

Triple Shot Betty

him. Now all we have to do is combine the brainpower and labor potential of seven extremely vengeful, super-caffeinated girls and we've got ourselves a coup d'etat.

4:30 P.M.

Equipment check:

Courtesy of Nikki's family's theater company, seven black robes with big, roomy hoods: check.

On loan from Marcy, a fabulous iPod docking station with four detachable speakers: check.

From Lexa's dad, who hopefully won't notice them missing, one pair of real handcuffs: check.

Torn from my old Halloween witch costume, a silk blindfold: check.

11:50 P.M.

Oh my God, what a night. *Dura lex, sed lex!* (For uninitiated plebeians: "The law is harsh, but it is the law!") I'm exhausted, but filled with righteous exhilaration. Maybe I should be a lawyer, or a judge, or a freelance feminist vigilante when I grow up.

Here's what happened: John picked Hero up at eight and, at her urging, drove to a spooky redwood forest kind of by Geevana Ridge. It's way out there, with no houses nearby, and the atmosphere at night is pure ghostliness. Amber, Marcy, Nikki, Kim, Lexa, and I were all waiting by a fairy ring at the heart of the forest, with Virg, Dog, and George lurking in the shadows armed with film equipment. The gods must have smiled on our questionable venture, because a thick, mysterious fog rolled in, slithering through the trees and licking at the ferns and generally adding to the creepiness of the place.

Pretty soon we heard Hero giggling as she walked through the forest, and a few seconds later we could just make out John's voice right behind her.

"Hero! I never knew you were so kinky."

"Don't take the blindfold off," Hero answered. "We're getting close. Just hold my hand—I'll lead you. Ooh, don't trip! Okay, I'm letting go now. Just follow my voice. We're almost there."

That was our cue to yank our hoods up over our heads and shrink deeper into the shadows. In less than a minute Hero had reached the fairy ring, and I tossed a robe at her, which she threw on immediately, pulling the hood over her hair like the rest of us.

"You're almost the-ere," she repeated in a flirty, singsong voice.

At last he stumbled into our trap, blindfolded, a wide smile on his face, his hands stretched out before him like a child playing blindman's bluff. He was trying to be a good sport, that much was clear, and I could tell he found her little cat-and-mouse game titillating, but I thought I could see little lines of anxiety starting to form around the edges of his smile already. Good. Anxiety was part of the plan.

Hero took his hand and led him gently to the redwood I was crouching behind. "Here," she coaxed, "just put your hands behind you—yep, behind the tree like that. Oh, you're being such a good boy."

Once we had his arms wrapped backwards around the

trunk, I clamped the handcuffs onto his wrists, and the sound of the metal clicking shut seemed to echo through the trees.

"Oh my God. Is that what I think it is?" A little struggle confirmed his suspicions. He tried to keep his tone light. "I never guessed you were into bondage."

But Hero didn't answer him. She was no longer a flirty girl traipsing through the moonlit woods. She bent to pick up her candle in silence, and we all picked ours up too; Amber lit them one by one while John prattled on nervously.

"Hey—is someone else here? This isn't like a group thing, is it? I mean, kinky's cool, but I like to know what I'm getting into."

We had our candles lit, and we formed a wide circle around our captive, who twisted his head left to right, listening. I nodded at Marcy, and she pushed PLAY on the iPod, filling the air around us with the sound of John's malevolent voice.

"Purebred pussy . . . Best blow job in town . . . You think anyone suspects? You think anyone suspects? You think anyone suspects?" We looped this over and over again—his disembodied, hateful voice bouncing off the mist-shrouded redwoods.

"Okay, hold up. What's the deal? Who's there?"

We said nothing.

"Hello?" he was getting louder now. "Hero? Is this supposed to be funny?"

Still we were silent. Marcy edged the volume up slightly, and John had to yell to be heard.

"Because it's not funny, you know! I'm not laughing."

When he seemed suitably unnerved, I nodded at Marcy

and she immediately turned the iPod off. Then I turned to Hero, and she began to chant in Latin, her voice deeper and more commanding than I'd ever heard it.

"*Dura lex, sed lex.*"

"*Dura lex, sed lex,*" we echoed.

"*Quidquid latine dictum sit altum viditur.*"

"*Quidquid latine dictum sit altum viditur.*"

"*Da mihi sis crustum Etruscum cum omnibus in eo . . .*"

And so on. Even though we'd practiced this some, I wasn't prepared for how authentic it sounded, out here in the ancient forest, with only the misshapen moon as our witness. (Okay, technically, the stofers were our witnesses too, but they were so stoned I hardly think they count.)

John wasn't saying a word now. Our candles cast flickering pools of light on his face, and I could see he was sweating. The Latin was getting to him. If only he knew we were saying things like, "Everything sounds profound in Latin," and "I'll have a pizza with everything on it."

When I sensed we'd milked all we could from the demented Druid act, I slid my finger across my throat, and the BAM committee fell silent. When I looked at Amber, she pulled the script I'd written from the inside of her robe and recited in a somber tone, "John Jamieson, hast thou sinned against the daughters of Eve?"

"Daughters of Eve? What the—?"

"I repeat: Hast thou sinned against the daughters of Eve?" Amber was louder now, getting into it.

John tried hard to yank himself free of the handcuffs, but it was futile. "I don't think so."

"You don't *think* so?" Amber was the very embodiment of

righteousness. "Sir, in the eyes of this committee, your answer is insufficient."

As if to punctuate Amber's statement, Hero led us in another chant: *"Dura lex, sed lex, dura lex, sed lex!"* Our voices intertwined and spiraled up through the trees, getting louder and louder. An owl hooted from somewhere above us, as if egging us on.

Finally, when our mantra sounded so maniacal it was scaring even me, Amber broke in with, "Sisters, he's not getting it. Bring me the cleaver."

She was improvising now, but I didn't mind.

John cried out, "Okay, okay, yes!"

"Yes, what?"

"Yes, I guess I've sinned. Against Eve, or whoever."

Amber glanced down at her script. "Please, sir, tell the committee what crimes you have committed against the Bettys here assembled."

John actually cracked a smile. "Wait a minute—is that Beezie?"

In a flash, Amber had her knee against his crotch. She wasn't inflicting any pain, but he cringed just the same, and she kept it in place as she spoke. "I recommend you refrain from using that name, now and forever. Do I make myself clear?"

"Yes," he grunted.

"What?"

"Yes!"

She stepped away from him and went on, referring to her script once again. "Sir, we have gathered here today to illuminate for public record the crimes you have committed against those assembled. You will hear the testimonies against you, and plead innocent or guilty, as your conscience demands. Do you understand?"

He just nodded, his face twisted into a tight grimace.

One by one, each of the BAMs stepped forward, removed her hood, and stated her grievance. Nikki had gone out with John three times, and when she refused to have sex on the third date, he'd told all his friends she had chlamydia. Lexa had gone to the prom with him and was blown away by the legendary yacht; unfortunately, he couldn't get it up when they tried to do it, and the next thing she knew people were spray-painting "whore" on her locker. Marcy had only gone out with him once, and because she told him to his face he was a sloppy kisser, she'd been plagued by rumors about her alleged sluttiness ever since. Kim hung out with him for a month, let him videotape her kickboxing in a T-shirt and boxers, but was horrified when the footage starting popping up all over the Internet.

Each of their testimonies only made me hate the guy more. He was charismatic, persuasive, charming, intelligent, and what did he do with those gifts? He chewed us up and spit us out, as if every girl with a drop of self-esteem was a direct threat to his manhood.

It was Hero's turn now. She stepped forward, shrugged off her hood, and said in a low, dangerous voice, "You ruined my birthday. You turned my first love against me. That's all, but it's enough."

Nobody knew better than me how important that birthday party was to her. It might sound silly to people who don't know Hero, but destroying her pink Glitterland fantasy was brutal;

it was like taking a child's favorite doll and slashing it to bits.

As Hero withdrew into the shadows of her hood, Amber removed hers and stood up taller. Her red hair looked fierier than ever in the candlelight. I thought Botticelli would be happy to paint her as she stood there, gazing at John with a look that mixed love and hatred in equal measures. He could call it *Venus Gets Her Revenge.*

"God, John. What can I even say to you? I was so happy; then you turned everything black." Her voice broke, and I stepped forward to squeeze her hand. She squeezed my fingers in return and took a deep breath. Then she walked over to John and carefully, tenderly, removed his blindfold. She looked him right in the eye and whispered, "You know how to make people love you, John. To use that against them is just cruel."

She pulled her hood up and walked back to her place in our circle, leaving John to gape at us, seven hooded figures in candlelight. It was my turn. I shook off my hood.

"What was your crime against me? You messed with my cousin and my best friend. That, I'm afraid, was a big mistake."

"Bitch." He said it under his breath, but we all heard it in the still, foggy night.

Amber started toward him, her eyes blazing, but I grabbed her arm and she stood still.

"I'm sorry," I said pleasantly. "What did you say?"

I wondered too late if we should have left his blindfold on. He had his bearings now, and though he was still handcuffed to a tree, the element of surprise was no longer ours. He focused on me, his eyes glittering with rage.

"You heard me. I know you're behind this, you stupid cunt. And I know where you live."

I felt a shiver travel down my spine, but I made myself address him in a commanding voice. "Sir, do you plead guilty to the charges leveled against you tonight?"

He laughed. "What? I went out with these girls, sure. All except you. I wouldn't touch you if you were the last skanky, disease-ridden whore in the world."

"Shut up!" Amber barked.

"The question remains: *Cum tacent, clamant.*" Hero got up in his face suddenly. I suspect Latin fueled her courage; it was like her superpower. "Are you guilty?"

He narrowed his eyes at her. "Yeah. Guilty and proud."

"Excellent. Then our work here is done." I produced a Triple Shot Betty to-go cup from the inner pocket of my robe. As I stood before him, I rattled it so he could hear the metal object inside. It was sealed with a plastic lid.

"What's that?" he sneered.

"The key. Specifically, the key that could keep you from remaining here for the rest of your life, and possibly starving to death." I shook my head. "Not a good way to go."

He just scoffed.

I bent down and placed the cup near his feet. "We think it'll take you a little while to get to it. Maybe a little longer to actually unlock the cuffs. But we imagine those hours of quiet reflection will serve you well. Given the crimes you've so freely confessed to, providing you with a little time to think things over is letting you off pretty easy, don't you agree?"

"Don't do me like that." His face turned from vindictive to imploring so abruptly, I had to admire his emotional agility.

"Mmm, sorry," I told him, "your charm's not going to work this time. It's late, we're tired, and frankly, we're a little disappointed in your lack of remorse. We'll sleep better knowing you're out here in these cold, dark woods, pissing yourself with fright."

We gathered the iPod and speakers before making our way back through the woods toward the car. It's funny; I expected us to be running and laughing at this point, exhilarated by our own daring. Instead we walked in silence. There was a somber mood hanging between us, like what we'd done wasn't a prank at all, but an actual ritual. We could hear John crying out to us, pleading at first, then getting angrier and angrier as he realized we weren't turning around.

Once we were out of John's line of vision, we waited for the stofers. They met us on the path a little while later, camera in hand, smoking up as usual. "Man," Dog said, "what a blowhard."

John's furious shouts grew harder to hear with every step, but we could still make out the gist of it. "You think anyone's going to believe you, stupid whores? No! Nobody will believe you! Get back here!"

"Maybe nobody will believe you girls . . ." Virg patted his camera affectionately. "But everyone will believe Baby."

Friday, August 15

10:10 A.M.

Woke up wondering if I dreamed last night's escapades. Checked my e-mail and knew I hadn't—there were twenty messages, all from the BAMs, all plotting and scheming about the final stage of our plan. Hopefully we'll pull it off cum laude magnum.

3:30 P.M.

Classic! A zit. I can't believe this. It's the size of a golf ball. Why must the gods taunt me so?

5:40 P.M.

Tonight's the big night: dinner with the guys, then off to the midnight screening of *Blood Moon*. I've been so nervous and fidgety, I could hardly apply my makeup.

Of course Hero looks fabu. All that shopping with Bronwyn has updated her look—she's gone from a princess to Bohemian babe. She still favors bridesmaid pastels, but she's gone in for a little leather fringe here and there, beaded halter tops, that sort of thing. Tonight she's wearing these killer suede flares with a celery green baby doll tank. Amber's wearing her signature denim mini with one of Hero's hand-me-down cashmere tees. I've got on a pale orange baby-T with Bronwyn's buttery suede skirt. All in all, we look pretty hot, except that I resemble the "before" shot in a Clearasil commercial. Why, why, why?

At Uncle Leo's suggestion, we got dressed early and sat out on the patio, sipping Pinot as we nibbled on cheese, crackers, and Elodie's amazing bacon-wrapped green beans. The valley below was bathed in creamy, golden light, and little wisps of fog were lining up above the far hills, ready to be stained pink come sunset. It's one of those evenings that makes you wish summer would last forever.

To my surprise, the EUWW was there—her name's Sharon, evidently—and every time she praised Uncle Leo's Pinot or complimented Elodie's appetizers, his eyes gleamed with pleasure.

I pulled Hero aside and whispered, "You think they're dating?"

She sighed. "I think so."

"Are you horrified?"

She tilted her head to one side, considering. "Not really. I'm not in love with her, but I want Dad to be happy. He's all alone here now."

I nodded, feeling a quick pang of guilt about my deep-seated bimbo bias. If only I could be as accepting and serene as my cousin.

The doorbell chimed, startling me. "They're not here yet, are they?"

Amber's face was puzzled too, but Hero bit back a knowing smile. "Dad and I invited a friend."

Uncle Leo stood up as Esperanza ushered in Alistair Drake. He was wearing black leather pants and a red silk shirt with dragons painted down the front. His blue-black hair was slicked into a ponytail.

"G'day," he said in his thick Aussie accent.

"Alistair! Glad you could make it." Leo clapped him on the shoulder and showed him to a chair. "Pinot all right?"

"Sounds great. But just a sip—can't stay long—got to pick someone up at the airport soon."

I snuck a look at Amber; her face was veering dangerously between ecstasy and terror.

"Hello, girls," he said to us before leaning forward and smiling at Amber. His teeth were slightly crooked, but it was a good, genuine smile. "You must be Amber. I've heard about you."

Amber's eyes widened. "Really?"

"Oh, yeah. Your friend Hero's been telling me you're quite an artist. Sorry to be so abrupt, but I've only got a couple minutes. I was wondering if you might have some samples of your work on you?"

Amber swallowed and nodded. She reached into her bag—a hand-me-down Louis Vuitton tote from Hero—and pulled out the little sketchbook she takes everywhere. She passed it to him and I saw that her hand was shaking a little.

He took it from her and flipped through the pages, sipping his wine as he perused. None of us spoke. Sometimes he paused and squinted at a page for a long time. "I love this rocket. The planets are brilliant." He flipped more pages. "Wow, the passion flower's quite detailed. Very evocative. And the Skater Girl looks just like your friend here." He nodded at me; then he locked his hawklike eyes on her face. "I'm gathering staff for my shop, you know—we open our doors next month. If you want to help out, I'd love to have you."

"I—oh, my God—yeah, absolutely."

I've never seen Amber so tongue-tied.

"Nothing glamorous, and the pay's not great, but if you help out with the phones and inventory, I guarantee you'll apprentice with the best. We're bringing in Seiji Unisuga from Kyoto—have you seen his work?"

"Have I seen it? Yeah—I mean, yes. He's amazing."

The side of Alistair's mouth quirked up in a bemused grin. "Excellent. Then it's decided." He reached into his shirt pocket and handed her a bright red card. "Call me next week, we'll set it up."

"Thank you." Amber's eyes were shining.

When he'd gone, she covered her mouth with both hands. "Holy—Jesus—God!"

Leo poured more wine. "Sounds like you're having a religious experience over there, Amber."

She looked back and forth between Leo and Hero. "You guys. Oh my God! Thank you, thank you, thank you!"

Hero shrugged, but I could tell she was pleased with herself. All she said was, "A deal's a deal."

Saturday, August 16
2:20 A.M.

Oh my God, I'll never sleep! I feel like I've been pounding triple shots with Red Bull chasers.

Ben, PJ, and Claudio showed up right at six. When we heard a car in the drive we ran to the window, expecting to see Ben's ancient relic of a Volvo, since we'd never fit into PJ's truck. Instead we found ourselves staring at a huge silver limo.

After we finished screaming, Hero looked at her father. "Did you do this?"

He was noncommittal. "I think it's a great idea."

"Because it was yours, wasn't it?"

"I might have suggested it." He loaded a cracker with brie and took a bite. "Studies show, the more teenagers you pile into a car, the greater your chance of having an accident. In order to eliminate that variable, it's easy enough to—"

Amber tackled him mid-sentence with a running hug. "Leo, you're so damn cool! I wish you were my dad."

"Thanks, honey," he said when he could breathe again. "You're welcome." He patted her back awkwardly, still chewing.

The doorbell rang.

Hero, Amber, and I looked at each other, suddenly rigid with nerves. "Okay, don't panic," I said as we made our way into the foyer.

Amber said, "What's the Betty Code of Conduct, girls?"

"Stick together," Hero and I answered in unison.

"That's right," she said. "Watch each other's backs."

"If a Betty has something in her teeth," Hero said, "notify her immediately."

"And don't get vomitously drunk," I added.

Amber came back with, "That's your rule." When I threw her a look she said, "But it's a good one. Gum, anyone?" Hero and I nodded, and Amber handed us each a stick of Big Red.

"Girls?" Uncle Leo called from the living room. "Esperanza's gone home. You waiting for me to get the door?"

"No!" Hero called.

"Okay, chicas," I whispered. "Let's do this." Then I yanked the door open.

God, they looked good.

The trio of boyness standing on those steps was a perfect Abercrombie & Fitch tableau. Talk about three flavors of yum! There was PJ leaning against the house in his black wraparound shades, his short, dark hair styled with just enough gel to look groomed but not frozen. He had on baggy cargo pants and a black T-shirt that stretched across his pecs rather nicely. Next to him was Claudio, looking Euro-chic in pressed chinos and a pale cotton sweater. He'd cut his hair so it was out of his eyes, but still looked slightly shaggy in that tousled, Italian way.

And then there was Ben.

If I think too much about him I'm *never* going to sleep.

Working from the bottom up: suede wingtips, faded jeans, olive green button-down shirt, tortoiseshell sunglasses, perfect black hair worn au natural as usual. In a word, totally edible. (Okay, that's two words, but if you saw him, you'd agree.)

"Bella!" Claudio took a step forward and drank in the sight of Hero. "You're here."

She gazed at him coyly from under mascaraed lashes. "I wouldn't leave without saying good-bye."

He wrapped his arms around her tiny waist and lifted her into the air, laughing as ecstatic Italian poured from his lips. Then they kissed—not the European nice-to-meet-you cheek-kisses, but the full-on French variety. Of course, Uncle Leo chose that moment to come out and see how things were going.

"I—oh—" he said, stopping.

They didn't even come up for air. Amber and I jerked our heads in the direction of the limo; PJ and Ben took the hint and started corralling the lovebirds toward the car. It was no easy feat getting them to move, since they were still sucking face like a couple of bottom-feeders. I was sure one of them would dislocate their jaw if they kept at it like that.

"Uncle Leo," I said, squeezing his hands and trying to block his view. "Thank you so much for everything."

"Two fifteen," was all he said.

As we drove off, I stuck my head out the sunroof and blew my uncle a kiss.

○ ● ● ○ ● ○

Dinner was delicious. We ate at Ysabel's, the restaurant PJ's dad named after his mother. Since we were family, the waiters let us split a bottle of their best champagne. The bubbles were so golden in the glass, so fizzy in my throat, I thought for sure I'd float away from the table and end up pressed against the ceiling like a helium balloon.

Though the tapas we ordered were totally delish, it was hard to eat much with the swarm of butterflies fluttering madly in my stomach. At least 80 percent of my nerves were about Operation BAM. It had to go well—it just had to, or I would be the next girl on John Jamieson's hit list. The other 20 percent of my anxiety was about Ben Bettaglia, who hardly took his eyes off me the whole evening.

"What?" I said finally, turning to him with a bashful smile.

He looked away and studied his flute of champagne. "Nothing."

"You can't say nothing." I tried to rearrange my hair so it covered my zit.

Our eyes caught and held. "You look amazing, is all."

"Oh yeah?"

"Yeah. You got a problem with that?"

I took a sip of my water. "Not at all."

"You know, I just want to tell you, when we're seniors, and I'm finally the undisputed valedictorian, I'll still talk to you."

I turned to him, my face incredulous. "I can't believe you're bringing this up."

He pressed on. "Although, given your record in algebra, I sometimes wonder if you'll even be number two."

I smirked. "Does that fetal pig haunt you much, Ben?"

Instead of answering, he put his hand on my knee and I felt shivers spreading to places I didn't even know could get the shivers. "You're great, Sloane. You know that?"

I laughed nervously. "The funny thing is, we wouldn't even be here right now if we weren't tricked."

"I wasn't tricked," he said.

I opened my mouth in shock. "Oh come on, you were too!"

"Well, okay, sort of."

"See! You didn't even like me before."

He shook his head. "The trick wasn't making me like you." His hand moved slowly up my leg. "It was getting me to admit what I felt all along."

○ ● ● ○ ●

When we got to the plaza, the place was mobbed. The line to get into the Sebastiani Theater wrapped clear around the block. We stepped out of the limo and everyone turned to gape at us like we were famous or something. It was a little embarrassing, and I noticed that Hero sort of bent her head so her hair hid her face, but Amber swaggered in the lime-light, smiling like she owned the world. It occurred to me that very soon we'd be the center of attention in a much bigger way, and I gave an involuntary shudder. The lights of the marquee pulsed in time with the butterflies in my stomach.

We finally got inside a few minutes before midnight. Normally I'd be losing a little steam by then, but my body was so charged with adrenaline, it was hard to imagine I'd sleep again for as long as I lived. Walking through the carpeted halls, glancing up at the beautiful art deco ceilings, I remembered that I was supposed to be there tonight with Dad. He loved that place; 1930s architecture was his favorite.

"You doing okay?" Ben squeezed my hand.

"Yeah." I smiled at him. "I'm great."

We hadn't told the guys about our big plans for the evening. We were a little afraid they'd try to talk us out of it, and we were already jittery enough without the voice of reason complicating things. Now, holding Ben's hand, worrying that he could feel mine growing clammier by the second, I wondered what he'd think of me in half an hour.

The BAM committee had saved us seats. Nikki's brother ran concessions at the theater, and her cousin was a projectionist. They'd worked it so that Virg could set up his digital projector for our homegrown preview. They knew they might get in trouble—might even lose their jobs. They also knew that John had a reputation for exacting wicked revenge. But they hated what John had done to Nikki, and they wanted to see him discredited almost as badly as we did. Thank God John had accrued enough enemies to make his downfall possible.

John showed up with Natalie Coleman hanging on his arm. She was nearly as tall as he was, and you could tell she'd spent a long time making sure her hair was glossy, her makeup perfect. Her face glowed with pride and adoration every time she turned to gaze at her date.

"Think she'll still be wearing that smile later tonight?" Amber said into my ear.

"I doubt it. Check out John."

He didn't look too good. His face had a mug shot weariness I'd never seen on him before. Amazing what one night of sleepless terror can do to even the physically elite. His eyes were puffy, his skin looked sallow, and his shoulders were hunched over in a defensive slouch. When he saw us all sitting together, he looked away quickly. We made it a point to stare him down.

"You can run," Amber whispered, "but you can't hide."

I stifled a cackle.

"What are you guys whispering about?" Ben leaned his elbows onto his knees and studied us intently. "I sense a plot hatching."

Hero's head whipped around abruptly. "Plot? There's no plot. Why do you say plot?"

Ben squinted at all three of us, then let his eyes roam to the other BAMs, who were all giggling, whispering, and looking every bit as guilty as we must have. We'd never make it as a secret society, I'm afraid.

"If you say so." Ben was obviously not convinced, but he let it drop.

When the lights went out, the entire theater cheered. I breathed in the comforting scent of popcorn and willed myself not to have a nervous breakdown. After wiping the sweat from my palms, I linked my fingers with Ben's hand on one side and Amber's on the other. I turned my head just in time to see Amber grab Hero's hand. At last we were one long, unbreakable chain, and that made me smile. I couldn't remember any time in my life when I'd had so many real friends. Even the other BAMs were turning out to be pretty cool. Forty-eight hours ago I wouldn't have said hello to them in the grocery store, but what we'd gone through last night forged an unusual bond. I guess Amber was right; it really does help having a common enemy.

"I think I'm going to throw up, I'm so nervous," Amber said into my ear.

"I know," I said. "I just want it to be over."

Then the projector fired up and the screen flickered to life.

Though I'd spent the last twenty-four hours obsessing over this moment, I still wasn't prepared for the sight of us on the big screen. My God, we were huge! I was instantly mesmerized as I watched us move solemnly in the foggy forest, draped in our Grim Reaper robes. My heart felt like a bird flapping madly in its cage. It was so surreal. You could hear us perfectly, and the image quality was a hundred times more professional than I'd expected—Virg had done an astounding job capturing it all. We sounded sincerely spooky chanting in Latin. There was John, blindfolded, handcuffed, looking even more helpless and pathetic than I'd remembered. The crowd stirred in confusion; some people gasped in surprise.

I heard a girl call out "Oh my God!" from somewhere at the back of the theater.

Ben turned to look at me. "You've got to be kidding."

I just shrugged, and he turned back to the screen, transfixed.

I glanced at Amber; she was wide-eyed and motionless. I could feel my pulse throbbing in my throat.

When John called me a bitch, Virg zoomed in for a close-up. I saw the expression on his face, now two stories high, and my stomach curled into an angry knot. I don't think anyone sitting in that theater could fail to see what I saw. His eyes were slits and his lips took on an incredulous expression that held the shape of a grin, but was so filled with hatred and disdain you could never call it a smile. All of his charisma, his wit, his charm, his Beemer, and his borrowed yachts were stripped away right then and he was naked. We'd all been given front-row seats to his soul. And his soul was ugly.

Suddenly John stood up, and everyone turned in his direction. He was smack in the center of the theater, imprisoned by his fellow moviegoers on all sides. We could see his silhouette pivoting this way and that in a panic. He yelled in a spoiled, petulant voice, "Stop it! Turn it off!"

The movie continued to play.

John started scrambling for the exit, pushing people out of the way. No one was watching the screen now; all eyes were fixed on his dark shape as he tried to make his escape.

Then, to my utter shock and amazement, Hero stood up and said smoothly, "What's the matter, John? Can't take it?"

He'd made it to the aisle by now, and he spun around, pointing a finger at her. "Fuck off, bitch!"

"Don't talk to my cousin like that!" I was on my feet and yelling before I could even think about it.

Amber stood beside me. "Humiliation sucks, huh, buddy?"

John turned to the crowd imploringly. Virg must have cut the sound, because the theater went silent. "If you believe this shit you're crazy. It was just—I was just—acting! I'm an actor, remember?" Behind him, on the screen, he was inching down the tree, balancing carefully on his knees, then leaning forward, his face inches from the dirt, trying to pick up the paper cup between his teeth. The packed theater exploded with laughter.

John whirled around, saw himself on his knees in the dirt, and attempted a booming laugh of his own. To me it sounded utterly fake and hollow; though, come to think of it, his laugh always sounded that way.

"Not bad, huh?" John cried in a jovial tone.

The screen went black then. When the credits came up they were simple and to the point: *This message brought to you by Bettys Against the Man.*

For a horrifying moment, I actually wondered if he could pull it off. True, the odds were against him, but maybe John Jamieson had the power to defy the odds, to reverse the laws of nature. We were so used to buying his shit. He'd just flash that Aquafresh smile and get away with murder. I could feel the audience half wanting to believe him, in spite of the evidence. It's hard to see your god go down in flames.

The lights came on, and nobody seemed to know what to do. An awkward hush fell over the crowd.

Corky stood up and called out, "Way to go, man!" He started clapping and cheering. A few other John Jamieson wannabes called out encouragement. John smiled and nodded, the old confidence slowly ebbing back into his limbs. There was a smattering of applause from other parts of the theater, and it seemed to be spreading.

But then I heard a girl's voice from somewhere in the back of the theater. "Bullshit!"

The applause stopped and everyone turned, craning their necks to see who had spoken. She stood up; it was a tiny freshman girl with blue hair. I couldn't remember her name, if I'd ever learned it. She stood there, wide-eyed and trembling as she looked John straight in the eye. "He's a liar."

A look passed over John's face, an odd mixture of surprise and dread, but then he got his old bravado back. "You going to believe this freak? Please!"

Before he could even finish his sentence, another girl jumped to her feet; I was surprised to see it was Jana Clark. "He's also a disaster in bed."

People laughed, especially the BAMs. John's face turned tomato red.

"And he treats all girls like *putas*." It was Reina Garcia; I had no idea that John's enemies came from such a diverse range of social cliques. Apparently, he was an equal-opportunity man-slut.

Dog Berry stood, and in his usual baked drawl cried out, "I never slept with the dude, but I never liked him either." This prompted fresh peals of laughter.

Natalie Coleman stood up, and the laughter died down. I figured she was going to defend him; she was his date, after all. Then I noticed that her face was streaked with tears, with mascara running in rivulets down her cheeks. "He . . . he . . ." she faltered.

"Speak up!" someone called from the back.

"He dated me in secret for three years, and tonight's the first time he'd be seen with me in public." As she fixed him with her stare, her voice went from trembling to pissed. "I guess I'm the only girl in Sonoma still stupid enough to go out with him."

John's eyes were wide with horror. Anyone could see he was a condemned man. "I—wait," he stammered. "You don't . . ." But his voice trailed off, and he bit his lip like he might cry.

I glanced around at the crowd and saw my own disgust reflected in the faces around me. It was like we all knew in our hearts he was a snake—had known it all along. Now, for the first time, we had permission to say it aloud.

"Down with the Man!" I chanted. "Down with the Man!"

The BAMs picked up my battle cry immediately. "Down with the Man!"

Others joined in, yelling at the top of their lungs, until the whole theater pulsed with it.

John's face drained of color. He backed toward the exit, looking like a cornered animal. Then he turned away from us and ran full-tilt, disappearing out the door.

That was it. The crowd went wild. People were cheering and whistling, stomping their feet. It took us a minute to realize that everyone was turning in our direction.

Amber said, "I think they're clapping for us."

We stood up, all seven of us, and the applause got even louder—thunderous—until it was throbbing in my ears.

We held each other's hands and took a bow.

Friday, August 22
3:33 P.M.

Whew! What a whirlwind. Who would have guessed that exposing a high school prick would earn us instant underground celebrity status? I guess there just weren't enough YouTube videos to keep viewers entertained this week, because as soon as Virg posted his little opus there, people started e-mailing it to each other like crazy. When I got off work last Sunday and checked my e-mail, there were twenty messages from girls I'd never even met before telling me they'd heard about what the BAMs did, and they'd seen the film, and they knew John was a miserable *blank* all along because of *blankety-blank-blank*. I even got an e-mail from some girl in Petaluma telling me they had a sociopath at their school just like John, and could I give her advice about how to bring him down? Marcy Adams started a BAM Web site, and in three days it's had 13,000 hits.

But, despite all the excitement, summer refuses to last forever. Hero went back to Connecticut this morning. Amber and I headed over to Moon Mountain to see her off. We brought her a Triple Shot Betty travel mug filled with her favorite drink: an iced soy chai. She was dressed in a corduroy skirt and a sparkly halter top—part of her new look, I guess. She stood there with her lime green luggage set, trying to be brave, but it was no use; we were all tearing up by the time Uncle Leo started the car.

254 o •••• :⚬⚬⚬: confessions of a

Amber hugged her first. "Take care of yourself," she said. "Don't let those prep school boys get away with anything."

Hero rolled her eyes. "After they see me on YouTube, they'll be too scared to even talk to me."

"They'll be all over you," Amber said. "Just don't do anything I wouldn't do."

"I guess that means the sky's the limit!" Hero said, and they both laughed. "Although, actually, I could never cheat on Claudio."

"Oh, come on," Amber chided. "You won't even be on the same continent."

Hero grinned shyly. "Thank God for technology. We're going to IM every night."

"Well, what do I know? The hopeless romantic thing works for you, I guess."

It was my turn. I stepped forward and folded her slender, birdlike body into my arms. "I love you, Cuz."

"I love you too." She pulled back and looked into my eyes. "Thanks for letting me into your world again."

I swiped at a tear. "Anytime."

"Hey, girls!" Uncle Leo yelled. "You want to wrap this up sometime today? I'm wasting good gas here, waiting for you Chatty Cathys to put a sock in it."

Touching scene of girly good-byes officially over.

⚬ • • ⚬ • ⚬

Surprise surprise—the summer didn't turn out exactly like I'd planned.

1. Operation Girlfriend became Operation Virgin/Whore— at least for a while.

2. On the Fourth of July, I got to eat hunks of dead meat

with a bunch of fossils instead of camping in Santa Cruz with my dad.

3. On my first real date, I was plagued with a zit the size of Mount Kilimanjaro.

Still, the summer had its moments.

1. Hero and Amber finally became friends, and we did get to paint our toenails together.

2. We started a grass roots neo-feminist movement with the potential to drastically affect gender politics (not sure what that means, but if Bronwyn says so, it's probably true, right?).

3. I got tricked into falling for the hottest guy in Sonoma, and somehow he fell for me too.